"I know you're hurting, but let me help you. Don't push me away."

"Sorry." He shrugged. "I'm not blaming anyone but the man who stole my daughter. But what you wrote—"

"I wish I could change everything, Hunter," Shauna said, her pain magnified by his. She laid her hand on his bare arm. "But I need you to trust me—"

She stopped speaking as his eyes, trained on hers, suddenly turned from dull green to flashing jade. He bent down, took her into his arms and kissed her. Hard.

She knew it was simply to shut her up. Prevent her from finishing what she'd been saying. Because the fact was, he still didn't believe she could help him find his daughter.

But she kissed him back with a longing born of seven years of missing him.

He pulled back. Even as she knew he would. Even as she knew she *should*. This wasn't seven years ago, when they were lovers. This was today, and they were drawn together by circumstances too horrible to contemplate. And they didn't need any more regrets…

Available in October 2005 from Silhouette Sensation

Not a Moment Too Soon

LINDA O. JOHNSTON

SILHOUETTE®
Sensation™

*First published in Great Britain 2005
Silhouette Books, Eton House, 18-24 Paradise Road,
Richmond, Surrey TW9 1SR*

© Linda O Johnston 2004

ISBN 0 373 27401 7

18-1005

*Printed and bound in Spain
by Litografia Rosés S.A., Barcelona*

LINDA O JOHNSTON

A practising attorney, Linda juggles her busy schedule between mornings of writing briefs, contracts and other legalese, and afternoons of creating memorable tales of the paranormal, time travel, mystery, contemporary and romantic suspense. Armed with an undergraduate degree in journalism with an advertising emphasis from Pennsylvania State University, Linda began her versatile writing career running a small newspaper, then working in advertising and public relations, and later obtaining her JD degree from Duquesne University School of Law in Pittsburgh.

Linda belongs to Sisters in Crime and is actively involved with Romance Writers of America, participating in the Los Angeles, Orange County and Western Pennsylvania chapters. She lives near Universal Studios, Hollywood, with her husband, two sons and two cavalier King Charles spaniels.

To all fellow writers. We all sometimes wish
that what we write would come true, don't we?
Well, be careful what you wish for...

And, as always, to Fred, one writer's
dream who happily came true.

Prologue

Shauna O'Leary opened her eyes slowly. As she remained seated on her stiff desk chair, apprehension contracted her body into the same tight, quivering mass that it always did when she wrote something at her computer.

Most of the time, the tales that poured from her fingertips were fine, even delightful. Suitable for reading to the kids who came especially to her restaurant, Fantasy Fare, to hear them. She would laugh aloud as she read, in relief as much as enjoyment. Chastise herself gaily, push the print button and—

As she automatically began to scan the words on the screen, she gasped aloud. This was one of those rare, yet nevertheless too-frequent, *other* times.

"Oh, no," she whispered, though no one else was there, in her small, secluded home, to hear. "Oh, no. Oh, no. Oh, no." She repeated the words in a mantra born of despair as she continued to read:

Andee was scared. So scared. "Daddy," she cried.

But Daddy didn't come. Instead, the bad man came back into the room.

"Help me, Daddy!"

Shauna stared at the hand clutching the computer's mouse as if it belonged to someone else. The long, slim fingers with blunted, pink-polished nails—fingers that were so skilled on the computer keys—were trembling. Resolutely, she highlighted the entire file, prepared to push Delete. Get rid of it.

But that wouldn't get rid of the problem.

She did it nevertheless. Erased everything. Closed the file. Opened it again.

The story was still there. Of course.

With a small moaning sound, she pushed Print.

There would be a physical record of what had already been set into motion.

Shauna took two long, deep breaths, steeling herself for what was to come. Anxiously running fingers through the sides of her long, ash-blond hair, she looked at the telephone beside her computer. It sat on the antique door that had been taken from her grandmother's house and was now propped on wooden file cabinets, serving as her desk.

She studied the phone, delaying the inevitable.

And then, filled with dread, she lifted the portable receiver and pressed in a familiar number. Elayne Strahm's. She needed to speak with her immediately. Get another phone number from her.

For the little girl in her story was Elayne's grandchild.

Hunter Strahm's daughter.

Chapter 1

Hunter Strahm steered his speeding rental car off the Interstate and onto the main road toward his mother's home.

Oasis, Arizona. Lord, it seemed like ages since he'd been back. It was late afternoon, desert time, though he'd already put in a full day of work and travel. He ignored the pounding of his heart as he hurtled through town, trying to silence the inner voice that told him he was on a fool's mission. Wasting not just minutes, but hours of precious time.

He'd made the decision to come here first. He'd live with it.

Yeah, but would Andee…?

''Damn,'' he muttered aloud, forcing his thoughts from the direction that could only make him crazy.

He stared out the windshield. Oasis looked the same as he remembered. Except—where was the restaurant he knew Shauna O'Leary now owned?

He'd find out, if he had to. First, he'd go see his mother. Would Shauna still be there? If not, his mother would know how to find her.

He turned onto the street where his mother lived, and he looked around.

What kind of car did Shauna drive?

It had been more than five hours since that series of phone calls which made him want to lash out in total frustration and fear at whatever, whoever, was convenient.

He usually thrived on dealing with the worst of situations. Taking control, and resolving them.

But the calls had concerned his five-year-old daughter. Andee.

She'd gone missing from Margo's home in L.A. Wandered off from the backyard. Or at least that was what his ex had said in the first of those damnable calls.

Hunter, a private investigator, had been a thousand miles away on business, unable to do a blessed thing but head for the airport. He'd left a job unfinished. He had never done that before.

He'd never faced an emergency this urgent before.

Shauna's had been the second call. And Margo's next call had confirmed what Shauna had claimed.

Andee hadn't just gotten lost. She had been kidnapped.

Emergency, hell. It was a crisis of a magnitude he'd never imagined.

Shauna had called from his mother's, where she said she'd gone to be with Elayne. And though what she said reminded him too much of the past, he couldn't ignore it—just in case she could provide a clue, no matter how absurd, about where Andee was. That was the major reason he'd come here, instead of straight to L.A.

Surely Shauna would have gone home, or to her business, by now. Yet when he strode up the familiar walkway to Elayne Strahm's tan stucco hacienda, he figured it wouldn't necessarily be his mother who answered the door.

He rang the bell, reluctant to use his key after not being here for so long.

He heard footsteps inside. Light, quick ones.

And when the door opened, he found himself staring into soft brown eyes that were wide but not with surprise, the way her call had startled him. With…what? Uneasiness?

Pleasure?

No way.

She hadn't changed at all, except to become prettier. Her blond hair was a little longer, a little lighter. She was slim in her T-shirt and shorts, with shapely, endless legs.

Steeling himself for what was to come, he took a step toward her. Parroting the initial, friendly greeting she'd given him over the phone earlier—before she had dropped her bombshell—he said simply, ''Hello, Shauna.''

He looked so tall, standing there.

That was the first thing Shauna thought. She hadn't forgotten Hunter's imposing height. Though she was above average stature for a woman, he had always towered above her. Before, it had seemed exciting and masculine and very, very sexy.

Now his daunting size seemed magnified by his anger. Those flashing green eyes she remembered so well glared, as if she were to blame. But she was just the messenger.

''Hello, Hunter,'' she said softly. She consciously pulled her gaze from his, hoping to relieve some of the tension building between them.

His blue sport shirt, tucked into khaki trousers, wasn't tight, but she could tell that the young cop she'd fallen for all those years ago was now even more muscular. With his prominent, straight brows, his wide jaw, he still was the most handsome man she had ever seen. Maturity would have looked good on him, if it hadn't been combined with the other emotions spewing from him like water from a broken sprinkler.

Like the emotions of the nonfiction characters in her latest story…

Daddy!

Needing to break the building silence—and escape her own

heartrending thoughts—she said, "I'm surprised to see you here."

"This is my mother's house." His voice was even deeper in person than on the phone. Perhaps it was also amplified by his obvious fury. "Did you have to worry her, too? But of course you did. You wouldn't keep such a feat of realistic storytelling to yourself, now, would you?"

She reeled back as if he had struck her. In a way, he had.

Malice spewed from lips that had once kissed hers sometimes sweetly, sometimes passionately, but always caringly.

Years ago. But she had loved him. And lost him. And he had married another woman.

Elayne spoke from behind her, reiterating Shauna's earlier question. "Hunter? What are you doing here?"

Staying silent, Shauna retreated a few steps. Elayne burst by her, and in a moment mother and son were locked in a tight, emotional embrace. Even though Elayne, too, was so much smaller than Hunter, she seemed to be the one comforting him. Reaching up, she stroked his head, his back.

If only Shauna had the right to try to ease his pain that way…

No. Not now.

She had to escape the emotional involvement that would swamp her if she stayed here.

Elayne was the first to back away. The pale, drawn skin of her face contrasted with her short mop of curly hair that was probably too dark to be natural for a woman in her late fifties. It had looked the same from the time Shauna had met her eight years ago. In fact, little had changed about Elayne's appearance during the time they'd been friends, except for the multiplication of tiny lines radiating from the edges of her eyelids and the deepening of the creases framing her mouth.

"You belong in California, son," she said, "looking for Andee." She held his arms and looked up, studying him.

"I'm here just for a couple of hours, Mom, on a stopover between planes." His sweeping gaze seemed equally con-

cerned about his mother. "Meantime, I called my best oper-
ative, and he's started our search for her. He's already talked
to Margo and the cops. I'll jump in soon, but for now I came
to see how you're holding up."

Maybe. But though he might not admit it, Shauna figured
he was also there to see if she had information that could help
him.

"I'll survive," Elayne said. "Shauna promised to stay with
me until I heard again from you. I guess you don't have any
news." She didn't wait for his answer. She undoubtedly could
read it in his stark expression as easily as Shauna could. "As
long as you're here, come in." She turned her back and motioned for him to follow her toward the kitchen. "I've got
steaks in the freezer. It won't take me—"

"No need to feed me," Hunter said. "A cup of coffee
would be great." He put one arm on his mother's shoulder
as he accompanied her down the hall.

Shauna remained in the entry, feeling so alone that tears
welled in her eyes. She had once been close enough to both
of them that she would have tagged along and gotten drinks
for them in their own house. During that time in the past,
Elayne had been like a mother to her, for Shauna had lost her
own when she was very young.

Now, mother and son needed time together to deal with a
situation that could have no happy ending. Shauna had suggested so in what she'd said to each of them.

Neither knew just how bad it was…

Help me, Daddy!

Damn. The tears she'd held back flowed down her cheeks.
She reached into her pocket for a tissue and swiped them
away, even as she pulled the front door open again. She had
done what she had to. It was time to leave.

"Shauna?" Hunter's voice stopped her. He filled the end
of the hallway.

He still was such a good-looking man…

"Join us." It wasn't an invitation, but a command. "We need to talk."

She owed him that, at least. Not that she could describe what had happened, at least not coherently. And she absolutely didn't want to provide any details about the ending of the story she had written.

But she was a psychologist. Her practice was very limited, of course. She made her living from Fantasy Fare. But she had gotten her license, become a therapist, to help people in crisis.

To help a select group of patients. Patients selected for her, by her stories. Though she had been sought out by former school colleagues to join their practices, she never took them up on it.

She maintained her license for the counseling she did intensely, but as infrequently as possible, when her writing called for it—mostly to work with strangers whose stories had swept through her without warning.

She had craved that kind of help when Hunter had left seven years ago, and when, soon after, another story had spewed from her fingertips, a tale as unbidden as the ones that had driven him away. As unbidden as the one she had written today. As unbidden as so many of them…

In that one, her father had died of cancer.

She hadn't been able to help Hunter before. Or her dad. Not even herself.

Now she had the resources to at least try to make it a little less agonizing for Hunter.

"Okay," she said. "We'll talk."

He stood still until she had passed him. After all this time, she was finally so close to Hunter that she could have touched him. *Wanted* to…but didn't. He followed her down the hall. For an instant, panic throbbed through her. She felt trapped. She couldn't get out.

But then they reached Elayne's cheerful, bright kitchen. She had remodeled it since Shauna had last visited her. The painted cabinets along the wall had been replaced by light pine ones that didn't quite reach the ceiling. Along their tops was a collection of antique pans. The new kitchen table was pine, too, with matching chairs on wheels pushed under it. The refrigerator was the same as before—a gold side-by-side.

On the new tile counter closest to the table, framed photographs, some of Hunter, were arranged in irregular rows. Nearest Shauna was a picture of an absolutely adorable cherub, a small girl with hair as dark as Hunter's and as curly as Elayne's. This had to be Andee. Her eyes were the same shade of green as her father's and grandmother's, too.

Shauna looked away quickly, her eyes dampening again. Her attention landed on Hunter. He was watching her. She turned away quickly, to help Elayne with their refreshments.

Soon all three sat at the table. The herbal tea Elayne and she had sipped earlier as they had talked had been refreshed several times, so Shauna opted to join Hunter in drinking fresh-brewed, strong coffee from large mugs.

And mother and son, black haired and with symmetrical facial features that resembled each other, trained similar emerald eyes on Shauna.

She looked back. Waited. Made herself remember every iota of her training as a psychologist. Compassion, yes.

But also detachment. Distance.

Please…

"Tell me more about this story you called me about," Hunter commanded.

"All right," Shauna began. "It came unexpectedly." She watched those brilliant green eyes study her critically. Otherwise, he seemed emotionless. Cool.

Cold.

"They're always unexpected, aren't they?" Elayne asked. "This kind of story."

"Pretty much so," Shauna acknowledged, looking at her friend's pale face instead of at Hunter.

Elayne, at least, believed in Shauna, for they had first met when a story had, long ago, caused Shauna to contact Phoenix's Human Services Department. Elayne, a social worker, had been Shauna's contact, and her kindness and curiosity had led Shauna to let down her guard and reveal—accidentally— the source of her knowledge about domestic violence in a child's home.

Which was what had made it particularly hard to call Hunter's mother today. Shauna hadn't divulged the story's contents over the phone but had come right over to be with Elayne. To stay with her.

To get Hunter's current phone number from her so she could call him, for she alone had to be the one to relay this horrible news to him.

Even though she knew full well, because of the way he had acted in the past, that he wouldn't buy it. Or at least he wouldn't want to.

"Where were you when this story came to you?" Elayne asked.

"Better yet, why don't you just tell us what it said?" Hunter's arms were folded as he sat back on his chair. His blunt chin was raised belligerently. Talk about expressive body language. Shauna sighed inwardly. Sure, he would listen to her, but he would fight any belief in what she said with all his innate stubbornness. That, apparently, had not changed.

Trying for therapeutic distance, Shauna briefly responded to Elayne's question first, needing to work into the rest. She explained that she'd sat down at her computer fully expecting—hoping—to write something especially for one of the kids who frequented the story time at her family restaurant, Fantasy Fare.

Instead, that hellish narrative had spewed from her fingers.

Looking unwaveringly into Hunter's skeptical stare, she finally responded to his demand. She described the story but only sketchily.

"I realized at once who the kidnapped child was," she finished, "and knew I had to notify you."

"The story said she was my child?"

"Not exactly." She had kept up with what was happening in Hunter's life in a manner she did not want to mention, so she didn't explain how she knew who Andee was. Instead, she asked questions for which she already knew the answer. Otherwise, why would Hunter have come here? "Hunter, have you called whoever's supposed to be watching your daughter in L.A.? Maybe this story is wrong." From experience, though, she knew better. "Do you know where she is?"

His strong features went as blank as if he had suddenly turned to stone. "She was with her mother. We're divorced. I have primary physical custody, but Margo watches Andee when I travel. And yes, I've spoken with Margo." His tone sounded bleak. "But no, I don't know where Andee is." He paused as if marshaling his internal forces, then demanded, "Is there anything helpful in your story, like something to identify the kidnapper?"

"There's one thing," she said slowly, rehashing the narrative in her mind. "The person—a man—thinks of himself as 'Big T.'"

"That's all?" Hunter sounded scornful. Damn, but his scorn, the same derision he had leveled on her just before he had exited her life for what she had believed would be forever, still had the power to wound her. "It's got to be a pretty short story. I want to see it."

"No, you don't," she replied quietly.

She hadn't intended to injure him by a thrust of her own, but pain briefly shadowed his face, and Elayne's, too.

"Shauna, don't you think—?" Elayne murmured.

Her son interrupted. "Did you arrange to have Andee taken so you could impress me, after all this time, by proving one of your damned stories was coming true?"

Shauna's sudden intake of breath was echoed by Elayne's gasp. Another direct hit, right to her gut.

Similar accusations had been hurled at her by strangers when she issued warnings about other situations she had written about. She was a psychologist. She understood that people lashed out in fear and hurt. She had remained calm and soothing and understanding.

But seven years had passed since her last confrontation with Hunter. Seven years, two months, and—

Enough.

She stood. "Why on earth would I? I wouldn't do anything to hurt a child. Or you, for that matter. Not now. And certainly not Elayne." Hunter opened his mouth as if ready to interrupt, but she pressed forward, not letting him. "I know you didn't believe in my stories years ago, and what I did at the end wouldn't exactly encourage you to trust me. But I didn't set out to write a story that'd come true this time, any more than I did then. I never do. This one involved you and your daughter, so I had to let you know. That's all. Except that I'm very, very sorry."

Hunter also rose. "Hell, me too. I was out of line." He shook his head slowly. "I only wish the solution was that easy. If you took my daughter, I could just ask you to give her back." The anguished smile he gave Shauna nearly broke her heart.

"You know I would if I could," she responded softly, her voice hoarse with the moisture she held back. She turned away. Elayne, too, was standing, and tears flowed down the older woman's cheeks. "I'll leave, now that you won't be alone," Shauna told her. "If it's not too hard for you, I'd like to keep in touch so I can learn how things turn out. And if there's anything I can do—"

"There is," Hunter interrupted. "Let me read your story."

"Hunter, I'm not sure you—"

He didn't let her speak. "You asked what you can do. Well, that's the *only* thing you can do. Let me read it, Shauna. If it's as you've always said, something that comes to you from the emotions of the participants, maybe it'll have something to help me find my daughter. Let me see it now, so I can get on my way to L.A."

Chapter 2

Shauna had argued with him, of course. Hunter, expecting it, hadn't budged. He'd won. His mother had understood and said she'd had a bridge game planned with friends that evening. Not that she'd play, but at least she wouldn't be by herself. She had encouraged them both to leave.

Hunter was so antsy to get on his way to L.A. that he ground his teeth together in frustration. Still he followed Shauna, in his rental car, along the streets of Oasis toward her home.

In the old days, he had enjoyed arguing with her. Shouts had led to surrender. Surrender had led to—

Damn. This was the present. His daughter's life was in danger. That, and only that, was his focus.

Shauna had even tried to convince him that, for his own good, he should just trust her. She'd told him she'd written the damned story and had given him the only possible clue in it. Wasn't that enough?

Hardly. She might be a professional shrink now—his mother had let that slip a few years ago—but he was the professional investigator. Shauna might have overlooked something that could lead to his daughter.

Except…others on the force had believed wholeheartedly in Shauna's stories when Hunter was with the Phoenix Police Department. And sometimes even he couldn't discount them entirely.

But Andee was all right. She had to be.

Hunter pounded one fist on the steering wheel of his rented sedan, then twisted it to follow Shauna's little blue sports model down a street on the outskirts of town. She turned into a driveway, and he pulled in behind her.

Nice house. One story, not very big, but pretty. It was the obligatory Arizona earth-tone color, but brighter in shade than customary, almost red, like rich clay.

The garage door opened automatically, and Shauna pulled in. He parked outside and grabbed his cell phone for one more call.

"Simon? What's happening?" Simon Wells, a Rolls-Royce of a British import, was Hunter's second-in-command at Strahm Solutions, his P.I. agency. Hunter had called him first thing when he'd learned about Andee, got him started doing all the things he'd do himself if he was in L.A. His complete trust in Simon was the only reason he'd been able to convince himself to indulge in this delay.

"Nothing new yet," Simon replied in his unabashedly English accent. "Soon, though. Banger's on his way." Strahm Solutions had developed an excellent working relationship with Los Angeles Police Detective Arthur Banner, whose nickname, perversely, was "Banger." Straitlaced and all cop, he was the furthest thing imaginable from a gangbanger, though his nickname was also used to refer to those street toughs.

"He's from LAPD's West Bureau," Hunter pointed out. "You sure he can deal with this? Margo's place is in Sunland. That's Valley Bureau. Foothill Division, I think."

"You know Banger. He'll figure it out. He understands this

is high priority and low profile, so he's called one of the best FBI agents he knows. A rare one who's discreet. So far, the press hasn't gotten wind of what's happened. Where are you?''

Hunter told him. ''I'll be here for another hour or so, then grab a flight back to L.A.'' A thousand instructions slammed through his head, but he left them there. Simon was smart. He worked well with minimal direction, and the others on Hunter's staff at Strahm Solutions knew to listen to him.

''Good. I'll let you know if I learn anything more in the meantime.''

''Thanks.'' Pushing the flap down on his cell phone to hang up, Hunter looked toward the garage. Shauna had exited her car and stood beside a door that opened into the house. Slender and poised and utterly sexy, she was watching him. Warily. As if she expected him to pounce on her the moment they got inside.

Didn't he just wish...?

Instead, he got out of the car, cursing himself silently for still wanting her. Cursing *her*. For looking so good. For inciting ideas inside him that he had no business feeling.

She stirred him still, as no woman had. Not even Margo. He wanted Shauna.

Was there some other way that Shauna had really known something had happened to Andee? So much about her stories had always seemed true, too much to be coincidental. Yet he'd always prided himself on being a realist, had never wanted to buy in to the idea.

Yeah? Well, if he hadn't bought in to it, why was he here, when what he really wanted was to be home, looking for his daughter?

He closed the car door and hurried toward Shauna. He'd accused her earlier of having something to do with the kidnapping. That had just been his anxiety lashing out, and they'd all known it. Apologies didn't come easily to him, but he'd owed it to her.

Years ago, though, he wouldn't have put such a terrible hoax past her, not if it would have gotten him to admit that she had the power to write stories, out of the blue, that came true. She'd always been upset when he didn't believe her.

And maybe if he had been more accepting, he'd still be living here in Oasis, his job with the Phoenix Police Department intact.

"Were you talking to someone in L.A.?" she asked when he drew near her. Her scent was much as he remembered it. Something too soft to be exotic, too spicy to be sweet and feminine. But very appealing. It suited the mystery of her.

"Yes," he said. "My assistant, Simon. He's with my ex-wife, trying to get better information. So far, there's nothing of use." He let his tone turn scornful. "Your story's as likely to tell me something helpful as Margo is."

Shauna's eyes blazed, but only for an instant. Saying nothing, she led him inside.

They entered the house through her kitchen. It was a lot smaller than his mother's. A lot more like a small, homey forest. Shauna had plants everywhere—on her tiny kitchen table, along her gold-tile counters, even on top of the refrigerator. A few had flowers. Most were simply large and leafy and green. The place smelled more like a garden than a kitchen.

"Sit down there." Shauna pointed to a chair beside her table. "I'll get you more coffee and…Hunter, I have to warn you again. I don't think you should read the story."

"Yeah, I got that. Is it because Andee's father is described in it as an ugly old goat who doesn't believe in magical stories that come true?"

She leveled her gaze on his. This time, what he read in her wide brown eyes, the tilt of her head that allowed her long, blond hair to cascade to one side, wasn't hurt or anger. It was pity.

Damn. Now *that* hurt. He had never wanted Shauna's sympathy before. He sure as hell didn't want it now. Yet the expression again reminded him of the past, of what they had shared.

And not just that he'd thought he'd loved her.

The passion between them had been phenomenal. The thought of it once more sent his blood coursing, as if a floodgate had been opened. Sure, he could imagine himself making love to Shauna again. Hell, yes. She was every bit as beautiful and desirable as she'd been then.

But the sympathy in her eyes brought him back abruptly to why he was here.

She thought she knew the ending to Andee's story, and it made her feel sorry for him.

He had to learn all she'd written, so he would know what she figured he'd be up against. And then he'd dash home.

Wearily he did as she asked and sat down on a chair. Covered by a thick, fringed pillow, it was more comfortable than his mother's kitchen chairs.

"What is it, Shauna? I know I never wanted to believe your stories came true, no matter what I saw. Some of the other guys swore by what you told them. Hell, maybe you've been right every time." That was why he'd taken precious time to come here before hurrying home, why his hastily crafted strategy had included seeing Shauna—just in case. "Maybe whatever you've written now is real and there won't be a damned thing I can do about it. But I've got to know, in case there's anything to help me find my daughter. If it's bad stuff, I'll fight it."

"I know you will, Hunter," she said with a sigh. "And you're right. If nothing else, I can at least let you prepare for it. But, honestly, the only clue to who the kidnapper is, is that he thinks of himself as 'Big T,' assuming that's actually his thoughts, not my imagination."

He couldn't help raising his eyebrows. This *all* was her imagination…except that Margo had confirmed that Andee had been taken.

"And no hints about how to find this so-called 'Big T'?"

She shook her head. "Hunter, the thing is…" She hesitated, then turned her back and opened the refrigerator door.

"Andee dies at the end," he supplied through gritted teeth. Prepare himself? Hell. Nothing could prepare him for that. "Right? Why else wouldn't you want to tell me?"

He heard a sound that might have been a sob. But when she turned back to him, a package of coffee in her hands, she looked composed. "Yes, Hunter. That's the end of my story."

Big T swooped down and reached behind a couch in the middle of the warehouse floor, lifting his Uzi. Before he could begin spraying bullets, Hunter ducked, rolled and came up shooting. His first volley got the guy in the gut.

The kidnapper fell to the hard concrete floor, moaning, as Hunter ran to kneel beside him, his weapon still leveled on him.

"Tell me where Andee is, you perverted bastard. Now."

Blood spurted from between Big T's fingers as he clutched his middle. "Too late." His gasp was a ghastly laugh. "Good luck finding her."

His eyes closed. He was dead.

Somewhere close by, but not near enough for Hunter to find her, Andee weakly cried "Daddy" for the last time.

Of course Hunter had guessed the ending, despite Shauna's reluctance about telling him. And maybe that had been what she wanted—not to have to say the words herself.

Still, when she acknowledged he had guessed correctly, she winced inside at the pain that crossed his face, only to be replaced an instant later by stoic blankness.

"I still want to see it." His voice held as much emotion as if he had requested the day's weather report.

What he didn't know yet was all Andee went through, all *he* went through, before that awful end. The story wasn't always specific, but their torment was stark and real.

But she knew he wasn't about to give up. He would fight

it. Hunter always fought everything, and everyone, that didn't comply with what he perceived as right and just and the way things should be. He wrestled with wrongs till he had them fixed, or at least wrapped up and within his control. That was why he'd made such a good cop.

And why things had gone so wrong for him at the end of his job with the Phoenix police.

"Okay," she said quietly, realizing she had no choice. "I'll get it in a minute." She took the coffee carafe over to fill it at the sink first, buying herself a little more time.

"Forget about the damned coffee," Hunter exploded.

She took a deep breath and put the carafe down. "Okay."

She glanced at him before she left the kitchen. He was watching her, brows locked in a glower she remembered too well from their last days together. It signaled his impatience. The way he blamed her for not listening to him.

Oh, she had listened then. She'd heard too much, most of it things he was thinking, not saying. She didn't need her special gift to tell her—only her eyes searching his, the mirrors to his very troubled, very angry soul.

Damn, how that had hurt her then.

It wouldn't now, no matter what he thought or said or didn't say. She wouldn't let it.

The inside door to the kitchen opened onto a long, narrow room that was supposed to be used as a dining room. Shauna seldom entertained at home, since it was much easier to throw parties at Fantasy Fare. That allowed her to maintain the privacy of her home more easily, too. As a result, she had turned the would-be dining room into her office. She loved spending time in it, writing in it—except when her fingers spewed her tales of painful prediction—with its wall of multipaned windows overlooking the desert garden that was her backyard. Her antique door-desk sat right in the middle, on a wood panel that protected the room's pale berber carpeting.

Ignoring her reflection in the large mirror along the inside wall, she sat at her desk chair and pulled open the top right drawer in one of the wooden file cabinets that acted as her desk's legs. She had put the printout of the story in a folder right in front, and as she pulled it out, she couldn't help scanning through it again. Surely she'd missed something, some glimmer of hope at the end that would mean—

"Is that it?"

Startled, she looked up. Hunter had sneaked into the room without her hearing him. Right behind her, he appeared to be reading the story over her shoulder. He stood so close he could have ripped the papers from her hands. So close that, if she rose, she could easily throw herself into his arms....

He was the one who would need comforting, not her. She wasn't to get emotionally involved.

"Yes," she said quietly. "Here it is." She turned enough in her seat to hand him the papers. "It'll be more comfortable in the kitchen. The only seat in here is my desk chair. You can use it if you'd like but—"

He muttered something that she took as refusal to move. His straight black brows were furrowed in concentration as he read the story.

She studied him as he studied the words on the page. She could tell what part he was reading by the alternating anger and scorn and concern in his expression. Not that those changes were obvious. When she'd known him before, when he'd been a cop, he'd prided himself on his ability to keep his face blank, unreadable. And it had been, to everyone but her.

But she knew the scornful twitch at the edge of his lips— lips she had once licked and tasted and kissed so often that she'd known their texture better than her own. The almost imperceptible hardening of his cool stare that signified fury.

Concern hadn't always been readable on his face, but was there in the briefest of caresses from those strong hands, the way he held her in his arms.

And now, she recognized pain in the way he closed green eyes that didn't flash but flickered and died, then opened again to read more. If only she could hold him, could comfort him…

"Are you okay?" she asked.

"Yeah." He barely responded. "Sure." And then he looked at her, his scowl fierce.

Once, her heart would have shriveled beneath that scowl. Today, despite her efforts to the contrary, it still hurt.

"I don't believe things will happen this way," he spit. "They can't." The last two words were lower, evincing grief.

Stay detached. Yet Shauna wondered if there was a way she could physically restrain herself from trying to ease his pain. The way she wished someone had helped her…

And then Hunter demanded, "I want you to get on your computer and write a different ending. Maybe that'll convince you what you wrote is nonsense. It can't possibly come true. Then I've got to get the hell out of here, to go look for her."

"All right," she said calmly. "I'll write a different ending." *But it won't be* me *who'll be convinced.*

She turned on her computer, a laptop she left set up on her desk connected to a printer, then waited while it booted up and Hunter paced impatiently. In a minute, she got into the file where the story had been saved.

"Look over my shoulder as I do this." She scrolled till she came to a part near the end that was a turning point, where Andee had nearly been found. She deleted everything after that and quickly wrote a new, happy ending. What would Grandma O'Leary say about it if Shauna could talk to her? Nothing good, she was sure. "Okay with that?" she asked Hunter.

"Good enough." Hunter's voice sounded grudging. "Go ahead and save it."

Her brief laugh was ironic as she tried to do just that. She closed the file, then opened it again, going right to the page where she'd made her changes.

The old ending was still there.

"This isn't something new, Hunter. The computer—any

computer I use—won't save a different ending. Or any other changes, for that matter.''

"Let me try."

"Sure."

She had barely gotten out of her seat before Hunter slid into it. It was too tall for him, but he didn't take time to adjust it. He looked like an adorable giant, his legs cramped beneath the desk. His fingers flew over the keyboard. She knew he was skilled in the use of computers—as well as in the use of things less cerebral. Like firearms and other weapons. She'd seen him in training when he'd been a cop. And his hands on her body…his skill in that had driven her mindless so often, so passionately, with wanting him.

How could she let herself think of that now?

"There." He sounded satisfied. Her thoughts back under control, she read over his shoulder. Though his new ending was different from hers, a lot shorter, it was similar, and of course Andee was fine at the conclusion. The biggest change was that he had added some directions for finding Big T—information that would let Hunter track him down when it was all over. "Do you have a floppy disk or CD that we can save onto?" She silently removed a floppy from a file cabinet drawer. Hunter both saved his story on the hard drive and used the "save as" command to copy the revised story onto the disk.

And when he checked both the hard drive and the floppy, the old version of the story was there.

"Damn. This can't be."

Shauna watched as he tried again. And then tried something else.

To no avail, of course. She knew better.

"What have you done to your damned computer?" He rose and towered over her threateningly. The slight scent emanating from him wasn't simply the aroma she recognized, of man and soap and Hunter. It was sharper, more bitter—like feral fear.

She'd never been afraid of Hunter, not even at his angriest. Even now, she did not believe he would hurt her…physically.

But he shouldn't have the power to wound her emotionally, either. Not today. *He doesn't,* she told herself.

Yet that didn't stop pain worse than if he'd actually assaulted her.

"I'm sorry, Hunter." She reached out and gently touched his arm. It was hard, tensed by his anger. And warm.

She remembered when he had held her in his arms tenderly. When tenderness had turned to lust. *Don't go there,* she reminded herself again.

"I know you don't want to believe it," she continued. "Neither do I. But I've lived with this a very long time. These stories can't be changed. In fact, my Grandma O'Leary warned me, when she was alive, that I shouldn't even try." Of course Shauna had tried anyway, especially with her father. "It could be too dangerous."

"For you? Well, what about the victims of your stories?"

She couldn't stand much more of this. She knew he was lashing out because of his own misery. *You're a therapist. Counsel him. Better yet, counsel yourself.*

Her mind fished frantically for the right words. *Don't take it personally* came to mind.

As if she could help it. But she managed to move her hand from his arm and take a step back.

"Tell you what," she said a lot more calmly than she felt. "Leave now. Take the story, if you think there are clues in it or that it'll help you some other way. Keep in touch, and if anything different happens from what's written, let me know. I'll enter it, then let you know if it saves on the computer and changes the ending. Okay?"

A phone rang. Hunter's cell, which he yanked from the back pocket of his khaki trousers. "Yeah?" Shauna couldn't hear what was being said, but Hunter's expression turned tormented before going blank again. "Yeah. I'm on my way." He flipped the phone closed. "That was my assistant Simon.

My ex-wife, Margo, is in hysterics about Andee. She's upset that Simon's brought in the cops, even someone we know and trust. The kidnapper told her not to, like that kind always does, so she's distraught. Simon thinks I'd better get there fast to see if I can calm her down.'' He snorted. ''Fat chance.''

''But you have to try, of course. I'll be thinking about you, wishing you—and Andee—well.''

''You'll be thinking about me, all right. You're coming along.''

She stared. ''Why would I do that?''

''Because of your story. You say you can't change it. Fine. I know you believe that. I don't have time to argue.'' His laugh was bitter. ''I don't want to believe *any* of it. But I can't take chances.''

Shauna closed her eyes. ''I can't help you, Hunter.'' But she knew she was lying. She had become a licensed therapist for just this kind of situation.

She knew how to help people in crisis situations.

Especially those whose crises were the subjects of her stories.

But most were strangers. Hunter wasn't, despite the years they hadn't seen each other. She would be too emotionally involved.

Going with him would be a mistake.

''Come with me, Shauna. You'll tell me everything possible about your damned stories. And you'll work with me to make sure this one doesn't come true. Got it?''

''Hunter, I can't.'' She regretted bringing him to her house. If they were anywhere else, she'd have fled.

For that wasn't the end of it. If he'd continued to demand, or even threatened, she'd have stood her ground.

But he closed the space between them, reached out and took her hands in his much larger ones, gripping them tightly. She remembered when he'd held her hands before…lovingly.

His voice, too, sounded full of emotion as he said, ''Please,

Shauna. Please help me. For Andee's sake. I'll beg if I have to, but—''

She couldn't stand that. She looked up into his sorrowful green eyes and said something she regretted even as she spoke it. ''All right, damn it, Hunter. I'll come.''

Chapter 3

Shauna stared resignedly into the passenger's side-view mirror. The familiar small-town streets of Oasis receded behind them and, with their disappearance, all sense of serenity and comfort receded from her mind.

But this wasn't about her.

She turned to watch the man sitting beside her. It *was* about him. His posture was stiff and taut, as if he maintained such discipline over himself that moving a muscle except to steer the car would snap him like a rubber band stretched to the breaking point.

His expression was as bleak as the rolling desert vista that abutted the highway, and he kept his eyes straight ahead, not even glancing toward her.

She struggled to think of something to say that would not sound too much like psychobabble, yet be of some help to this man who had once meant so much to her.

But what was there to say? His daughter had been kidnapped. A five-year-old child. And whether or not Hunter believed her, she had already told him there could be no happy ending.

And despite his earlier apology, she knew he somehow blamed her for this, as he once had blamed her for another situation she had written about that had gotten so terribly out of control.

She had packed and changed clothes quickly before leaving home. Now she wore a pink buttoned shirt tucked into navy slacks, a matching navy vest and sandals. L.A. wouldn't be as warm as Arizona, so she'd stuffed a sweater into a small suitcase with a couple of changes of clothes and her night paraphernalia.

She considered turning on the radio, for the only sounds were the growl of the engine and the unending road noise of tires humming on pavement.

First, though, she needed to make a call. She pulled her cell phone from the bottom of the burlap tote bag that doubled as her purse and pressed buttons until the number she called most frequently showed on the display screen.

It was answered on the second ring. "Fantasy Fare. Hi, Shauna. Are you okay? Where are you going?"

"Hello to you, too, Kaitlin."

Shauna smiled to herself in bittersweet irony. Kaitlin Verona, a lithe and exuberant dynamo, was her closest friend, and the manager she'd blessedly hired to assist her with running Fantasy Fare.

Kaitlin had dropped in one day when a child had fallen at the restaurant and his father was threatening a lawsuit. Not only that, but food deliveries were late. In short, when things had been particularly hellish.

Kaitlin had simply taken over, made both the kid and his parents laugh, and used her sense of humor to persuade the superintendent of the food warehouse where Shauna bought supplies to send her order after hours.

Later she had told Shauna she'd heard her cries for help

and responded. Of course, Shauna's pleas had been strictly internal.

As they'd gotten to know each other better, Shauna understood that they had something in common: they shared abilities that most people would believe bizarre and unreal, though each one's manifestation was unique.

They both perceived when someone else's emotions roiled.

Shauna's abilities translated to her fingertips, from which her stories spilled onto computer keyboards.

Kaitlin simply *knew* and reacted. Like now.

"It's him, isn't it?" Kaitlin demanded over the phone. "That guy from your past, Hunter."

This was one time Shauna wished Kaitlin didn't have her uncanny perception. "Yes," she said briefly.

"You wrote a story about him and now you're back together."

"Not exactly. Look, I need for you to—"

"Manage Fantasy Fare on my own for a while. Yes, I've got that. But tell me what's going on."

"Some other time."

"You're with him."

"Yes," Shauna acknowledged.

"And it's not because you want to be. Oh, heck, it's really bad, isn't it? I'm so sorry, Shauna. Can I help?"

"Just take care of things for me. I'll be back as soon as I can. Okay?"

"Sure. You take good care of yourself, you hear? Don't take any unnecessary risks. And call me when you can talk."

As Kaitlin hung up, a shower of shimmering rainbows suddenly appeared in Shauna's mind, gently tumbling toward the ground. As they fell, they turned upside down till they formed a myriad of colorful, happy smiles.

Despite herself, Shauna laughed aloud. That was one ability she didn't share with her friend. Kaitlin had the power to implant images into the minds of those whose emotions she sensed, the better to soothe them. Shauna had frequently enlisted Kaitlin's help in the therapy sessions she held to assist those whose stories she had written.

But where had that warning come from? It wasn't characteristic of what Kaitlin usually did. Did she see something that Shauna—

"What was that all about?" came a chilly masculine voice from beside her.

Shauna glanced toward Hunter. He still sat stiffly as he watched the road, gripping the steering wheel, as if by manipulating it he could reverse the diabolical incident that had suddenly taken control of his life.

"I had to tell my manager at the restaurant that I was going away for a while and that she'd need to take care of things."

He finally darted a look at her, his green eyes quizzical but not as icy as before. "It didn't sound like you did much talking, let alone giving directions."

Shauna replayed her end of the conversation in her mind. He was right. But knowing Hunter's antipathy toward anything that smacked of extraordinary abilities, she said simply, "I'm sorry you haven't met Kaitlin. She's been my manager for a couple of years, and we're good friends. To other people it might sound like we talk in code, but we're close enough that we understand each other."

"Yeah." He didn't sound convinced, but Shauna doubted he'd push this issue further. She had known Hunter to be intelligent and intuitive in the past. Otherwise, he wouldn't have made such a good cop. He had also been stubborn, refusing to acknowledge what he chose not to accept or understand. Right now, she suspected he'd gotten the gist of what she *wasn't* saying.

But at least he was talking to her again.

"We're not far from the airport now," she said, eager for some conversation—any conversation—to avoid their former uncomfortable silence.

He nodded. "I haven't been away long enough to forget my way around."

Just long enough to forget *her,* Shauna thought. Or so he must have wished.

If only their reunion could have been under other circumstances. But there would have been no reunion between them if she hadn't written that horrifying story.

And now they could only both wish they had never seen each other again.

The plane was finally in the air. The trip to Los Angeles International Airport, abbreviated LAX by most Angelenos, would take about an hour.

An hour too long.

Ignoring the aircraft's typical loud engine noise, Hunter forced himself to lean back in his narrow seat that, despite the height of its backrest, was too short to cradle his head comfortably. He had to concentrate on something other than his edginess. He had become an adopted Angeleno, like so many other immigrants to the sprawling urban complex. Yet, despite his reason for being there, he'd felt a sense of nostalgia visiting Oasis and his mother. And—though he despised himself for admitting it—seeing Shauna again.

L.A. was home now. His business was there.

His daughter was there…

His restlessness was a demon sitting on his shoulder and taunting him to stare at the still-lit seat-belt sign. He looked at Shauna, who occupied the window seat. He had the aisle, and they were fortunate, in their row of three, that the middle seat was vacant. Shauna had obviously decided to take advantage. She'd pulled her carry-on bag from beneath the seat in front of her and rested it between them. She wrested her laptop from it, opened her tray table and placed the computer on it.

After she turned it on, a look of concentration etched a small furrow between the soft arches of her brows. They were darker than the deepest blond shade of her long hair, which was still highlighted in soft streaks by the Arizona sun. Her unique hair color was something he had found extraordinarily appealing about her long ago. One of many things.

If there hadn't been a vacant seat, Hunter wondered if he'd have offered to trade with the person unlucky enough to have been assigned the uncomfortable middle. Would he have wanted to spend this hour separated from Shauna that way?

Not that he had any desire to be close to her…although *desire* was a poor choice of words. Hell, yes, he still desired her. But long ago he'd made self-control an unbreakable habit. It was the only way his P.I. business could survive.

The only way *he* could survive.

Without so much as a glance toward him, Shauna began to type. Was she writing another of her damned stories that she would use to drive some other poor jerk mad by claiming it would come true?

Muttering something without quite knowing what, Hunter bent to retrieve his small briefcase from under the seat in front of him and yanked out Shauna's story. He started to read it…until pain forced him to close his eyes.

When he opened them again, Shauna was watching him.

"Hunter, do you want to talk about—"

He hadn't brought her along to practice her psychology mumbo jumbo on him. "Is that another of your fortune-telling fairy tales?" His words spit out as he nodded toward her computer. Her graceful fingers still rested on the keyboard as if poised to peck out more nonsense.

"That's not your business." Her tone was conversational, but the glint in her eyes told him she was peeved.

She was right. It wasn't his business, unless it concerned Andee. That didn't make him any less curious. Or less peeved with himself, too, for taking his anxiety out on her. Again.

Maybe she couldn't help writing that story. How would he know? It wasn't like he'd bombarded her with questions before, when they'd been together.

He looked around. At least with all the plane noise, no one could have heard what he'd said.

When he turned back, Shauna's smile was forced. "Actually, I'm writing the story I started out to do when…when the story about Andee came out. I do that, you know—write little tales I read aloud at story time at Fantasy Fare. Kids who come in tell me what they want to hear, and most often that's what comes out when I sit at the computer. A boy whose parents bring him about once a week asked for a story about his dog Duke, and that's what I'm working on."

"Why didn't you just write your shaggy-dog story before and leave Andee alone?"

He didn't mean to ask that. Worse, though he could have taken another of her indignant glares, he hated the renewed look of sympathy she turned on him.

Shauna reached over with her closest hand and pulled his from where it clutched the armrest. He didn't fight her as she rested it on top of her bag on the seat between them, and squeezed gently. Her hand was much smaller than his, but it was strong. He stared at the point of contact between them, at the light polish on her short nails, her slender, curled fingers, feeling as if her strength suddenly radiated through his skin and up his arm.

But it wasn't her strength that singed him with that deceptively innocent touch.

"So tell me," he said, trying to sound conversational as he restrained his anger with this woman and her sympathy and her seemingly unconscious seduction.

Or was he angrier with himself? He had been the one to coerce her into accompanying him. And now that they were together, he acknowledged to himself that he wanted her.

He'd missed her.

"Tell you…?"

"About your stories." He kept his voice even. "You sit down to write something about a dog and a kidnapping comes out instead?"

Her eyes grew huge. Why were they dampening that way?

Was she trying to lay a guilt trip on him for just asking a simple—well, maybe not so simple. Even if he believed it.

"You never asked before," she said in a soft, husky voice. More forcefully, she continued, "And I know how hard it is for you to even pretend to give credence to my...my—"

"Let's just use 'fairy tale' again," he said wryly. "It's all-purpose enough to suit many situations, right?"

The smile on her full, kiss-me-quick-or-die-from-wanting lips quivered for an instant, then grew wistful. "Sure," she said. "You know I don't ask for that kind of...fairy tale to come out. The firstborn woman in each generation of my family has the ability. It's easier in some ways for me since I've grown up having computers. My Grandma O'Leary would just be sitting at a table somewhere, go involuntarily into...well, let's call it a trance, and when she woke up, she found she'd engaged in automatic writing, pen to paper. My mother used a typewriter. I just sit at the computer and what I write is there on the screen when I...when I become conscious of it. I don't know if I actually go into a trance, but my eyes close."

"And these stories always come true?" He made little attempt to hide his scorn, especially since he knew what she was going to say. He'd heard this part of her claims before.

"You know the answer," she said quietly, trying to withdraw her hand for the first time. He didn't let her, exchanging her firm grip for his own. "It's not so much that they *come* true. They *are* true."

"Because you sense someone's emotions? How bizarre is that? Is that why you became a shrink as well as a restaurant owner? To come up with an explanation of how those supposed emotions come from people you don't even know, like this 'Big T'? And Andee." His voice grew hoarse on those last couple of words, and he cleared his throat.

"I never said I could explain why, Hunter. And I became a therapist for other reasons. But, yes, the stories emanate from someone else's strong emotions while they're feeling them. Like the people in this one. And those years ago when I picked up on those vicious bank robbers you were after.''

"I didn't ask about that," Hunter snapped.

"No, you never did." Shauna's voice was sad. "Or at least not in any helpful way. You didn't want to hear about it then, but if you'd like to now—"

Hunter used the excuse of a slight rumbling behind him to turn his head. A flight attendant asked someone what he wanted to drink. "Some other time," he said to Shauna. Yeah, like the twenty-second century. Pulling down his tray table, he considered ordering an alcoholic drink but discarded the idea. He needed his wits about him.

"Coffee," he growled when the flight attendant asked what he wanted. "Black. Thanks."

But what did he really want?

To be in L.A. a lot faster than this plane was going.

And then, his daughter.

Peace.

And Shauna back in Oasis. Out of his life again.

Every time she was in it, she messed with his mind. Made him feel like he'd lost control of everything important to him.

And that wasn't all. Even now that he wasn't touching her, he felt uncomfortable. Physically.

For now, and much too frequently since he'd been in her presence again, the involuntary reactions of his much too impulsive body reminded him vividly of some of the reasons Shauna had once been such an important part of his life.

Shauna took a sip of apple juice, then returned the plastic glass to the tray table of the seat between Hunter and her.

He was sipping his coffee.

And reading, again, her story about Andee's kidnapping.

Anguish knit his thick, dark brows into a single tortured line. Anguish that she, however unintentionally, had helped to paint there.

She couldn't change the story. But maybe she could ease the rest of this flight for him, if only a little.

"Tell me about Andee, Hunter," she said.

He glanced at her. "I thought you were writing about a dog."

She nodded. "But I'd like to hear about your daughter." She'd known when Andee was born—and not just because Elayne had proudly yet sympathetically revealed to Shauna that she'd become a grandmother.

In fact, Shauna hadn't had to see photos of Hunter at Elayne's over the years to recall poignantly how vibrantly male he was—and how painfully missing from her life. Now and then, stories about him had flowed through her fingertips, generated by his own rampant emotions.

Like the day he had opened his own private investigation agency. The day he'd married.

The day Andee was born.

The day his divorce was final.

She had printed those stories and stuck them in one of her file cabinets. With improvements in technology, she'd changed computers over the years, so she'd had to save the stories onto disks before discarding the old equipment. In any event, she hadn't looked at any of them afterward, on paper or on computer.

"Andee's a great kid," Hunter said. "She's beautiful. Smart. She can even read a little already. She doesn't deserve what's in this damn story. And even if it's not true and she hasn't been kidnapped, she doesn't deserve to be lost. Or scared. She's only five years old."

His voice cracked. Shauna reached toward him and touched his shoulder in comfort, but he flinched.

That hurt as much as if he had slapped her.

"Of course she doesn't deserve it." Inside, Shauna was screaming. What good did it do anyone for her to write those stories? Maybe it was better for people not to know what they'd be facing.

But *that* was why she had become a therapist: To help the friends and strangers she wrote about through this kind of horror.

But what good was she if she couldn't, in some manner, help the man she had once loved?

She racked her brain for something she'd learned to balance her own painful emotions and came up with nothing.

"Okay, Shauna," Hunter said after a long moment. "I never wanted to believe your stories were real, but sometimes things in them seemed uncanny. So let's work this through, just in case. We tried to fix the ending on your computer but couldn't save changes. But we hadn't done anything different from what was on the pages. The story says I start my own search for my daughter. What if, when I return to L.A., I turn it over to the police and stay out of it? If you wrote that into your story, could the changes be saved? Maybe that would fix the ending." He grabbed his forehead with one of his large hands. "Listen to me," he muttered. "Talk about buying into craziness…"

"Okay, let's engage in 'what ifs.' You've already told the police, and that's in the story, even though you mentioned your—your ex-wife—said, when she called the second time, that she'd heard from the kidnapper and he said not to involve the authorities. That doesn't change the story. You could just let the police look for Andee. But that's not logical for you. You're a former cop, a private investigator, so of course you'd look for her, like the story says."

"But what if I didn't?" he insisted.

Shauna drew in a deep breath. "I've learned that even changing in a logical way what happens in real life from the way it's written in my stories…well, I was never able to save the changes. And the ending always stayed the same." She'd tried to speak matter-of-factly. It didn't work. Her respiration increased, and tears closed her throat. She turned to study the now-blank computer screen.

"You're talking about your father, aren't you?"

Amazingly, Hunter's voice was filled with sympathy. Surprised, she darted a glance toward him. This time, he took her hand.

She nodded, wanting to talk about it. *Not* wanting to talk about it. Not now.

She was relieved when the sound of the aircraft's engines changed and its altitude decreased. The captain announced the final descent into Los Angeles. She used the distraction to pull her hand back, shut down her computer and start putting it away.

She was not sure whether to be glad or sorry this ride was nearly over. She sensed a truce between Hunter and her.

He still wouldn't admit to believing her stories…exactly. Nor did he shove his disbelief in her face.

But how would things go in Los Angeles while he searched for Andee?

And when it was all over, and the ending of the story had come to pass?

He might be ambivalent now. But then he would hate her.

So, for now, she had to dredge up every nuance of her psychology classes, everything she'd learned, to help Hunter. And his ex-wife.

And herself.

For, despite everything she had told herself in the past seven years, being with Hunter now made clear one very important thing: she had never completely gotten over him.

Chapter 4

Because it was summer, daylight still glowed when they arrived at Margo Masters's home.

Shauna noticed right away that the light blue stucco house was larger than the others on its crowded residential block in Sunland, an area in the northern San Fernando Valley. It was the only one with a second floor. Had it had been added by Margo, or had she bought it that way?

Or had this been where Hunter, too, had lived when they were married?

That thought snatched all the charm she'd noticed from the home as she preceded Hunter along the winding front walk between patches of well-manicured lawn.

There hadn't been a detailed description in her story of where the kidnapping occurred. But then, there never were great descriptions. Sometimes, she had to use intuition to determine the origin of the emotions that set her stories into play.

This time, because it had involved Hunter's family, the origin had been obvious.

If only *all* connections with Hunter had been severed when he'd left. That was a laugh, after all those stories she'd written in the interim.

Hunter had driven them here in his sporty silver GTO, which he'd parked near LAX while away on business. Now Shauna waited while he stepped around her and rang the bell. Margo pulled the door open in less than a minute. Shauna recognized her. She'd looked the struggling actress up on the Internet after writing her story about Hunter's marriage.

"Thank heavens you're finally here," she exclaimed, her low, throaty voice conveying simultaneously both relief and criticism. She glanced at Shauna without saying anything. "Oh, Hunter, it's been terrible." Tears glittered in her eyes.

"Yeah," he said, that single word conveying both acknowledgment of her pain and the expression of his own. "Anything new?"

"Yes," Margo wailed. "You need to control your assistant. And make sure that policeman he called doesn't do anything to put Andee in worse danger—if it isn't already too late."

Shauna, inhaling the strong and probably expensive scent wafting around the woman, forced herself not to stare at her flawless beauty: high cheekbones, smooth skin, softly pouting lips, shoulder-length light brown hair shimmering with auburn highlights. She wore a short white shirt and slim black slacks. Margo wasn't a tall woman, but even in her wired emotional state she held herself regally, and the movement of her hand as she motioned them inside was as graceful as a model's.

Her eyes were pale brown. Shauna had no doubt that the way they'd been enhanced with makeup sometime earlier that day would have rendered them outstanding and gorgeous. But Margo's crying had caused her makeup to run, turning her beauty fragile and sad.

Margo preceded them into her living room. Three men seated in the conversation area around a low, polished coffee table rose at their entrance. A woman, too.

Hunter made the first introductions. "Everyone, this is

Shauna O'Leary. Shauna, you met Margo Masters at the door. This is Detective Arthur Banner.'' He gestured toward one of the two men who'd been seated on chairs. ''And Simon Wells.'' Hunter pointed to the guy beside Banner.

Shauna knew that Simon was Hunter's assistant at Strahm Solutions. He was not quite as tall as Hunter and barrel-chested, and had a brown mustache darker than the longish hair on his head. He wore a tweed sport jacket over a brown mock turtleneck. As he bowed his head in greeting, Shauna had the incongruous impression of old-world courtliness. If they'd been closer, she'd not have been surprised if he'd kissed her hand.

Arthur Banner, on the other hand, was tall, thin, reserved, and seemed to memorize everything about Shauna in a single, prolonged look with small but omniscient gray eyes. Hunter had told her about the police detective, whose nickname ''Banger'' was a joke, for he was trustworthy, an all-cop cop.

Margo had slipped past Hunter and now stood between the other two people in the room. ''My friends BillieAnn Callahan and John Keenan Aitken,'' she said, finishing the introductions. Not that Margo had said, but Shauna figured that BillieAnn and John were fellow actors. Though both were dressed casually, their self-possession suggested they awaited their next cue. BillieAnn was taller than Margo, but still resembled a pixie, with her short, wispy cap of dark brown hair around ears that protruded a little too much, pouty lips painted deep red with shiny gloss, and short, clingy blouse with flowing sleeves.

Aitken put a protective arm around Margo. He was of moderate height, slim, a Cary Grant type with an air of savoir faire punctuated by his raised chin and cool smile. The impression was destroyed, though, by his clothes: blue jeans and a muscle shirt adorned with the logo of a Hollywood theater.

''Can I get everyone something to drink?'' Margo asked, as if this was a social gathering.

"I'll get it," BillieAnn said. But no one took them up on the offer, though Shauna was tempted. Her mouth felt dry.

Hunter sat down at the edge of one of two matched antique-looking sofas that faced one another, both with beige damask upholstery and carved backs and legs. He was brawny enough to look as out of place as the proverbial bull in a china shop. But maybe he liked this kind of furniture now.

Shauna noticed how he'd made himself right at home. And why not? Even though he was no longer married to Margo, he undoubtedly spent time here with their daughter.

Shauna ignored the hurt that constricted her throat. She was long past that particular pain.

As Shauna joined him, Margo's friends resumed their seats on the sofa matching the one where Hunter and Shauna sat, and Margo slid between them. Simon and Banger sat once more on the high-back chairs they had vacated at the same end of the coffee table.

Vases, figurines and other knickknacks graced the table and glass shelves at the room's corners. They looked old, too, and valuable.

A five-year-old child had played here? The place didn't look childproof to Shauna, who made sure there were no sharp corners or anything she valued too much to get broken around Fantasy Fare, particularly in the small room where she told stories three nights a week. Just a lot of plants.

Margo rose again, as if too full of energy to stay seated. She walked to the side of the sofa where Hunter sat. And why not? She had every right to share his pain and partake in mutual comfort.

Instead, shaking her head, she moaned, "What are you try-ing to do, Hunter?"

She swayed, and BillieAnn and John immediately took their places again at her sides. She tossed them thankful smiles. "I promised to stay calm, so I will. But I told Hunter the kid-napper said we weren't to tell anyone. And did he listen? No, he sent his assistant." Pursing her lips, she blinked at Simon.

"*He* called the police, which is even more against the rules."
Banger received her next fearful glower. "I couldn't take any
more, so I called BillieAnn and John. I know I can trust them,
at least." Her demeanor changing from anxious to angry, she
took a step toward Hunter. "And then you bring this woman
here." Her glare at Shauna oozed malice. "Your old girlfriend. You told me about her before, and I recognized her
name. Do you think this is a joke? Do you want Andee
killed?"

Fighting the urge to wince, Shauna shifted her gaze to
Hunter, to see his response to the verbal assault.

Cold fury gleamed in his green eyes. He stood and walked
behind the sofa, glaring not at Margo but across the room,
between Simon's and Banger's shoulders. When he spoke his
voice was ominously quiet—a tone Shauna remembered well,
from the end of their relationship. Then, when it was directed
at her, it had churned her stomach, drawn tears into her eyes.

"I was out of town when you called, Margo. You know
that. I didn't want to wait to get a search for Andee started.
That's why I asked Simon to talk to you. He did the right
thing by requesting police assistance. He called Arthur because we've worked with him before and know he's a good
guy."

"But why *her?*" Margo cried. "She's not a cop or an investigator. You told me she ran a restaurant. How will that
help us find Andee?"

Shauna wasn't about to explain her involvement. In fact,
Hunter and she had discussed whether to tell anyone about
her story. Their decision: no one but Simon. Hunter had insisted on telling him, since Simon was his closest friend, all-
around assistant and near-partner in Strahm Solutions. He
wouldn't have to believe what he was told, but it would explain why Hunter had already asked him to start investigating
stuff that otherwise would look off base.

And Margo? No way would Shauna want Hunter's former
wife to think of his long-ago lover as weird, an unnatural

creature. Even if the thing she did that sounded weird was true.

Before Hunter attempted a reply to Margo, Shauna stood. "I understand how hard this must be for you, Ms. Masters. Hunter asked me to come here expressly to help *you*. I do own a restaurant. But I'm also a licensed psychologist and my specialty is working with people in crisis situations." She felt the sting of Hunter's glare but ignored it. Who knew? Maybe she could be of help that way. "I'm here for you to talk to, and if you'd like I can offer advice on coping with the stress."

Ignoring Shauna, Margo moved from the circle of her friends. At Hunter's side, she threw her head back and looked up into his face. "You brought your old girlfriend here to give me advice? That's sick, Hunter. Get her out of here. Now."

"I would welcome your advice anytime, Shauna," said Simon in a British accent as upper-crust as his rigid posture as he stood and joined her. Shauna smiled gratefully at his teasing expression. Had Hunter told him about her story yet?

"Okay," she said, in a tone that suggested she was bantering back, "I'd advise you to come outside with me while Hunter and Margo—"

"Bad idea." Banger rose and strode toward Margo. "You don't have to talk to Shauna or anyone about how you feel. But you've delayed enough. Now, we are going to talk. You insisted on waiting till Hunter got here before answering my questions."

"I talked to Simon before," Margo protested, "but—"

Banger continued as if she hadn't spoken. "It's time you cooperated with the police. So, we'll sit down, Shauna included, and chat. Not your friends, though. They can come back later if you need company."

"If she stays," Margo hissed, "my friends can, too."

Wondering why Banger, who didn't know her background, wasn't kicking her out, too, Shauna opened her mouth to say that was fine, she'd go—but Hunter gave a quick shake of his head. She didn't want to argue with him.

She didn't want to argue with anyone.

Least of all Margo Masters, whose emotions seemed to mutate moment by moment, from sad to accusatory, to who knew what?

Give her a break. The woman's child was missing.

Hers and Hunter's.

Once, Shauna had thought *she* would have Hunter's child someday....

Dragging defeatedly, Margo retreated to the sofa and sat. BillieAnn joined her, and John took his place behind them both, one hand on Margo's shoulder.

Margo aimed a baleful glance toward Shauna.

"Now, if you two would excuse us." Hunter looked from John to BillieAnn and back again.

"We're not going anywhere if Margo wants us here," BillieAnn protested.

"I agree." John's voice was modulated but firm. "Although I've an audition coming up, so I can't stay much longer."

Then Shauna had been right; Margo's friends were actors, or at least one was.

"It's okay." Margo's tone was cheerfully courageous. "I'll call you both later. Thanks so much for coming." She followed them, presumably to see them to the door.

As the three left the room, Shauna said, "If it's going to cause problems for me to be here—"

"Stay here," Hunter commanded. And then, more softly, he added, "Please."

She might wind up having to pick her battles with the man. This one was a no-brainer. Shauna stayed where she was.

A minute later, Margo returned. "All right," she said, a catch in her voice. "I don't like being ganged up on like this, but what do you want?"

"It's our intention to find Andee for you, Ms. Masters,"

said Simon, "yet we need your guidance. You are the closest to an eyewitness that we have." His aristocratic accent added once more to the formality of his words.

"Start at the beginning," Hunter told Margo. "I know you told me before, but I want everyone to hear. Tell us exactly what happened when Andee disappeared."

Hunter wanted to get on the move to find Andee, if he only had a clue where to look.

He also wanted to throttle his ex-wife. She should be tossing them clues. That was in the strategy Hunter had started developing, since it made sense.

Hell, nothing made sense right now.

He'd seen the pain in Shauna's expression when Margo attacked her. Found himself admiring Shauna for her composure under fire. She was here only because he'd dragged her along, in case she could be of help. Not as a shrink, of course, but no one else needed to know the real reason.

And though he would never admit it to her—didn't want even to admit it to himself—as a psychologist or not, her presence was of some comfort, at least to him.

Banger must have picked up on it, or at least on something regarding Shauna, since he hadn't told her to leave as he had Margo's drama-society support system. Or maybe he just liked the looks of her. Who wouldn't?

Right now, Margo's cluelessness and nastiness were only a fraction of why Hunter wanted to wring her neck.

On top of everything else, now that she had an audience, her description of how she'd reacted to Andee's disappearance was heartrending, as if Margo, and not their missing daughter, should be at the center of their concerns.

"I was only inside for a couple of minutes," she said. She was seated now, her face in her hands, her voice muffled. "I—I expected a call about an audition, but I'd forgotten to carry the portable phone. Andee was outside, waving one of those wands that blow giant bubbles. I grabbed the phone and went right out again, but when I returned to the backyard, the wand was there but Andee wasn't."

Her voice broke, and she shuddered as she cried into her hands. "I'm so sorry," she sobbed. "I know I haven't always been a good mother, but I love Andee. We have to find her."

If she hadn't been Margo, an actress whose stock-in-trade of over-the-top emotion Hunter had seen all too often as she'd manipulated him, he'd have felt sorry for her. Might have held her, to ease her pain.

But as he'd gotten to know her, after they were married, he had lost all certainty as to what was feigned and what was real.

She'd given him custody of Andee easily enough. Having a kid burdened an up-and-coming unmarried actress.

On the other hand, even if she admittedly wasn't an ideal mother, Andee was her child, too.

"Tell us how you attempted to find her." Simon, bless him, had gone to Margo's side and rested a hand consolingly on her back.

She looked up, and her eyes actually were red, swollen and wet—and they looked directly at Hunter.

Which made him feel about three inches tall. What a louse he was. Of course she cared that their daughter was missing.

"I'm sorry, Hunter," she said. "It's all my fault. The gate was shut, so at first I thought she'd followed me into the house without my noticing. I called her and looked around before I started getting really worried. But I couldn't find her."

More sobs. This time Hunter did approach her. Awkwardly, he touched her head.

In moments, she had stood and was crying against his chest.

Automatically his arms went around her. Even though it didn't feel natural to have her so close. Especially now.

His eyes involuntarily darted toward Shauna. She was watching them, a look of compassion on her face. And sadness.

And pain.

For Andee, of course. And, in sympathy for him, whether he wanted it or not.

He had no doubt it felt awkward to her to be in the same room as her onetime lover and his ex-wife. She had made it clear, though, she no longer cared for him. Any more than he still cared for her.

But he *did* still care for her…sort of. Nostalgically.

Even so, he gently pulled away from Margo, his eyes on Shauna. He could see her struggle to hide any emotion. Did she, perhaps, still have some feelings for him—other than to despise him for leaving all those years ago?

He looked deliberately away from her and into Margo's eyes. "We need to hear the rest," he told his ex-wife. Even though he had heard it from her before, on the phone.

Her story didn't change. She'd continued looking for Andee, then assumed she had somehow gotten out the gate and started wandering the neighborhood. Margo's backyard abutted a narrow alley, as did most other houses along her street and the one behind it. She didn't see anyone there, so she went up one road and down the next, knocked on a few doors. But no one had seen Andee. That was when she had first called Hunter.

The second time was after she had received a call from the kidnapper.

"It was a man. He said that if I told anyone besides her father, he'd kill her." She looked straight at Banger. "I wasn't to talk to the police. He said I could pay for her safe return and promised he'd be in touch to tell me what to do. And if I didn't follow his instructions, I'd never see my daughter again. If he saw anything in the media, or one of those Amber alerts, or anything public, it would be all over for Andee." Tears ran down her cheeks. Her gaze returned to Hunter. "I may have been at fault in the first place, but you brought in all these other people." She darted another brief, disapproving glance toward Shauna. "We've got to do as he says, Hunter."

He nodded, then turned to Banger. "Glad you're here," he said. "You've taken charge of this case, I hope, even though it's outside your division."

Banger's narrow, solemn head nodded. "That's right."

"Do I dare ask how you're managing it?"

"Not if you value your P.I. license," Banger growled, though a corner of his mouth quirked up as though it attempted a grin without his permission.

"Okay, then, here's something I do dare to ask. How about putting a listening device on Margo's phone?"

"What do you mean?" His ex sounded horrified.

"To trace the kidnapper when he calls again," Banger explained.

"Don't you need a warrant or something for that?" she asked.

"Only if the subject of the wiretap isn't aware or doesn't agree," Banger said. "Do you have any problem with it?"

"Of course not," Margo said. "Not if it will help get Andee back. But that means more people will know. And if word gets out—"

"We'll be careful," Banger said. "I've already got an investigation started. Mostly Foothill Division guys." He looked at Hunter. "They're okay. I know all the detectives on the case. They'll keep a low profile, don't worry."

For once, though, Hunter sided with Margo. "You'll have to be damned careful," he told the detective. "We can't take the chance of a leak. Any publicity will spook the kidnapper. In fact, I want to handle the canvassing of this neighborhood myself. Do you have any problem with that?"

Banger didn't look happy. "You know that if it wasn't your kid, I'd tell you to go pound sand and not interfere with a police investigation. But you and I have a history, so I'll cut you some slack and call off the guys I've got on the way—

for now. We'll work the case from some other angles. But I don't like it. I won't give you more than a day.''

"But that's not—'' Hunter protested.

"One day,'' Banger repeated. "And only regarding asking questions around here. The rest of the routine is already underway. I checked out Margo's yard personally when I got here, looked for evidence of the abduction, kept a log of what we did and what we found, dusted the gate's latch for prints, took a zillion photos of stuff big and small, that kind of thing. Not that it's regular procedure, but Simon assisted. Good thing you both were cops once and know the drill.''

Blessing Banger for having enough seniority and guts to take any heat for doing things his own way, Hunter asked, "Anything helpful?''

"Nada, so far. Not even Margo's prints on the latch. Looked like it was wiped clean. But we gathered print samples from the house and yard, plus some of Andee's things and other items from outside. Started a standard—more or less—report, including collection and chain of custody of evidence. I'll send what little we found to the lab for analysis soon as I get back to my office.'' He shook his head. "I'll let you take the initial swipe at asking questions around here, but you'll need to butt out otherwise. Though I'll keep our investigation as quiet as I can, a kidnapping's high priority. I've already called my most trusted FBI contact—maybe you know him, Lou Tennyson?''

"I know *of* him,'' Hunter said. "The feds all tend to be heavy-handed. The kidnapper has made it clear he'll harm his victim—'' He almost choked on the last—it seemed like such a detached way to refer to his sweet Andee. "—if there's any publicity at all. And the more people you get involved on this case, the more likelihood there is it'll leak out.''

Banger's slow nod made his long, thin face look even more doleful. "I'm doing my best, but you know I can't do *nothing*. While you're looking around here, my guys'll be asking questions at Andee's school, talking to parents of kids there, your neighbors, whatever. We'll give 'em a good cover story, like they're investigating you for a security clearance or something. Even so, word'll get out, count on it. A day, two days—'' He raised his hand to silence Hunter, who'd opened his mouth to protest. ''That's assuming we don't get her back right away, which we hope to do. But I'll keep a lid on it as long as I can—as much of a lid as can be on a kidnapping investigation.''

Through this discussion, Shauna appeared to be attentive, taking in every word. Only when they were nearly done did she venture a question to Margo. ''Can you think of anyone who might have taken your daughter?''

Margo, who'd cried quietly into her hands during the discussion, looked up tearily. Her tone was disdainful as she replied, ''I'd have told these men if I did.''

That had been a clue in Shauna's story, if it was true. Andee apparently knew her kidnapper. It was something Hunter intended to pursue, just in case. Right now, he gave Shauna credit for not flinching under Margo's contemptuous stare.

''Of course you'd tell them,'' she said soothingly. ''Tell me this, then. Do any of your friends or acquaintances go by nicknames that refer to letters, like their initials?''

Interesting question. Hunter had been racking his own brain for who this ''Big T'' could be but had come up with no one.

''What are you talking about?'' Margo's tone suggested bewilderment—unsurprisingly. It was a rather offbeat question.

''Just answer, please.'' Shauna could hardly say it was a clue that came to her out of the blue, or Banger would demand to know what she meant. And Shauna and Hunter had already agreed to avoid mentioning her story to the official investigators.

Looking at Hunter with exaggerated tolerance, Margo said, ''No, I don't know anyone who uses initials for their nicknames.''

"How about friends or acquaintances whose names—first or last—begin with the letter *T?*"

"What—?" Banger began.

"Just humor her," Hunter said. He jotted down the few names Margo mentioned, but they were mostly women. Shauna hadn't specified men, but her story, and Margo, had indicated that the kidnapper was male. A couple of the men Margo named were clearly name-dropping—big Hollywood celebrities whom his ex might have met at large industry parties.

When Margo threw up her hands and proclaimed she couldn't think of anyone else, Hunter suggested that they map out investigation tactics.

They continued their discussion until it became clear they could accomplish no more that night. Though what he wanted to do was to start pounding on doors right now, Hunter knew he'd only freak people out. He'd do what he could tonight on his computer, mapping out strategy, doing what research he could, directing Simon on the rest. Time for Shauna and him to leave.

Once they were in his car, Hunter headed for the San Diego Freeway, which he would take south toward his home. And his personal computer, which would serve him just as well, for now, as his office computer.

Then there was the other thing he intended to do. Or, rather, he intended Shauna to do.

"Are you okay?" Shauna asked.

"No. Are you? You should be pretty pleased with yourself. Everything's following your story so far, isn't it?"

"Yes," she said quietly. "Andee disappeared, and the kidnapper called her mother. Her father did the right thing and told the authorities, and enlisted their cooperation while he starts the search for his missing daughter."

"I'll change things—the outcome, at least," Hunter insisted. "Everything that's come true did so without my input, or I did it because it made sense."

"Don't blame yourself for mostly following the story," Shauna said. "Though I can't tell you why, I don't think you have much choice. And I can say from experience that even if you do things differently, it doesn't change anything."

"So you said." He knew he sounded irritable, but, hell, he believed in free will. No damned story was going to be so engraved in stone that real life would follow it.

His daughter would be fine.

"I'm still changing your story, Shauna," he finished. Fortunately, they were stopped at a red light near the freeway entrance. He looked at her.

The time was close to midnight, but they were under a streetlight. Shauna's brown eyes were wide and puzzled and even a little irritated. "Hunter, I've already explained—"

"Yeah, I know you think that changing something won't make a damned bit of difference. And even if I alter events and you enter the changes onto the computer, it won't save them. But I won't give up before I've even tried. Got it? And you've got to work with me, like it or not. That's why you came, isn't it—to help me?"

She was silent, biting her bottom lip as she obviously thought how to respond.

He once had nibbled on that same full, sexy lip. The top one, too.

And other places on her silky, sexy body—

But that was before. He'd keep his hands off her now, even if it killed him.

Because if he didn't, if he upset Shauna enough to make her leave, it might imperil his daughter's life even more.

Of course, that gave credence to the credibility of her damned story. But like it or not, he'd already given it credence. Ignoring it wasn't an option.

He'd learned his lesson the hard way before.

"Okay, Hunter," she said quietly. "I'll stay, at least for a while. If I can do anything at all to help Andee, you know I will. And if the best I can do is to help you accept—"

"I'll never accept that," he retorted, his voice raised. "Don't play shrink with me." He noticed that the light had turned green. Fortunately, there was no one behind them.

"All right," Shauna said sadly. Her hand touched his cheek. His eyes closed as his senses drank in the contact— the softness of her skin, her unique scent, which was neither too sweet nor too spicy. His entire body responded with awareness of Shauna and her touch, her closeness to him after so many long years. Good thing they were still stopped.

His eyes popped open, and he turned to look at her. She withdrew her hand, but it still hovered between them. He'd have shoved it away if all he'd seen was sympathy on her face. It wasn't. Yet…was it desire darkening the brown of her eyes?

Did she feel it, too?

Lord, how he wanted to take her into his arms, the way he once did. Make love with her, to forget all that was happening, if only for a few, wonderful minutes.

She looked away first. "You missed the light."

He glanced in that direction. "Yeah."

"I don't have reservations, but are there any hotels around here?" She swiveled in her seat. They'd driven a ways from Margo's into a rougher area of town. There was no way he would leave Shauna here.

"You're staying with me," he said.

"I can't, Hunter." Her voice was low, husky, but this time, as the light changed, he didn't look at her.

"Yeah, you can. I'll keep my hands off you, don't worry." He *had* to.

"Like I said, I'm changing your story, Shauna. And for that you need to hang around. You'll come with me when I ask questions. Help me brainstorm what else to do. You can gather new and different stuff to type in while you're along for the ride. In the story, I investigate alone. Now, I'll have an assistant along. If enough is thrown into your story that's different, maybe the ending will change. And having you with me, when in the story I go it alone, will be a good start. Deal?''

They were on the freeway, and the best he could do in the silence was to glance momentarily at her. She was staring straight ahead. Her upper teeth were again worrying her lower lip in that same, sexy manner.

He wouldn't let it affect him.

"Well?" he prompted.

"Okay, Hunter," she finally said. "Deal."

Chapter 5

Though Hunter's house was in Brentwood, an area on the west side of Los Angeles that Shauna knew was upscale, it seemed even more low-key for its area than Margo's.

She could see in the lights along the wide street that his place was the smallest on the block, not the largest—white stucco and boxy looking, a modest, well-tended yard around it. Hunter drove his GTO down the driveway to the back of the house. The door inside the attached garage opened right into the kitchen, which was compact, outdated and cluttered.

A cookie jar shaped like a smiling pig sat on the counter beside the side-by-side refrigerator. On top of the butcher-block table was a box of sweetened kiddy cereal and under it was a bright plastic child's step stool.

All signs that a child lived here, and was loved. The little everyday items left in homey disarray nearly broke Shauna's heart.

Hunter had insisted on bringing in both her small suitcase and his, though she toted her own laptop. "I'll show you to the guest room." He led her through the kitchen and down a narrow hall decorated with framed pictures of Andee alone, Andee and Elayne, and Andee with Hunter. But none with Andee and her mother. Not a surprise, since Hunter and Margo had been divorced two years or more, but recognizing that fact helped Shauna relax a little. Not that it should matter.

Hunter turned on the light in the guest room and put down her suitcase. Beyond were a couple more doors—his room and Andee's, Shauna assumed.

The uncluttered guest room was small, with a twin bed in the center. The quilt appeared old and well used. There was a sliding closet door on one side and a bare table on the other, with a chair pushed up under it.

Shauna walked inside. A slightly musty smell hung in the air, as if the room was seldom used. But when she opened the closet to hang up the few clothes she had brought, she saw hanging there a white terry-cloth robe in Elayne's size and favorite style. This must be the room where she stayed when she visited her son and granddaughter in L.A.

"I know it's late," Hunter said from the doorway. "You're probably beat, and I intend to get going early tomorrow, but I'd still like you to do one thing before you get ready for bed."

"What's that?"

"Boot up your computer and see if we changed things enough today to let you save any modifications to the story."

Feeling stricken, Shauna stared at him. Other than a pulse working at the side of his broad jaw, he showed no emotion. Even the expression in his eyes, which often revealed his feelings to her, looked impassive.

Inside him, however, she sensed a whole lot more going on.

"I know that's why you wanted me to come, Hunter, but—"

He waved one arm to erase what she might be planning to say. He had rolled up the sleeves of his casual blue shirt, revealing sinewy forearms sprinkled with hair as dark as that on his head.

She didn't know why a glimpse of something as innocuous as partially bared arms should send a rush of heat through her, but it did. She ignored it. Sort of.

"Humor me," he said. "It's not like I've forgotten you've said your stories don't change. Whatever other signs of aging might have overtaken me in the last seven years, memory loss isn't one of them. At least not enough to worry me—yet." Amazingly, he smiled. Not one of the huge, hearty, life-embracing smiles he'd once bestowed on Shauna, but definitely an improvement over the scowls and other dark expressions she had almost grown used to since he'd appeared at his mother's earlier that day. Had it really only been a few hours ago?

"All right, Hunter." In a minute, she'd removed her computer from her carry-on and set it up on the table. Unsure how much battery power remained, she plugged it into an electric outlet along the wall and booted it up.

She opened the file containing the story, and held her breath as she scrolled to where she assumed the timing of the story intersected where they were right now—the end of the same day as the kidnapping:

Why was the bad man T acting so mean? He'd always been nice to Andee before. And now he was even making her stay in a room by herself.

As soon as the bad man shut the door, Andee got down off the bed. He had told her to go to sleep, but how could she? She was so scared. "Daddy," she whimpered into the darkness. A tiny bit of light shone from under the door. Andee turned the knob.

It was locked.

The window in the room was too high for Andee to reach. From underneath, she pulled the drapes to the side and looked up.

It was dark outside, too. No moon, or even stars, in the little bit of sky she could see.

Sadly she let go of the drapes, crawled back up into bed.

"Please fly home from your trip now, Daddy," she whispered, *"and come get me."* And then she began to cry.

Shauna felt Hunter's hands grip her upper arms as he read over her shoulder. He must be reading the same part, too.

Andee wasn't the only one crying. But through her tears, Shauna continued reading, determined to finish this part. Again.

And outside the room, Big T turned on the television and put on the news, just to be sure his orders had not been disobeyed. He smiled as he heard the usual things about terrorist attacks, politicians and the weather report. Fair and sunny.

Nothing about a missing child.

So Big T went to bed, too.

Shauna turned and looked up at Hunter when she had finished reading this segment. He didn't release her arms. To encourage her, or to help his own emotional condition? She didn't know.

She only knew how conscious she was of his touch.

"I'll try to change it now," she told him, her voice cracking. She gently eased her arms away from him. She needed unfettered access to the keyboard, after all.

Though there was no type of modification she hadn't attempted when she'd prayed to save her father's life, she figured that if she could change anything, it would be something small. She decided to type in a change that reflected today's reality. It wouldn't hurt, even if it wouldn't help.

She put her cursor on the paragraph that described Andee's getting back into bed. She changed what the child said. Instead of, *Please fly home from your trip now, Daddy, and come get me,* she entered, *I know you're home from your trip now, Daddy. Please come get me.*

"Okay?" she asked Hunter.

"Sure. Why not?" His tone was even huskier than hers, and though his words were nonchalant, she was well aware that his attitude wasn't.

Shauna put the cursor on the Save icon, watched for an instant while the little hourglass on the screen tipped and emptied, then closed the document.

She inhaled and exhaled a couple of long, uneasy breaths. "Ready?" she asked.

"Do it," he said, his voice tight.

The file opened on the beginning of the story again. Shauna scrolled through it until she got to where she'd made the change.

And gasped.

The words attributed to Andee on the page said, *I know you're home from your trip now, Daddy. Please come get me.*

"It worked!" Hunter shouted from above her.

The tears that Shauna had shed only a minute earlier seemed like a drizzle compared with the downfall that now wet her cheeks. She couldn't believe it.

It had never happened before.

She must have said those words aloud, for Hunter said, "But it happened now. It happened now!"

Her hands shaking, Shauna reached into her bag and extracted a blank disk. She shoved it into the computer and again went through the routine to get it to save, this time onto the A drive.

Once again, when the computer was through, she closed the file. And once again, when she opened it, the change was there.

Shauna scrolled slowly through the document. She hadn't tried to change anything else, so it wasn't a surprise that the rest of the story read the same as before.

But this time, something she had changed had actually remained there. How had it happened? *Look at that, Grandma!* Shauna thought jubilantly.

"Let me try," Hunter said. His intense expression looked

elated—the kind of expression that had once given Shauna chills of desire when it had resulted from something she had done or said. Something they had participated in together. Dinner at one of their favorite dives. A walk through a desert museum. A slow, sensuous dance in the dark at a club they both loved.

Now Hunter all but pushed her out of the way, sat on the chair she vacated and went to the end of the document.

As he had tried earlier that day, at Shauna's house, he deleted the entire ending and replaced it with something shorter. Happier. Andee was saved, Big T was captured, and all was well.

That change didn't save.

"Damn." The single word was bitter. "You do it," he told Shauna. "Just the way you made it work before."

As she slid into the chair again, her eyes were on him. He held one hand to his head as if in pain and disbelief. "It doesn't matter," he muttered. "Stories that come true, my ass. Why the hell do I even worry about this one?"

"Because you've seen my stories come true enough that you can't discount them," Shauna said quietly. "Otherwise, you'd have ignored my call, not come to Oasis, not brought me along."

Anguish doused the light in his green eyes. "Then fix it, Shauna. You've changed some of it. Change the rest."

"I'll try," she said softly. She had no idea why she was able to save that small change. And she wasn't surprised when her new modification to the end didn't save. "I'm sorry, Hunter."

"Good night, Shauna." He headed for the door. His broad shoulders, usually thrust back as if in unconscious pride, were bent like a much older man's. His stride was slow, pained. Tortured.

Without thinking, Shauna raced to his side. "Wait."

"I've got work to do." He didn't look at her.

She had spent years conducting therapy sessions with people in crisis, to help in situations like this. She couldn't let him leave without trying to help him deal with his pain.

She took his arm. "It'll help if you talk about how you're feeling."

"No thanks." He shook off her grip.

"Please let me—"

"You've done enough for one night," he snarled. Then, he said, more sadly, "You gave me hope, then took it away."

She shriveled at his words and beneath his tormented gaze before he tore it away. "That's not fair. You've been acting as if you blame me for what's happened. I know you're hurting, but let me help you. Don't push me away."

"Sorry." He shrugged. "You're right. I'm not blaming anyone but the piece of crud who stole my daughter. But what you wrote—"

"My stories don't cause what happens," Shauna interrupted defensively.

"Maybe," he replied. "I don't know if what you did years ago was on purpose. It doesn't matter. I don't think what you did *tonight* was intentional. And you're right—after what I saw in the past, I can't discount the possibility that you write stories that come true. That's why it's almost worse now. You changed a few words after claiming all those times that you couldn't even modify something minor. But the ending stayed the same." He closed his eyes, and when he opened them again he continued toward the door.

"I wish I could change everything, Hunter," Shauna said, her pain magnified by his. She couldn't help him. She couldn't help herself. Yet once more she laid her hand on the bared, warm skin of his arm. "We'll try again, I promise." She hesitated. "Even though I can't promise that—"

She stopped speaking as his eyes, trained on hers, suddenly turned from dull green to flashing jade. He bent down, took her into his arms and kissed her. Hard.

She knew it was simply to shut her up. Prevent her from finishing what she'd been saying.

But her knees nearly collapsed beneath her as he held her.

She remembered the feel of his lips on hers, had longed for it. And now that she experienced it once again, she knew nothing in all those heated, fiery recollections had been exaggerated by time, or her imagination.

She kissed him back with a longing born of seven years of missing him.

With passion that she knew should instead, for now, be compassion. But she was no more able to stop herself from tasting him, reaching up along his back, moving her hands down to grip his tight buttocks, than she could prevent her lungs from drawing in air.

But he pulled back. Even as she knew he would. Even as she knew *she* should. This wasn't years ago, when they were lovers. This was today, and they were drawn together by circumstances too horrible to contemplate.

Too dreadful to be sublimated in a few moments of heat that they would both only regret later.

Hunter stared down at her for a long second, the dull bleakness returning to his eyes.

''Good night, Shauna,'' he said again.

And this time he was gone.

He had to be out of his ever-lovin' mind.

Hunter was certain of it the next morning as he sat across from Shauna in the fast-food restaurant where he'd taken her for breakfast. Though he intended to make this a quick meal, get on the road as soon as possible, it was only six-thirty, still too early to knock on doors without nervous people calling the cops on him. His legs itching to move, he pretended to read the sports section of the *Los Angeles Times* so he wouldn't have to talk.

Shauna was reading the front page. Or maybe she was feigning it, too.

Bad enough that he'd given her a hard time for stuff he really couldn't blame her for.

What was worse was the way he'd grabbed her, with no warning—not even to himself. And then he'd given her a kiss. One that could have knocked not only his socks off, but his shoes, his pants, his boxers…Lord, how he'd wanted to touch her more. Kiss her everywhere. And then—

Only then had he decided to play it cool.

Just like the weak coffee he now sipped from a decorated foam cup.

He had to get control of himself. Of everything.

He took a bite of his breakfast sandwich. He'd only been gone a few days, but all he had to eat at his place was stuff Andee liked. But now his daughter was missing. Kidnapped.

He crumpled the edges of the newspaper in his fingers before he chilled out enough to relax, just a little.

He had been up all night, working at the computer he kept in the corner of his bedroom, taking what little control he could of the situation. That was how he dealt with his cases: by organizing. He devised a detailed investigation plan for each, and followed it. Got results, then he turned them over to the client—along with a healthy invoice.

But how the hell could he take control of his daughter's kidnapping?

By using Shauna and her story? How? So what if some piddly detail had changed? It was the end that mattered. If *anything* mattered.

When he'd gotten his arms around Shauna years ago, it had been physically, which had him crazy from pleasure. But he'd never gotten his arms around what she claimed to do with her writing. And that had driven him really crazy.

Across from him now, she calmly sipped her coffee. He visualized himself as that cup, meeting her pliant, hungry lips again.

Shauna glanced up from the paper and caught his eye. He looked back at the article on the Dodgers he'd been trying to read for the past three minutes. But it wasn't the team that turned his breathing so fast and irregular that he could have been running bases himself.

"I don't see anything in the news about Andee, thank heavens," Shauna said quietly. She wore a gold Arizona State University T-shirt this morning, and he liked the way it looked, with waves of her blond hair spilling over the shoulders.

He liked the way it hugged her curves, too.

"That's a good thing," he agreed.

He shouldn't be noticing the way the clinging material molded around her lovely, firm breasts. But he'd thought about those curves a lot last night, after he'd felt them against him before he stomped from her room, even while concentrating on his investigation plan.

Thought about her slim, sexy shape even more as he heard her puttering around in Andee's bathroom as she got ready for bed last night. And as he took his own cool shower before dawn that morning, in the master bathroom off his bedroom, to ensure his continued wakefulness. Oh, yeah, those thoughts kept him, and his strategic body parts, awake.

"Finished eating?" he asked abruptly. "We'll get coffee refills and take them along."

"Sure."

He didn't head his GTO to his office as he usually did first thing. Instead, he drove north on the San Diego Freeway, got on the 118 and took the 210 east toward Sunland. He called Margo on the way, let her know they were coming.

"What's your plan, Hunter?" Shauna asked after he hung up.

"What?"

"Your plan. I know you must have one."

"You remember that?" he asked, pleased despite himself. He glanced at her. She smiled, but her eyes looked wistful. Even sad. He had an urge to stroke the side of her face, touch her soft skin and smooth the sadness away.

He kept driving.

"Of course I remember," she replied. "You always had a plan for every case you worked on as a cop. You'd tell me about them, at least what wasn't confidential. You used to say that anyone who worked without a plan could never accomplish anything."

"Yeah. You used to tease me, ask to see the plan I'd made about us."

"Good thing you didn't really do one," she said.

"Yeah," he said. The fact was, he had started a plan about them, not long after they'd met. He'd put it aside, since it felt so damned good to be erotically out of control with her.

Later, he had been glad he'd never gone back to it. Once he devised a plan, he liked to see it through until the end.

But he didn't want to get into that now. Instead, he told her about the plan he really had devised last night.

He had first decided exactly how to search for Andee today, utilizing Simon. Then, he had researched Margo's neighbors on the databases Strahm Solutions subscribed to on the Internet, plus the few people Margo had mentioned whose first or last names began with *T,* and some of those Hunter thought of who might get a thrill out of hurting him. He'd communicated with Simon, who was a whole lot more skilled in using those databases—probably because the guy had the patience of a cathedral full of saints, unlike Hunter, who had none.

He had told Simon to work fast, since Banger had offered only a day until cops would overrun the investigation. Well-meaning cops, sure, but that wouldn't help if word was out and the kidnapper got steamed about seeing his ugly crime plastered all over the media.

Thank God for Banger's willingness to low-key the situation initially in the hope they'd find Andee first.

Shauna offered a couple of suggestions, which pleased Hunter, especially when she told him, "Good plan. It makes great use of your time and resources."

It didn't incorporate her story, though. How could it? The

plans he came up with were real, based on facts, reasoning and strategy. Shauna's stories came out of the blue, from emotions and imagination and pixie dust. He wouldn't mention that now, though. His attitude about the differences was one of the many things they'd argued about years ago.

A while later, at the curb in front of Margo's house, Shauna said, "I'll wait here."

"No, according to my plan, you come, too." His firm tone shouldn't have left room for further discussion, but Shauna didn't take the hint.

She remained in the passenger seat after he opened his door. "I thought you were going to talk to Margo about who she spoke with yesterday when Andee disappeared."

"That's right." That was item number one.

"It'll go faster if I'm not there."

"Maybe, but you're coming. You weren't in your story at all, so having you joined at the hip with me, so to speak, might help you change it again, like last night." That was the best use he could make of it: to figure out how to change it. "And you should hear what Margo says about the neighbors so I won't have to repeat it."

"All right." Though Shauna sounded reluctant, she left the car.

The first thing he asked—again—when Margo opened the door was "Any word from the kidnapper?"

"No," Margo wailed. "I'd have called you if I'd heard anything else. Oh, Hunter, I can't stand this." Tears rolled down her cheeks, and she dabbed them away with a tissue.

Margo was dressed, as usual, to be camera-ready. Her yellow shirt was well ironed and tucked into light pants. Her light brown hair appeared newly combed, and her face remained actress-gorgeous despite the redness around her eyes.

"Well, come in." She aimed a brave smile at Hunter, which turned as cold as one of Andee's favorite frozen fruit bars when she looked at Shauna, before waving them both into the house. She showed them again into her living room, and Shauna and he sat on one sofa, facing Margo on the other. Margo had a photo of Andee on the coffee table in front of her.

Both women remained civil despite the wary way they watched each other. But Margo, despite the continued moisture in her eyes, got on *his* case. She'd done that a lot while they were married. Still did it about matters concerning Andee, and the money he gave Margo to care for their daughter as he traveled. It had to be enough to keep Andee in the style to which she had been accustomed. Of course expensive creature comforts really didn't matter to a five-year-old.

As to Margo's tastes, this was a community-property state, so when they'd split, she got half of all he'd earned while they were together—a lot more than she'd earned from her occasional acting gigs, and he hadn't asked for his half of that. If she couldn't maintain the lifestyle she wanted from it, and from whatever she earned now on her own, it was no longer his problem.

And whether or not he had to be so generous, he gave her plenty of money to take care of Andee when she watched their child.

Trying tactfully to keep her from becoming defensive, Hunter quizzed an uncharacteristically quiet Margo again about what she had done after finding Andee missing and who in the area she had spoken with. "What about people who might have a grudge against you?" he finished. "Have you thought of anyone else?"

"I'm not exactly the type to make enemies," Margo said. "There are a couple of other actresses considered to be of a similar type to me that I rather despise, but I don't think either would kidnap my child to get back at me. Do you, lady shrink?" She turned toward Shauna, her expression challenging.

"Without talking with them, I can't really offer an opinion," Shauna replied.

"And do you offer opinions on other things?" An angry

gleam lit Margo's eyes for a moment before she smiled ironically. "Of course you do. That's your job. Well, as to my
rivals, both are working right now—small roles on shoots that
I tried out for, too. I don't even think they're in town."

"Give me whatever information you have on them,"
Hunter said. "I agree it's a long shot, but we'll eliminate them
as potential suspects."

"What about *you?*" Margo demanded. "In your line of
work, you must make enemies. Maybe one is the kidnapper.
Our poor little Andee." Her tone rose, and she picked up
Andee's picture from the table and looked at it tearfully.

"There are a couple," Hunter allowed. "I've got Simon
and my staff checking them out, just in case."

"And you'll let me know if anyone looks suspicious?"

"Banger first," Hunter said. "Then you, if it makes sense
to tell you."

"Andee is my daughter, too," Margo cried. "Of course it
makes sense. I have to know what's going on. You can't keep
me in the dark, Hunter." She hugged the photo closer.

"He won't," Shauna said. "I won't let him."

Margo turned a damp but haughty stare on her. "Do you
really think you can get my dear ex-husband to do anything?"
She stressed "ex-husband," as if rubbing their former relationship in Shauna's face.

As if Shauna gave a damn any longer.

Shauna responded, "No, I can't get Hunter to act. But if I
learn of anything that Andee's mother should know and he
doesn't tell you, I will."

She'd spoken mildly, and her gaze shifted from Margo's to
his. He didn't contradict her. But if he learned of something
Margo *shouldn't* know about, he'd make good and sure that
Shauna didn't learn of it, either.

Unless it showed up in her story…

And that wouldn't happen, no matter the tiny triumph
they'd had over it last night.

"Thank you," Margo said to Shauna, sounding sincere for

the first time. "As a psychologist, is there anything you can tell us about the awful man who took our daughter? I mean, I know you haven't talked to him. But I've told Hunter about the conversations I've had with him—he sounds so horrible. So threatening, especially if we go to the police. Do you think it is one of Hunter's enemies?" More tears welled in her eyes.

"I wish I knew," Shauna replied softly. "I have an impression that he's a person Hunter or you know, though, so if anything he said, or may say in future calls, reminds you of someone, be sure to tell Hunter."

"Really?" Margo shrilled as wetness spilled down her cheeks again. "You actually think it's someone we know?"

Hunter heard a hint of hysteria in his ex-wife's tone. And a hysterical Margo was not a pleasant thing.

"It's only a guess at this point," he said to Margo. "Just keep it in mind as a possibility, like Shauna said."

"All right," Margo said, calming a little.

When they were finished talking to Margo, Hunter went into the backyard again to look around, now that it was daylight but still a little too early to call on neighbors. Not that it was likely that Banger and Simon would have missed anything, but taking a look himself was in his plan. Shauna didn't follow.

When he returned inside a few minutes later, Shauna was in the living room alone. "Where's Margo?" Hunter asked.

"She didn't tell me," Shauna said with a wry smile.

"I'll find her." He headed for the door to the rest of the house. "It's time for us to go."

Shauna murmured something like "amen," but when he glanced back, she was sitting there with an innocent expression on her face. A sweet face. Much more appealing than Margo's, despite his ex's star-of-stage-and-screen enhanced gorgeousness, for Shauna was naturally pretty, without a lot of fuss and makeup.

And sexy? Hell, she only had to aim her most innocent

gaze at him to remind him of how good they'd been together once.

And when a hint of her own recollection of hot, steamy
nights they'd once shared surfaced in her eyes, in that kiss
they'd…

With a mutter of his own, he went to find Margo. She was
on the phone in her bedroom and hung up as Hunter walked
in.

"That wasn't the kidnapper?" he demanded.

"No." Her laugh was brittle. "I just can't believe that
Shauna thinks anyone I'm even acquainted with would do
such a horrible thing." Her expression crumpled. "My poor
baby."

"We'll get her back, Margo. Believe me." No matter what
Shauna's story said. "Right now, we're going to canvass the
neighbors."

"You won't tell them Andee has been kidnapped?"
Margo's pale brown eyes went round as her voice again grew
shrill.

"What do you think? No, what I'll tell those you talked to
yesterday is that when you spoke with them, Andee had somehow slipped out the back gate. I'll say you found her and
she's fine, but I'm asking around to get better information on
how she got out, where she went, so we can prevent its happening again."

She relaxed. "Fine. And you'll tell me what you learn?"

"Sure," he said with a straight face.

He retrieved Shauna and they left. "We'll start in the alley
behind the house," he told her, "although just because it's
about the same time of day Andee disappeared yesterday
doesn't mean the same people will be outside. Then we'll
head up and down both the street Margo's house faces and
the one at the far side of the alley."

She nodded her assent, and they both walked toward the
alley.

* * *

Shauna had no problem with the course of action that came next in Hunter's plan, for it had been described similarly in her story—even if she hadn't been part of it:

Because Andee had been taken from her house, her father decided to question the neighbors, in case they'd seen anything. But he learned little that was useful.

A neighbor was irritable.

A neighbor was too nosy.

A neighbor had actually seen something useful but didn't realize it.

Yet another neighbor offered help and sympathy.

Shauna wouldn't remind Hunter of those written words. She probably didn't have to.

And *she* certainly would keep them in mind as they spoke with the people who lived near Andee Strahm's mother.

Chapter 6

Although the alley behind Margo's was only wide enough for one car to comfortably ease through at a time, it wasn't one-way. Otherwise, it was fairly pleasant, Shauna thought. Early-morning sunlight streamed between garages and along the well-maintained paving. No litter or graffiti in sight.

Or anything else that looked ominous to her. To Hunter, though, a few steps behind, it might be another story. Perhaps his trained investigator's eye saw something she didn't, for when she looked back, his mouth was a grim line of concentration. He turned his head slowly, looking not at her but beyond.

It was all too easy to imagine a young, confused child being propelled into an idling car in this narrow, secluded alley. But its constriction had a good side, too. If anyone had been here, the abduction shouldn't have gone unnoticed.

Right now, only one garage door was open, catty-corner from Margo's. Shauna hurried in that direction, then made herself breathe shallowly. The vehicle inside was running, a large old car with fins that appeared to be from the early 1960s. Its exhaust smelled terrible.

As Shauna drew near, a door opened at the far side of that garage and a man came through. He opened the driver's door and started to get in.

Shauna hurried forward. "Good morning," she called.

The man stopped and looked around, his eyes finally lighting on her. He grinned. "Good morning."

He was maybe seventy years old or more, dressed in a nice sport shirt and dressy slacks. His hair was more gray than black, cut very short. His nose was prominent, and he had deep crow's-feet at the edges of his eyes behind his glasses.

Shauna heard Hunter's footsteps behind her but didn't wait for him to catch up. Was this man the irritable neighbor, the nosy one, the sympathetic one—or the one who knew something helpful about Andee's abduction without being aware of it?

When she started to speak, Hunter put his hand on her shoulder and squeezed, silencing her. She stayed aware of the contact, wanting to shrug him away while at the same time feeling an odd reassurance by the connection, as though they were acting as a team.

As they once had…until it became clear that their team of two was incapable of functioning as a unit.

"Hi." Hunter released Shauna and approached the man with his hand outstretched. "I'm Hunter Strahm. Andee's dad. Do you know my daughter, or her mother Margo Masters? Margo lives there." He pointed to Margo's yard.

As Hunter spoke, Shauna realized he was right. It made more sense for him to start conversations with Margo's neighbors than for her to jump in.

"Sure, I know them." The man's voice was deeper than Shauna expected. "I'm Conrad Chiles."

"Margo said she spoke with you yesterday," Hunter said. His shirt today was soft plaid, and its lines made the breadth of his back seem even more impressive. But that didn't mean

Shauna intended to stay behind him. She eased to the side to watch Conrad Chiles's face.

"Is the little girl okay?" Conrad asked. "Margo said she'd wandered off and got lost. I told her I'd check with people on my street, but no one saw her. I called and let Margo know."

He sounded sympathetic. Maybe he was *that* neighbor.

"That's what she told me," Hunter said. "I hope she let you know that Andee's fine. A friend's mother recognized her, took her in and called Margo."

Conrad reached into his car and turned it off before shaking his head. Its fumes didn't immediately dissipate. "Nope. She didn't tell me, but I'm glad to hear it. Who was the friend? I know pretty much all the kids in the neighborhood."

"Someone she knows from school," Hunter replied.

"But I thought she didn't go to school around here. She lives with you most of the time, doesn't she?"

This man apparently knew Margo fairly well. Or was he simply the nosy neighbor?

"That's right," Hunter said.

"Your story isn't making sense." Conrad peered at Hunter suspiciously. "My first thought when Margo asked me was that Andee's dad was trying to make trouble. That happens in divorces. I like kids. Don't like to see them in trouble. When they're young, I have neighborhood kids over for lemonade in the summer. Hire them to mow my lawn when they're older. You sure everything's okay with Andee?"

Right now, he sounded like the irritable neighbor.

"Have you ever invited her over for lemonade?"

Did Hunter suspect Conrad in Andee's abduction?

"Of course. Margo, too. I like them, and if you're trying to hurt them in any way—"

"All I'm trying to do is find out if anyone saw her get out of Margo's yard so I can prevent it from happening again."

"Sure. Well, I'm not one to stand back and let kids get hurt. Their mothers, either."

"What do you mean?" Shauna blurted.

"Not a thing, miss. But if you're this man's lady friend, tell him that if he's going to try to keep Andee from seeing her mother because of one little incident, I'll have something to say about it."

He got into his car again, turned the key in the ignition and backed out without looking at them again.

"That guy was jumping to some ridiculous conclusions," Hunter said as they continued down the alley. "I don't like him, but I think he'd have called the cops if he saw anything suspicious." No one else was around, but Hunter kept peering into windows and between garages. Nothing helpful jumped out and shouted, *Here's how to find your daughter.* Damn it.

"I agree," Shauna said. "I mean about his letting someone know if he saw anything. And he didn't like you, either."

"In terms of your story, he's got to be the irritable neighbor—assuming that part of what you wrote is right."

"Till we see otherwise, I'm assuming everything is right."

He heard what she didn't say: Each detail in her damned stories was *always* correct. Including the endings.

At the end of the alley, he strode down the street perpendicular to Margo's block. "We'll hit them all, one by one." He had a list of owners from a reverse directory.

Chatting with someone at every house, for a block in each direction, was in his plan.

No one was at home at the first house. The older lady in the second one hadn't spoken with Margo and wasn't aware that Andee had supposedly gotten out of her yard.

At the third house, two doors down from Margo's, a tired-looking young woman answered, a baby in her arms. "Mrs. Kelly?" Hunter asked.

After his prepared speech, Mrs. Kelly said, "I'm so glad Andee is all right. I saw Margo looking for her and asked what the matter was. She looked upset, and no wonder. I told her to let me know if I could help. I called some neighbors for her, but no one was home.''

She hadn't seen anything to help them prevent Andee from getting out again—Hunter's continued cover story. He felt sure if she'd seen someone with the child, she'd have said so.

''She's got to be the helpful and sympathetic one,'' Shauna said as they continued down the street.

Hunter referred often to the notes he'd taken during his conversations with Margo, cross-checking names and addresses of the neighbors with what his ex had said about each. A couple could have fit the designation of ''nosy neighbor.'' Several seemed sympathetic, and another couple bordered on irritable at being interrupted from whatever they were doing to discuss a situation that Hunter claimed was already resolved.

None had noticed anything out of the ordinary around the time that Andee had been taken. Or at least no one said so.

Standing on the street corner while Shauna strolled ahead, he called his office, but Simon hadn't yet reached everyone Hunter considered possible enemies, Simon's assignment that day. Next, Hunter called Banger. The police detective grumbled about having one heck of a time conducting an important investigation surreptitiously, but he and the other cops had succeeded in avoiding media attention. So far.

As Hunter ended his last call, he found Shauna back at his side.

''I'd hoped we'd get someone, just one person, to say they saw Andee with someone who didn't belong here,'' he said.

''That wasn't what you asked them,'' she reminded him quietly.

''You think I was too subtle?''

''I think you did what you felt was best.''

''Spoken like a true psychologist.''

''I *am* a—''

''—true psychologist,'' he finished with what he hoped passed as a grin. He walked in the direction of Margo's house, though he wasn't through here. Someone must have seen *something*.

Yeah, like that unidentified neighbor in Shauna's story who'd seen something without recognizing its importance.

"So you think Conrad Chiles is the neighbor who was irritable," he said to Shauna, "and Mrs. Kelly was the sympathetic one. A couple could have been the nosy ones."

"I'd put my bet on the one who seemed really put out to have been shopping at the time Andee got out. She sounded as if otherwise she'd have been observing the entire neighborhood through her field glasses."

Hunter didn't want to smile at that, but he did. "The intrepid Mrs. Bremer."

"Exactly." Shauna's return smile reminded Hunter too much of the old days, when they'd shared a similar sense of humor—among other things.

Abruptly he said, "I'll try a few houses in the blocks behind the alley, just in case." That wasn't in his plan, but he *had* intended to get information from someone here. And hadn't. Yet.

"Do you really think anyone that far from the alley would see something no one here did?"

"I won't know unless I ask them."

"Well, I'll go talk to Margo a little more. Maybe she saw something important that she didn't recognize."

Hunter couldn't help lifting his brow skeptically. "And you think she'll spill that to you?"

"Not if I don't ask her."

Shauna knocked on the door, hoping Hunter's ex-wife would let her in without him along.

Not unexpectedly, Margo frowned when she opened the door, then glanced past Shauna as if looking for someone.

"Hunter's talking to some neighbors around the block," Shauna said. "I hoped you and I could chat for a while about Andee."

Margo's reddened eyes narrowed, but there was a hint of curiosity. "Come in," she said. "I don't suppose you've found her." She sounded dejected.

Shauna shook her head, and Margo's lips quivered before she turned away.

This time she showed Shauna to her kitchen, obviously not intending to entertain her as formally as she had with Hunter and their friends. Like the other room in Margo's home that Shauna had seen, this one was a decorator's delight, with dark wood cabinets trimmed with ornate carving, a lighter wood floor and rust-colored counters devoid of clutter. No sign of food beloved by a child here.

Margo motioned Shauna toward a small drop-leaf table against one wall. There were chairs at either end. Shauna pulled out the nearest and sat on its embroidered upholstery.

"Would you like some iced tea?" Margo's tone suggested she asked only because it was the polite thing to do.

"If it's not too much trouble."

"I wouldn't offer if it was."

Shauna smiled. "I figured."

A few minutes later, Shauna took a sip from the tall glass Margo had placed on a stone coaster in front of her. "This is delicious!" she exclaimed. "Do I taste peach in it?"

"That's right. A little tangerine, too. My own mixture. I leave out the tea and add a little sugar for Andee. She loves it…" Her voice broke. "I'm sorry."

"Don't be. I understand your worry for your daughter."

"I'd be out there looking for her myself, asking questions, but I was told to wait here in case the kidnapper calls again." Margo sat down and faced Shauna. "Why are you really here, in L.A.?"

Shauna took a deep breath. "I know Hunter's mother," she said vaguely. "I heard about Andee from her after Hunter and she talked, and I thought I could help."

"Because you're a shrink?" Margo asked deprecatingly.

"Yes." But Shauna knew Margo wasn't convinced, so she

blurted, "Besides, I was curious about the woman Hunter cared enough about to marry—and to have his child."

A look of something Shauna couldn't quite identify shot over Margo's expression—deeper sadness? Vulnerability? But it was replaced immediately by a cynical look.

"It was a mistake," Margo said with a sigh. "He came to town all hungry to make changes in his life. Find himself. We met at a bar and I liked him right away. Showed him around, helped him locate what he needed to get started. I even introduced him to the private investigator he worked for while he got his license. I'd met the guy while he worked security on a movie shoot I was on."

"I'll bet Hunter really appreciated it." Shauna pictured the young, angry man who had stormed away from Oasis and the Phoenix Police Department in disgrace, partly because of her.

Had stormed away from *her*.

"So he said. And I really appreciated him. He was different from the guys I meet in the industry."

Shauna translated: the *entertainment* industry.

"He was the strong, sexy type—not silent, though. He never kept his opinions to himself."

Shauna knew that well.

"Anyway, one thing led to another. I fell hard for him. Guess he cared for me a little, too."

"I'm sure he did. He married you."

"Yes, but though he didn't tell me what made him leave Arizona, I knew a woman was involved. A woman he hadn't gotten over. He told me about you and what had happened later, a little at a time."

Panic zapped through Shauna. Did Margo know the whole story? *Story.* An inadvertent yet perfect choice of words.

"I'm sure his feelings for me weren't exactly fond by then," Shauna said. "What did he tell you?" She held her breath.

"Only that he'd been seeing a woman who sometimes consulted with the police department," Margo said with a shrug of her slim shoulders beneath her yellow blouse. "She'd learned something that could have helped him on a case, but kept it to herself long enough to make things harder to resolve. He got canned for it and didn't forgive her. Didn't forgive *you*. But he didn't forget you, either."

Of course not. People don't forget those they feel have done them grave injury.

The ironic thing was, Shauna had been trying to help Hunter.

She'd met Elayne first, while following up a story she'd written about a frightened child in a domestic-abuse situation—that child's emotions had projected themselves through her onto the computer. She had worked with Elayne, the social worker assigned to the case—and Elayne had somehow extracted from Shauna the truth of how she'd learned about the sad situation. Elayne then referred her to the Phoenix police.

Introduced her to Hunter.

Shauna had made friends with a couple of other officers, too. She had never hesitated to let them know when a story she'd written described a criminal situation.

Hunter hadn't wanted to believe in her stories. Despite their love, their passionate relationship, he'd seemed embarrassed by her claims of writing tales that came true—even when they did. He had tried to get her to stop writing them, as if she could. But she'd learned by then how much Hunter needed to feel in control.

Which did not help their relationship. Her ability—gift or curse—remained uncontrollable.

Then had come the rash of bank robberies. Vicious ones. Ones in which she had somehow sensed the violent emotions of the perpetrators.

Hunter had been put in charge of the investigation.

In the first story she'd written about a robbery in progress, the location wasn't clear, and she'd guessed wrong. Later, Hunter had ridiculed her story. And her.

The next time, the location was more certain, but she'd hesitated about telling him. A bank employee and two patrons were killed. The other police officers who knew of Shauna's stories and who had relied on them to solve other cases had made life hell for Hunter. Without telling his source, they'd asserted in official reports that he'd ignored a credible tip, to the public's detriment.

He had stonewalled the investigation, keeping quiet about Shauna and her stories, protecting her from media scrutiny and public ridicule while resenting the entire situation. He had been reprimanded for his lack of cooperation, which had made him angry enough to resign from the Phoenix P.D.

Had quit Shauna and their relationship…

"Hunter never cared for me the way he cared for you," Margo was saying. "Even though he had the hots for me. That's the main reason he married me. And because he wanted kids."

Shauna hoped her expression did not reflect the anguish she felt—and not just from her recollection of the past. Of course Hunter would have fallen for this beautiful woman, wanted her.

And Margo had given birth to his beloved Andee.

He'd been out of Shauna's life. He'd had every right to go his own way and to seek happiness.

"And I wanted Hunter," Margo went on. "Though he's not the easiest man. I don't think the word 'compromise' is in his vocabulary, you know?"

Shauna nodded. Oh, yes, she knew. But still—

"Once we were married, things got a little…well, difficult. But I tried, and so did he. Mostly, to make him happy, I agreed to have a child, though I worried what it would do to my career. It certainly didn't help. But Andee's such a great kid." A look of pain passed over her face, and she buried it in her hands. When she spoke again, her voice was muffled. "I'm so worried about her."

"Of course you are," Shauna said sadly. "I doubt there's

anything I can do to help you, any more than I'm helping Hunter, but if you think of anything, please let me know.''

Margo looked up, tears in her eyes. "Here's one thing you can do—tell me why he's really got you with him. He won't admit it, but there's something between you again, isn't there?" She choked a little, as if the idea of Hunter being with another woman was painful, even though he wasn't with her any longer.

"Not what you think," Shauna said. "What's between us is—"

She was interrupted by the ringing of the phone.

"Excuse me," Margo said. Approaching the set mounted on the wall, she picked up the receiver. "Hello?"

Her eyes widened and her mouth opened as if in shock.

"It's him," she mouthed.

"The kidnapper?" Shauna whispered.

Margo, who had gone pasty, nodded.

Shauna got close to Margo, tried to put her ear close enough to hear, but only got a sense of a garbled, too-cheerful voice.

She hoped Banger had already put the recording equipment in place. She watched Margo nod, tears streaming down her face, making her look like a mother whose child was abducted, and who suffered for it.

Shauna's heart raced in her chest. *Please,* she whispered to whatever demon inside her forced her to create her stories. *If not for my sake, or even for Hunter's or Margo's—for little Andee Strahm's sake, let this one be wrong.*

Hurrying up Margo's front walk, Hunter wondered if he'd made a mistake by leaving Shauna alone in Margo's presence this long.

Maybe not. But as he'd gone impatiently from one house to the next, to the homes of people whose names he hadn't even attempted to find in advance, he'd wound up dragging his feet—mostly because he hoped someone would remember something, come running out and give him news of Andee.

But also, he admitted to himself, because the way Margo had given Shauna the cold shoulder felt a little like punishment. For both of them, maybe, but mostly for Shauna, for writing that damned story and continuously putting roadblocks in the way of his hoping for a changed ending.

Yeah, like changing the story would—

The door to Margo's house burst open and Shauna flew out. "Hunter, thank heavens you're here. The kidnapper's on the phone with Margo. I couldn't hear—"

Hunter pushed past her. Ran into the house. Where was Margo? He heard a sound in the kitchen and rushed in.

Margo stood near the wall phone, hanging on as if it was all that kept her from falling down. Her face was white, her eyes strained.

He quickly maneuvered the phone so he could hear, too.

The voice had been electronically altered. He couldn't tell whether it was male or female, though Margo had thought the kidnapper male.

"I'll let you know when and where," the voice said. "I want to make sure you have enough time to get all that nice money together. But you still understand, I hope, that telling the cops will be bad for Andee's health."

Hunter pushed the phone completely back into Margo's hand and nudged her.

"Y-yes," she said. "I understand."

Before Hunter got into position again to eavesdrop, Margo cried, "Wait! Please—" But it was too late. She stared at the receiver for a moment as if willing it to talk to her.

Hunter held the thing to his own ear, wanting to shout but staying quiet in case the kidnapper remained silently on the line.

In a moment, the female recorded voice that signaled the other person had hung up began to speak: "If you'd like to make a call, please hang up and try again."

Hunter slammed the receiver down, then demanded of Margo, "Do you have caller ID?"

She shook her head. She grasped the nearest counter as if ready to faint.

Pressing *69 wouldn't do any good, Hunter realized. If he got the kidnapper on the line, what then?

Instead, he used his cell phone to call Banger. "You able to trace a call that came to Margo's line yet?"

"Yeah," Arthur Banner said. "Why? The kidnapper call again?"

"Yes," Hunter hissed.

"I'll get right on it."

"Thanks." Hunter closed his cell phone, then turned to face the women. "Margo, tell me exactly what the guy said."

"He…he said the ransom will be one million dollars." The figure came out in a wail. "How can we get a million—?"

"Don't worry about that." Of course Hunter hadn't any better idea than she did. "What else did he say?"

"Only that he wanted to give us time to get the money together before telling me any more. At first, he just laughed, taunted me. I thought I heard Andee crying, but he didn't put her on the phone."

"Did she sound all right?" Hunter demanded.

"I don't know." Margo sobbed, then took a deep breath. "We have two days to get the money ready. He'll call again the day after tomorrow to let us know where to drop the ransom."

"Two days? Damn! That's too long. Andee…but at least it'll give us time to figure out a plan."

"Plan? Our plan should be to get the money."

"With luck, Banger'll figure out where the call came from. Maybe we'll catch the SOB and get Andee back without needing to get the ransom together. In any event, we're going to talk it over with Banger and his FBI friend so next time the kidnapper calls, you'll be able to dictate to him about when and where to make the ransom drop. He'll listen if he wants the money."

"Then you aren't going to get the money together?"

"I didn't say that," Hunter snapped. "Two days isn't enough for me to get a million dollars in cash, but I'll get my hands on all I can. We just need to be as ready as possible."

"I don't have much," Margo said, "but I'll put in what I can—a few thousand. Maybe I can borrow from my friends. But we have to get the money for him. We just have to!"

He looked away from the frightened expression on his ex-wife's face—and faced Shauna.

Her stricken expression told him exactly what she was thinking—remembering what was in her damned story about the ransom demand:

Big T was in it for the money. No more, no less.

As long as the kid's family came through, they'd see her again. If not...

Well, that was a situation that no one wanted to think about. Especially Big T.

Damn, but he would not allow anyone to make a fool of him like that.

And having blood on his hands was not his idea of a good time.

Chapter 7

The doorbell rang.

They were in Margo's house. Hunter's ex-wife, still crying, appeared in no condition to answer it. But Shauna didn't think it would be appropriate for her to go.

"Go check who's there, please, Shauna." Hunter's voice was calm, his expression impassive.

But Shauna again discerned subtle nuances in features so familiar that she had known them as much by touch and taste as by appearance. He was hurting.

The green of his eyes was dulled from pain, shadowed below from apparent lack of sleep. The creases framing his mouth had deepened. His posture bowed an iota at the shoulders.

"Sure," she responded, glad to flee, even for a moment, from the misery she could not ease.

As she hurried to the entry, her brain continued to reel from what she'd gleaned from the phone call from the kidnapper.

And her recollection of what her story had said about it:

As long as the kid's family came through, they'd see her again.

But a million dollars?

Shauna knew that Hunter's private investigation agency was small but successful. Even so, could he gather that much together—especially right away?

In her story, it hadn't been clear, when Hunter went to the ransom drop location, whether he'd been in possession of all the money that had been demanded.

If only that location had been specifically described in what she'd written, maybe they could prepare for it. Get the police to watch the area, ready to grab the kidnapper and get Andee back.

If only what she wrote was more specific altogether: about the kidnapper's identity. And where he had taken Andee.

But her stories, stoked by emotion, often were plentiful in allusion and sparse in details, and even those weren't always clear. Like the ones leading to her loss of Hunter. And in this one on Andee, only the ending seemed much too clear.

A sigh burst from her as she reached the door. The peephole was below her eye level, so she bent to peer out, just as the doorbell pealed again. And again.

She recognized Conrad Chiles. The irritated neighbor in her story? That would explain his impatience.

She opened the door. "Hi, Mr. Chiles. Margo's a little busy right now. Can I help you?"

"No, you can't. I want to see Margo right away." His eyes glittered behind his glasses, and despite the fact that he'd struck Shauna as more senior citizen than middle-aged, he rocked with pent-up energy on the balls of feet clad in athletic shoes beneath his dressy brown slacks.

"I'll tell her you're here." Shauna didn't want to be rude and shut the door in his face, but better that than let him slip uninvited into the house, behind her.

"It's okay. Let him in." Margo's voice was hoarse but

strong. Shauna turned. Margo stood framed by the open door way to the hall. She looked fragile yet brave.

Maybe that was because Hunter stood behind her. Shauna remembered having his strong, assertive presence as her own courage booster. Not that she'd needed a lot of courage then…until the end. When he hadn't been behind her at all.

"Hello, Conrad," Margo said more strongly. "Would you like to come in and join us for coffee?"

"No, but I'd like you to tell me what's really going on."

He stood inside the front door, thin arms crossed in his dressy shirt, and glared. "First, I see you yesterday in the alley and you're looking for Andee. Then your ex-husband and his girlfriend show up and claim Andee's fine but they want to know how she got out of your yard."

Shauna felt her face go pink under Conrad's stare—but not solely because of his accusatory look.

He'd called her Hunter's girlfriend.

Of course she had been, long ago, but Shauna didn't attempt to clarify their current relationship to this stranger.

She darted a glance at Hunter, who stood close to his ex-wife.

Conrad kept talking. "So you told me Andee's visiting a friend now, after the friend's mother found her and took her home. Well, I don't buy it. Tell me what's really going on."

Shauna's mind changed again. Conrad wasn't the irritated neighbor from her story; he was the nosy one.

How could they answer him? *Should* they answer him? Shauna donned her therapist's hat. "It's so nice of you to be concerned about her," she said carefully. Were Margo and he such good friends that he normally would know where Andee was at any time?

She glanced toward Margo, hoping for a clue.

Hunter's former wife seemed to rally as she came closer. "I know it seems a little odd, Conrad," she admitted, "but, well…" She gave a small laugh that Shauna figured this actress would never dare use while playing a role. It was so obviously false. Margo turned toward Hunter. "Conrad's been so sweet. When he sees us getting into the car in the garage, he always has a lollipop for Andee. They're friends."

Shauna throat constricted. How good friends were they?

Good enough that he would steal the child away, then hide his heinous act by pretending to be a concerned neighbor?

She had nothing to base that on, but she met Hunter's stare and knew he wondered the same thing.

Not that his expression had changed much from its former impassiveness. But she could tell, from the tiny flare to his nostrils, that he was as suspicious as she.

"I like kids," Conrad said to Margo. "You know that. And Andee's one of the best. That's why I want to know what's up."

Whether he was the caring neighbor that he seemed or an abductor, they had to tread carefully.

Hunter's mouth opened. Shauna guessed he was about to start an investigator's interrogation—and not a gentle one. Margo must have figured that, too, for she grabbed Hunter by the arm and took a step toward the door, which caused Conrad to fall back.

"Honestly, Conrad," Margo said, "Andee's fine. You're sweet to be concerned, but there's no need for you to worry."

"But something's going on," the man persisted. "You look like you've been crying." He'd allowed Margo to herd him toward the door but didn't go through it.

Shauna decided to resort to the truth—a modified version. "Okay, Mr. Chiles. You're right. There's something going on, and I think you guessed part of it." Three people's stares focused on her, and none felt friendly. She continued anyway. "I'm a psychologist, and an old friend of Hunter's. He was angry with Margo when he heard Andee got out of the yard, was considering not allowing her to stay here, when he traveled, if she wasn't being adequately supervised by her mother. I agreed to come to ask some questions, determine whether

Andee's sneaking out was a fluke or whether Margo's attention needed improvement. Obviously, she's upset about it."

"Oh?" Conrad maneuvered around Margo to confront
Shauna. She was taller, but he didn't seem intimidated. He
pointed an arthritic finger at her and said, "I've known Margo
for a while. She's a nice lady. Loves her daughter, even
though she doesn't have full custody. Andee's getting out of
the yard was an accident. Margo takes good care of her, and
don't let her former husband tell you otherwise." He took a
couple of steps in Hunter's direction, obviously intending to
seem menacing.

But Hunter was a lot taller, broader, younger and obviously
in much better shape than the older man. Conrad halted
abruptly when Hunter strode toward him.

Oh, heavens, Shauna thought. Not a good time for a confrontation. What if the man went to the police? Banger might
not be able to keep the situation quiet, even for a few more
hours.

Assuming Conrad wasn't the kidnapper.

But instead of accosting the man, Hunter held out his hand.
"Thanks for keeping a close watch on Andee, Mr. Chiles.
And for being a caring enough neighbor to check on the sit-
uation. Most people wouldn't give a damn. And you're right.
I've seen nothing to indicate that Margo did anything wrong."

Shauna's heart swelled with pride in Hunter. He'd kept his
cool despite the heat of the moment.

*You've no right to feel pride about anything Hunter Strahm
does.* Her reminder deflated her.

Conrad's chin lifted enough to straighten the folds of skin
beneath. He shook Hunter's hand brusquely, then let go. "All
right," he said sternly. Then, to Margo, he added, "Sorry if
I was out of line, but you know I'm on your side." He gave
a quick nod and finally headed out the door.

Margo closed the door behind him, leaning her head against
it with eyes closed, as if the confrontation had absorbed all

her remaining energy. "Lord save us from well-meaning butt-inskies," she intoned sadly.

"Yeah," Hunter agreed.

Shauna said nothing. Something about Conrad Chiles had bothered her.

Could he be the abductor? She no longer thought so, yet…

She wasn't surprised when Hunter slipped out the door after him.

"It's not him," Hunter said a while later, back in Margo's kitchen. He hazarded a glance across the kitchen. The cabinets were dark wood. Depressing.

So was his damned mood.

"Unless he's put Andee someplace else," he continued. "He'd need an accomplice for that, since he's been around here, and Andee's too little to leave by herself this long."

Unless, of course, his daughter was dead. And he refused to accept that. Besides, even Shauna's story described how Andee was alive…at least until the kidnapper was caught.

He felt even more frustrated than before. His brainstorm hadn't provided a breakthrough.

Attempting to pretend everything was normal, he got himself a drink of water from the dispenser on the refrigerator door.

"Who are you talking about?" Margo demanded. She stood by the sink, holding a dish towel decorated with flowers that went well with her yellow blouse. "Conrad? Of course he had nothing to do with Andee's disappearance. He's a pushy old guy, but he's harmless. Don't waste your time on him, Hunter, please. Find Andee!"

"How can you be sure it's not him?" Shauna asked softly. She stood by the door as if eager to leave. Her arms were crossed, emphasizing the distinct swells of her breasts beneath her gold T-shirt.

He had seen the momentary shocked expression that had widened her eyes earlier as she'd looked at him. Hunter had known what she was thinking, for his mind had glommed at the same time onto the same possibility: that Margo's grumpy but otherwise seemingly harmless, neighbor, whom they had interviewed before, could, after all, be the kidnapper.

Margo had been talking about Conrad's handing out lollipops at the time. That had made Hunter suspicious. Why did an old guy like that, apparently with no kids of his own, have treats to pass out to youngsters? Shauna's expression suggested she, too, had caught it—a kind act of a lonely man, or something more sinister? Her look had given Hunter the sudden, disconcertingly gratifying sensation of the past merging with the present.

They'd once been on the same wavelength about a lot of things. It was something he had particularly liked about her. And him. *Them.*

It was the things they hadn't seen eye-to-eye about that had been the killers. Literally.

"I followed Conrad home," Hunter said in response to Shauna's question. "Called Simon on the way and let him in on what I was up to. When Conrad got inside, I walked around, looking in windows. When I didn't see any sign of Andee, I rang his doorbell, asked about a neighbor who doesn't exist, and—surprise!—his phone rang. I let myself in while he answered it, looked around. It took a few minutes. Simon's good at things like keeping people talking. But there was no indication Andee had ever been there."

During this speech, he'd approached the table. Instead of sitting in the nearest chair, he lifted one foot and rested it on the seat. Margo immediately protested, as she always had when his comfort conflicted with her most prized things, which consisted of nearly everything she owned.

And excluded him. He'd wondered—till now—if it also excluded Andee. But Margo was obviously upset about their daughter's kidnapping. Maybe it took something as terrible as this to turn on her maternal gene.

"Sorry." He dropped the errant foot back to the floor.

"Look, I've got to make a call." He turned his back on both women and pushed buttons on his cell phone. Enough time had passed for the cops to trace the kidnapper's call.

"What do you mean 'no luck'?" Hunter demanded when he got Banger on the line and asked the trace's status.

"Well, we did trace the call—to a cell phone. Only problem is, the thing was stolen a couple of days ago. The owner checks out—a college girl who reported it."

"Great." Hunter felt his fist tighten around the phone and loosened it. He depended on the thing too much to crush it.

He pivoted. Shauna and Margo were now seated at the table. The two were conversing quietly, although Shauna's eyes met his for an instant.

Hunter hadn't tried to hide his frustration before, that he hadn't found Andee at Conrad's place. He didn't attempt to hide his anger now with what could be cop ineptitude but was more likely a smart kidnapper.

Shauna's gaze on him was sad and compassionate, everything a shrink's should be. She had come with him to L.A. to help…that way. Not the way he needed.

As if she could really fix things, her damned story or not. If he hadn't been so gut-punched by Andee's kidnapping, he'd never have given any credence to—

"I've got to get to the office," he said abruptly, "to start getting the ransom together."

Though he would much rather be tracking Andee and the kidnapper. That was the kind of thing he was good at. In fact, that was how he'd programmed things, in his plan.

But his plans always left room for flexibility and amendment. Right now, he had to make sure the money was available, in case it was the only way to get his daughter back.

He looked at his ex-wife. "About that cash you offered…?"

"I haven't had any jobs for a few months," she said, "but I received a couple of residual checks this month for almost five thousand dollars. For Andee, I'll give it all to you now, and I'll start calling friends about loans, too. A bunch of us actors are used to helping each other out in a pinch.''

''Thanks.'' He didn't reject it, but five thousand dollars wasn't going to do a lot of good. And he doubted that show-business friends of Margo's would be able to lend much more.

''I—'' Shauna began.

''You're coming to my office with me,'' he said, purposely interrupting her. He could guess what she'd been about to say. Even with her restaurant and shrink business, Shauna probably didn't have much money, but even if she'd been loaded he didn't want her to offer any to him.

Unless he got desperate.

''All right,'' she said. ''I'll come with you.''

Hunter strode to the back door and opened it. ''Call if you hear anything else,'' he told Margo. ''And I'll keep you informed about what's going on from my end.''

''Okay,'' she said. ''And Hunter, I know you understand, but *please* don't let word out about what's going on, for Andee's sake. I'm really sorry I can't help more with the money, but I know you'll do your best.''

Of course he would. But a million dollars cash, with his assets—a whole lot less—rolled up in his business and home the way they were, might as well be ten times that.

He'd need a hell of a lot of luck on his side to get the money together.

And he feared he'd need more than luck to get his daughter back.

Shauna, beside him at the door, said to Margo, ''Take care of yourself, and remember I'm always available to listen.''

''Thanks,'' Margo murmured, ''but I really can't talk about this.''

''It might help,'' Shauna urged.

''Only getting Andee back will help.'' Margo closed the door behind them.

A few minutes later, settled in his GTO beside Shauna, he

pretended to concentrate on his driving. "You don't always have to act like a psychologist," he finally blurted.

"And why is that?"

Infuriated that her response sounded like something a shrink would say, he glanced toward her—and saw her teasing smile.

She was pulling his leg. Despite his instinct to fight her, he liked it.

And if she were really pulling, touching, stroking his leg…

"You can't help anyone feel better about what's going on, you know," he said, trying to ignore what his randy thoughts about the woman in his passenger seat were doing to his body.

"I understand. Like Margo said, I'm sure nothing can make you feel better till you get Andee back."

What she thankfully didn't say was to remind him the condition she expected his daughter to be in when he got her back.

"That's right," he agreed. "And you were awfully nice to Margo."

"You don't sound entirely pleased by that."

He wasn't, though he wouldn't admit it to her. But a touch of jealousy would show she still cared.

Yeah, and why on earth should Shauna be as foolish as he was, thinking about the past too often, too nostalgically?

Too heatedly.

"Of course I'm pleased," he lied.

Because the reason he needed Shauna with him wasn't rooted in the past. It was in the future.

Andee's future.

Shauna was glad when Hunter turned on his radio—a soft-rock station that allowed her to think without talking.

Act like a shrink.

Don't act like a shrink.

Which was she to do?

For her own sake, she had to keep an emotional distance.

And that meant drawing on all she had learned in school and in her practice.

But could she really help Hunter?

He'd followed Conrad Chiles home. Exonerated him from Andee's kidnapping—maybe.

But there had still been something about the man that had formed an irritation in Shauna's mind, like the bite from a sand flea in a place she couldn't reach.

What was it…?

The song on the radio changed to news on the hour. Nothing, still, about Andee, thank heavens.

Traffic on the San Diego Freeway heading south through the Sepulveda Pass was always this bad during the day, or so Hunter informed her. At least talking about traffic, the misty marine layer due to come in over the Pacific, the scenery including the majestic off-white Getty Center perched on a ridge overlooking the road—these were neutral topics.

Still, it seemed forever until they reached Hunter's office. It was in a tall building in Westwood, not far from the UCLA campus, which Hunter pointed out to her.

The Strahm Solutions suite, on the sixth floor, wasn't very large—a reception area, combined kitchen and file room, and three offices for Hunter and his staff.

Hunter's office had a lot more pizzazz than his home did—modern sleek furniture and colorful oil paintings of an ocean sunset, a desert rainstorm—and his daughter.

Shauna stood with her back toward Hunter's desk, looking at Andee's portrait. "She's beautiful," she sighed. This portrait was probably even more recent than the ones in his home, for the child looked older. Her smile was huge, her black hair an adorable curly mass that framed her cherubic features.

"Yeah," Hunter said from behind her. "Smart, too. You'll love her when you meet her."

Shauna didn't let him see her sorrowful smile. He clearly didn't want her to help prepare him for what she feared was inevitable. He needed to keep his hope alive.

She cared too much about him still to do anything to shatter that hope—unless he precipitated it. Like trying again to get her story to change.

Yet it had changed....

"So, you're both here," boomed a familiar British voice. Shauna turned to see Simon Wells standing in the doorway. He was wearing a different sport jacket from the one she'd seen him in when they'd met at Margo's the day before. He approached and gripped her elbow as he pumped her hand with a firm grip. "Delighted to see you again, Shauna."

"You, too, Simon."

Hunter, still seated at his desk, took no time for amenities. "Have you been in touch with the bank? I'll use my house for partial collateral. How much money will they lend—fast?"

Shauna tuned her mind out and sat in one of the seats facing Hunter. She didn't need to hear them talk finances. She let her thoughts return to what had nettled them earlier: Conrad Chiles.

What was it about the man that—?

It hit her.

"Hunter!" she said excitedly. "I have an idea about something in my story."

Simon perked up. "Really? Hunter's told me a bit about it. I'd like to hear more, if you don't mind."

"I mind," Hunter growled.

Simon sighed dramatically. "Too nasty of you. Well, I believe I hear my telephone ringing." He left the room.

"What is it?" Hunter then demanded, rising from his chair.

"Well, you know we've been wondering which neighbor Conrad Chiles is—from my story, I mean. At least I have."

A small pulse began to throb at the side of Hunter's neck. Was he preparing to dispute her intuition before even hearing it?

She wouldn't give him the opportunity. "My story described four neighbors." She said quickly, then quoted, "A neighbor was irritable. A neighbor was too nosy. A neighbor had actually seen something useful but didn't realize it. Yet another neighbor offered help and sympathy." She rose, placing her hands on her hips and leaning over his desk just a little so he had to look at her. "That sounds as if it's four different people, but what if the first three descriptions refer to the same person—a neighbor who is irritable and nosy and has seen something useful? The fourth sentence begins, 'Yet another neighbor…' That can be interpreted to mean that the first three are all one neighbor, and the fourth is a separate person."

"So what are you saying?" Hunter's dark brows dipped in confusion.

"If the first three are one person, then irritable, nosy Conrad Chiles has seen something useful but doesn't realize it!" She waited for a long moment as Hunter appeared to ponder.

Then his handsome features lost their dourness. He rose and unexpectedly grabbed Shauna by the shoulders, giving them a squeeze. "You might be right. Good deduction, Detective O'Leary."

Shauna reveled in what he undoubtedly meant as a compliment. And the fact that the more time they spent together, the more relaxed, and the less remote and irritable he seemed to become with her, despite the terrible circumstances that generated their reunion.

She reveled even more at the sensations he generated in her hungry body when he touched her.

He looked down at her. Something more than admiration tinted his eyes a deeper, hotter green.

He had obviously noticed their proximity, too.

Shauna, feeing a flush rise up her face, resisted the urge to clear her throat and run to the far side of the room. She didn't want to notice how wonderful it felt to be so close to him.

She *shouldn't* want to…

Hunter's breathing was uneven as he released her and glanced at his watch. "It's getting close to rush hour." His tone was more gravelly than usual. "And on the San Diego, every hour is rush hour—but we can probably be back at Conrad's in forty-five minutes."

All business again, Shauna said, "I'll call and let him know we're coming, if you can get his phone number from Simon."

He did, and handed it to Shauna.

On the third ring, an answering machine picked up.

Shauna, disappointed, left a message that they needed to talk to Conrad about something. She made certain she didn't sound too excited, for that might cause the irritable man to avoid them.

But what did Conrad Chiles know that could help them find Andee Strahm?

Chapter 8

But Conrad didn't answer the phone the second time Shauna called from Hunter's office, either. Or the third.

Sighing, Shauna hung up once more.

"No answer?" Hunter asked, popping his head in the door.

"No," she said shortly. Conrad probably wasn't home, for she left messages each time for him to call her on her cell, emphasizing how important it was that she talk with him.

Frustrated, Shauna had agreed with Hunter when she hadn't reached Conrad the first time that it made no sense for them to dash back there on the off chance they'd find him. Not with all the other matters involved with Andee's kidnapping that needed immediate attention.

Rising from Hunter's desk chair, Shauna again went into Simon's office, where the two men had been meeting.

She'd sat there quietly earlier as Hunter and Simon discussed which financial institutions Hunter should call to start assembling the ransom money. Fortunately, his credit sounded excellent and he had substantial equity in his home to use as collateral. Even if he emptied his bank accounts for cash, he could probably get loans. Whether the amount he could amass would be enough to meet the demand…well, that they couldn't tell yet.

Then they went through the list Hunter had previously compiled, of people who might think they had reason to get even with him. Shauna's story had suggested that Big T knew one of Andee's parents and that the kidnapping could be retaliation for some perceived wrong, not just a random crime with a ransom demand its reason:

It wasn't just that Big T wanted big bucks out of snatching the kid. Oh, no. This was personal, too—against one of Andee's parents.

They'd shown her story to Simon, who, bless him, had treated it—and Shauna—like an additional resource, not a freak.

In addition to all that Hunter had accomplished on the computer, Shauna learned that Simon had used his infinite, sometimes undisclosable and not entirely legal sources to track down and verify current addresses, phone numbers, places of employment and car license numbers of people on Hunter's list. Quite a few were in the L.A. area.

They faxed all the info to Banger, in a condensed form that wouldn't give away any of Simon's indiscretions. When they'd called to alert him it was coming, Banger reported that, not unexpectedly, his own investigation was starting to burgeon, thanks to rapidly increasing numbers of law-enforcement personnel assigned to the matter. He'd made it clear to everyone, he said, that keeping the kidnapping hidden from the media was mandatory. Still, he'd warned Hunter, with the mushrooming numbers involved, the time the matter remained covert was quickly running out.

An indignant and tearful Margo had continued to profess, when they'd called her, that she was beloved by everyone— or at least that no one disliked her enough to kidnap her daughter in revenge, not even the other actresses she'd mentioned. And, no, she hadn't seen Conrad Chiles that day.

As a result, for now, at least, they would concentrate on Hunter's possible foes.

Simon had checked out several yesterday. No indication they had Andee. But there were others. And that was to be their quest that afternoon—Hunter's and Shauna's.

Shauna tried Conrad's number once again before they left. Still no answer.

A short while later, Shauna watched house numbers as Hunter drove his car slowly down the cramped Hollywood street. He parked in front of a place with a sagging fence and flaking wood trim in dire need of a paint job, half a block from the house they were looking for.

Shauna opened her car door and started to get out. She felt a hand firmly grab her upper arm, stopping her.

"What are you doing?" Hunter demanded.

She turned back to face him. "I'm going for a walk."

He looked perturbed. Exhausted. There were dark circles beneath his brilliant green eyes. He kept his hand on her shoulder, as if trying to control her movement.

She took it gently in her own, squeezed it reassuringly, then placed it back in his lap. "This fellow Salinger would recognize you if he hates you so much. He won't know me, so I can check things out at his home without his getting suspicious."

She saw the war inside Hunter reflected on his face, despite the way he continued to block any overt emotion. The merest glimmer of appreciation in his eyes told her he recognized the validity of what she said, maybe even admired her for it.

But he didn't like it. That was visible in the unyielding set of his broad jaw.

She recognized his decision in his scowl as he opened his mouth to respond. She beat him to it.

"I'm tired of doing nothing today, Hunter," she said. "Simon and you hardly let me get a word in during your strategy session at your office. Not that I had any problem with your tactics, but I felt invisible.''

''There's no way I'm letting you get anywhere near Jerome Salinger,'' Hunter said.

Even without a *t* in his name to suggest he was Big T, Hunter had stuck Salinger near the top of his list of avowed enemies who hated him enough to steal his daughter. On their way here, Hunter had explained that the guy lived in this run-down area because his wife brought all the money and brains into their marriage. Salinger had blown it by getting caught cheating—thanks to the surveillance Hunter had done for his wife a couple of years earlier. It wasn't the kind of case Hunter liked, but since Salinger's ex was an executive at one of the major studios, he'd agreed to the job.

Once Hunter had described the sleazy, potentially danger-ous guy, he'd apparently expected Shauna to stay in the car.

She had other ideas.

''If he's got Andee, he'll be suspicious of anyone checking out his place,'' Hunter argued now. ''He could be dangerous. I'll be as fast as I can, but if I don't get back here within half an hour, call Banger.''

Hoping to take him off guard, Shauna leaned toward him over the console and planted a kiss on his stern lips. To her surprise, they yielded, opening and welcoming hers. His tongue darted out and laved her mouth until it opened.

Heat and liquid desire raged through Shauna. Heck, that wasn't what she'd intended by her impulsive action.

Regretfully she pulled back. ''I'll be back soon,'' she called as she threw open her door again and hurried out. ''*You* call Banger if you don't see me in fifteen minutes.''

She heard his door open but figured she had enough of a head start that he'd have to back off. If he did anything to call attention to them, the element of surprise would be lost.

And he wouldn't do anything to jeopardize Andee if she was here.

* * *

Hunter did what he hadn't intended and parked in plain sight of the house.

That was the best way to keep an eye out for Shauna.

He was angry with her, though he had recognized the logic of what she'd said.

He was angrier with himself for letting her throw him for a loop that way—with a kiss that had almost made him forget where they were.

But not why they were there.

What if Salinger did have Andee?

What if the torment he was experiencing was compounded by the jerk harming Shauna, too?

He'd seen Shauna go to the front door, but no one had answered the bell. She'd slipped around the side.

Enough. He'd been twiddling his thumbs for five long minutes. Time to do something. He opened his door—and stopped.

Shauna was walking down the house's driveway toward him.

He got back inside the car. She joined him in a minute.

"Well?" he asked.

"She's not there. Jerome Salinger has remarried. His new wife was in the backyard with her three-year-old from a prior marriage. I told her I was thinking of moving to the neighborhood and that I was pregnant with my first baby, wanted to find out if there were other kids around." She shook her head sadly. "If there are any besides Salinger's new stepson, they don't include Andee. None has a *t* in their names. Oh, and Jerome was home all day yesterday, nursing a cold."

Shauna pregnant with her first baby.

Hunter knew she wasn't, that she had made it up to further her investigation, just as he did when he was on a job.

But as much as he tried to eject the thought from his mind as he drove them quickly toward the next place on his list, the more it implanted itself in his brain.

Now and then, as surreptitiously as if he had been hired to check her out, he let his gaze drift toward Shauna and her slacks and her formfitting T-shirt, dark blue today, that emphasized her slender, sexy curves. She was just hanging up her cell phone after another attempt to reach Conrad Chiles.

As far as he knew, she didn't even have a boyfriend.

Written strategy plan or not, he'd considered marrying her years ago, had envisioned planting his seed within her.

And then everything had gone to hell, and his daughter had been born to Margo instead.

"How far is the next place?" Shauna asked, thankfully interrupting his musings. She sounded a little grumpy after once more getting Chiles's answering machine.

"Not far. It's in the San Fernando Valley."

"My checking things out worked fine at Salinger's," she said. "I'll do it again, and you can—"

"Forget it."

They were on the San Diego Freeway again, traveling up one of its many hills in a herd of other cars speeding in the multiple lanes on either side of them. He made his glance toward Shauna a quick one.

The grin she'd aimed at him made his groin stand up and take notice. "Want me to distract you again the way I did last time?"

He couldn't help smiling back, though he kept his attention straight ahead. "You do, and we'll wind up smeared all over the freeway."

"I mean after we're parked."

He took his right hand off the steering wheel and placed it on her thigh, squeezing gently. "On the other hand, I could distract you this time."

"No fair."

The thing was, this wasn't a joking matter. Or one that could be gotten around by playing games.

"It's more than fair, Shauna," he said seriously, pulling his hand back. "You don't know what you're getting into. If it turns out that one of these creeps has Andee, you could get hurt. This isn't even your problem.''

"Yes, it is," she said quietly.

"Just because you wrote one of your stories?" He hadn't meant to raise his voice, so he said, "Sorry. I know I've given you a hard time about them. You have to realize it's not easy for someone to swallow—something that could rock his life is spilled out onto a computer by a woman miles away. And it's true."

"I've never said any of it was easy," she acknowledged. "Not for me, and not for the people I write about. Even as a therapist, all I can do is try to guide them so they survive the best they can."

"Yeah, I got that."

"And you don't like it. I understand that, too."

"You're just too damned understanding." He took a deep breath to regain control. "This was a bad idea, Shauna, bringing you here. Especially since I told you I didn't believe your stories were true. I'd have to be damned stupid after all that happened before to ignore that they do come true, at least sometimes. But you also said you can't change anything that gets saved, and last night you did. Right now, I don't know what to think."

"Neither do I. I'm sure I made it clear that has never happened before. But whether it'll change things at the end—"

"I know you don't think so. Look, I want you to go home tomorrow."

"What? Why?" Her brown eyes went wide with shock.

"Because I said so." He hadn't intended to say it till it burst from him, but now it made sense.

"All the more reason for me to stay."

Hunter gritted his teeth. Stubborn woman.

Tomorrow would be two long days since Andee had been snatched. Damn! Every minute she was gone was another minute his daughter remained in danger.

But Shauna was too distracting. He needed to focus every iota of his concentration on the critical search for his daughter, and on carefully evolving his strategy as each new bit of information got factored in.

Not on the woman beside him whose presence played havoc with his plans. All too often he had urges to touch her. Kiss her. More. When all he should be doing was looking for his daughter.

And now she had purposely distracted him with a kiss.

Plus, she never fell in line with what he told her to do. Yeah, her info-gathering at Salinger's had been helpful. He probably wouldn't have done as well, talking to the creep's new wife. But Shauna could have put herself in danger.

"You can play with the story on your computer at home," he reasoned, "and then I won't have to worry about your getting hurt, too."

"I'm not here for you to worry about me." For the first time in the conversation, Shauna raised her voice. "If I want to take chances to help out, that's my business. Despite my doubts, if there's anything in my power I can do to make things turn out different from the ending I wrote, I'm going to do it. I've no intention of running home because you're worrying about me. I'm not your concern. Andee is, since I wrote about her."

They'd reached the freeway exit. Hunter turned onto it in relief. Driving while distracted wasn't a good idea anywhere, and particularly not on one of L.A.'s busiest freeways.

As they stopped at the light at the bottom of the ramp, he looked at Shauna. "Tell you what. I won't worry about you. We'll scope out this place, and if it makes sense for you to help check it out, fine. But I'll be your backup. Tonight, we'll have a long talk. And tomorrow, you'll go home. Understand?"

"I hear you, Hunter," she said, and turned toward the passenger window.

*   *   *

As it happened, Shauna didn't have to argue with Hunter about tagging too close for her to learn anything at the next place they visited. The guy wasn't home.

For the following one, Shauna insisted on calling first on her cell phone. Hunter had argued. In case any of their prey was the real thing, he didn't want anything to broadcast a possible warning.

But she'd prevailed, in the interest of saving precious time—time in which Andee had not yet been found. And the dwindling time before Banger's official investigation would likely be picked up by the media.

Shauna had therefore used her cell phone, a number Sol Perina couldn't possibly recognize. When he'd answered, she'd identified herself as a representative of a local phone company calling about a wonderful new offer. Of course he'd hung up, but they'd confirmed he was home.

Only, he wasn't. And the result was inconclusive.

Perina lived in a large apartment complex surrounded by a fence. Shauna felt uncomfortable sneaking in after a tenant who'd used a key to open the door. She entered anyway, talking on her cell phone, ostensibly to a person in one of the apartments—but actually to dead air.

When she got to Perina's and rang his bell, a man came to the door—taller and chubbier than the guy Hunter had described as the subject of an embezzlement investigation he'd done for a local bank. The amount taken had been too small to spend company time and resources in having the guy tried for a crime, but there had been more than enough evidence to fire him immediately, with no references.

Perina hadn't been pleased, Hunter had said. And when this large, scowling man who didn't smell particularly good came to the door, Shauna hoped that this time Hunter had sneaked in, too, and was watching her back. And her front. She felt very uncomfortable under this man's stare.

"Hello, Mr. Perina," she said brightly. "Your name was chosen at random among the residents of this building to have a free apartment cleaning by Maid-of-the-Week. We just need to look at the condition of your place to determine how many people to send, and then we can set up a time and date. May I come in?"

"No," the man said curtly. "Sol's not here right now, and I know he doesn't want a damned maid coming in."

"Then you must be Mr.—" Shauna grasped for a name so the guy hopefully would correct her. Preferably with something that began with *T*. "Mr. Taylor?"

"Koffleman." The door was shut in Shauna's face.

She returned dejectedly to the parking lot beside the complex, where Hunter was to pick her up. She didn't see him at first, but then noticed him slip out the building's side door.

He *had* been inside, watching over her. Of course it was only because he falsely felt responsible for any jeopardy she might stumble into while helping to find Andee, but his protectiveness still washed a warm sense of security over her.

She smiled sadly as he approached.

"I gather by your expression that you didn't find her," he said. He took Shauna's elbow, a once-familiar gesture, and led her to the far side of the lot, where she soon spotted his car.

"I didn't eliminate him as a suspect, either," she said dejectedly. She explained that the man in the apartment, most likely the same one who'd answered the phone, wasn't Perina but Koffleman. That meant Perina could be anywhere.

Including somewhere holding Andee.

"Okay," Hunter said when they were in the car. "Another one to keep on the list, including the suspect who wasn't home. That's three we've gone through. Two more to go." He sounded neutral, a P.I. on a difficult case for a client he barely knew—if she ignored the way his hands trembled as he shuffled papers he'd withdrawn from beneath the seat. "I'll check with Simon while we're on our way."

His assistant's success rate had been about the same, Hunter reported to Shauna after a brief cell-phone conversation. One possibility had been pretty much eliminated by location, circumstances and probably witnesses. A couple hadn't been around for Shauna to check on, and a fourth, whose first name was Timothy, remained high on the list.

Of the final two Hunter and she planned to scope out that day, one didn't answer his phone. That left one more, who responded at his office number. He worked in Glendale.

While they were on the way there, Shauna's cell phone rang.

"I'm really sorry there's been no big breakthrough so far," said Kaitlin after Shauna answered. "And that you're feeling so miserable about it. But why were you so nervous about half an hour ago? I don't like that at all." Kaitlin's special sense was obviously still honed in on Shauna, who appreciated it.

"It's great to hear from you, Kaitlin," Shauna said, smiling. She had only been gone just over a day and knew her restaurant was in good hands—and that Kaitlin would call her in an instant if anything was wrong. Still, she had to ask, "Is everything okay at Fantasy Fare?"

"Have you written any horror stories about it? Of course you haven't. Everything's hunky-dory. But what's with this guy in your life? When I tuned in a while back, I also had a feeling of arguing, but it wasn't that. It was…oh, never mind. It's not my business."

Shauna knew just what she was talking about, though—her disagreement with Hunter that she had cut off with a kiss.

Kaitlin could sense even that from so far away? But Shauna already knew how attuned she was to emotions.

"No," Shauna agreed, "it's not. What happened is also not what you may think."

"Yeah, and I'm Buster the Barker. It wasn't even the first time, though I didn't call you then."

Buster was a big, polka-dot dog that Shauna had made up as a character for a lot of her Fantasy Fare stories—a character who meant well but sometimes got in trouble for going about helping others the wrong way.

The kids loved Buster, and often asked for stories about him that reflected their own concerns.

"Okay, Buster," Shauna said. "I'll fill you in on what really happened when I get back there. Which I expect will be tomorrow." She darted a glance at Hunter. He seemed to be concentrating hard on his freeway driving. Too hard. Obviously he was listening.

He had said he would send her home tomorrow. She recognized it would be better for both of them. But though she hadn't wanted to come here in the first place, now she didn't want to leave. And not solely because she hoped she could help him cope with whatever was going to happen to Andee.

She was enjoying, much too much, spending time with Hunter.

Which told her that he was absolutely right. She had to leave, the sooner the better.

"Sure. Well, kiddo, I'm keeping fingers crossed that everything works out great."

This time, as Shauna hung up, her field of vision behind her eyelids was filled with disembodied hands—cartoonlike, and white gloved. Some snapped fingers in rhythm, and the rest were all knotted up, with digits all crossed over one another.

Once again, Shauna had to smile at the image Kaitlin had sent her way.

"Your manager again?" Hunter asked. His expression seemed bemused.

"That's right."

"I figured," he said. "More shorthand."

"Uh-huh," Shauna agreed.

Hunter was silent, but Shauna could see, by the way his lips flattened then opened, that he wanted to say something.

She recalled their earlier kiss—feeling those lips on hers in what should have been only a distraction…and was a lot more. It prompted memories.

And longings.

Neither of which belonged in her beleaguered brain.

"Something wrong?" she asked hurriedly. She'd mentioned leaving tomorrow. It had been his idea, after all.

But had he changed his mind?

Did she want him to?

"No," he said. "Nothing at all."

They met Simon at the end of the day, at one of Hunter's favorite dives on Santa Monica Boulevard, in West Hollywood.

Whoever built the place had never heard of acoustics, for with the music and the crowd all shrieking at full volume, there was no way to hear oneself think.

But it was a good way to have conversations one didn't want overheard—too noisy.

He sat across from Simon and beside Shauna at a square table near the entrance. Flatware and napkins had been dumped unceremoniously into a heap by the single empty place. Simon had wrinkled his nose so much at the rudeness that his mustache, which usually looked a lot neater than his straight, dark hair, appeared wavy. He parceled the utensils around, then set his own precisely in front of him.

Hunter knew better than to smile at his right-hand's idiosyncrasies. Simon was a darned good P.I. That was what counted.

"Okay," Hunter said after they'd given their orders to a gum-chewing waiter, "let's compare notes."

They went over everyone on his list, describing what contact, if any, had been made with each.

"I think you can rule out Jerome Salinger," Shauna offered. "But not Sol Perina."

"So our fearless leader Hunter allowed you to participate in the investigation?"

"He didn't allow it," Shauna said, "but he didn't stop me." The conspiratorial glance she shared with Simon annoyed Hunter.

They continued their discussion over meals of enormous hamburgers and crispy fries. Not that Hunter had much appetite.

Though they had been able to whittle down the list a bit, not many suspects had been completely eliminated. Simply finding them at home alone wasn't enough. The kidnapper could have hidden Andee someplace else.

"All right," Hunter said. "Let's discuss what to do next."

"You know what that is," Simon said, so quietly that he almost couldn't be heard over the din.

Putting down his glass, from which he'd just taken a swig of cold, watered-down cola, Hunter glared. Of course he knew what Simon had in mind. He just didn't agree with it.

"What?" Shauna asked.

"I believe it is time to fully unleash our compatriot Banger," Simon replied. "Figuratively, of course."

Most of the time, Simon's use of language amused Hunter. But nothing about this discussion amused him now. "I know Banger hasn't liked keeping a lid on things," Hunter said, "and that he's had to work hard to do it and still get the ball rolling at LAPD. The day he gave me is nearly up. I'm going to ask for more time, even though he's already gone way out on a limb for me. If nothing else, it'll give me more time to get the money together."

"Caving in to an extortionist's demands is not necessarily the wisest way to catch him and end the situation," Simon replied. "I believe he's more likely to return Andee safely if he knows he is the subject of an intense manhunt, and his only chance of a light prison sentence is to give her up unharmed. Let the authorities loose, Hunter. It's what Banger wishes."

"But the newsmongers'll grab on to it," Hunter protested. "Having cops after the guy is one thing. But having the whole scenario the subject of a media circus is something I don't want to chance. It could scare him into doing something really bad."

"But Hunter..." His name tapered off on Shauna's lips. Obviously she didn't want to finish what she'd started to say.

That told him what it was.

The word had somehow gotten to the media in her story. Plus, the cops' all-out effort had expanded.

He knew how she thought that turned out.

Hell, it was how he figured it'd turn out, too.

"If we'd made more progress today," Shauna finally said, "I'd agree with you, Hunter. But we've barely eliminated anyone on your list. And that's even assuming you've remembered everyone."

"And that it is actually one of those many citizens who have vowed revenge on the owner of Strahm Solutions," Simon added.

They were right, of course. But he'd had to continue with his mapped-out strategy and follow up on whatever meager clues he had. No way would he just sit around twiddling his damned thumbs while the cops ran around in circles looking for his daughter.

But he couldn't even say with certainty that any of them— himself included—had made headway toward finding her.

Andee had been missing for almost thirty-six hours.

Shauna and Simon were both looking at him. Amazing how he wasn't much affected by Simon's expression of understanding, but the anxious compassion in Shauna's brown eyes made him want to roar in anger and give in to self-pity all at the same time.

"All right," he finally agreed. He pulled his cell phone from his pocket and called Banger.

"You find her?" his police detective friend asked immediately.

"No. You?"

"No, but we've been busy." Banger gave a rundown on all the guys he had out searching for Andee and for clues, what the Fibbies were up to, the works. They *had* been busy. And it was a miracle that the news hadn't grabbed it up by now. But he'd continued to talk to his troops in person, mostly early in the mornings, in the roll-call room. Or by phone to senior officers, instructed to keep their guys looking for a kidnapped kid but to keep it quiet. Nothing went out over police channels, where messages would be susceptible to media scanners. "But we're reaching that wall, Hunter. We need the public's help—tips and so forth."

"I know," Hunter replied. "That's why I called. Give me one more day, till tomorrow. If we haven't found her by then, go ahead and pull out all the stops…no matter what the SOB who has her has threatened." His insides went icy, but he knew he was doing the right thing.

To keep Andee alive, they needed media pressure. And more.

"I don't like it," Banger growled. "But…okay. No guarantees, but I'll try not to let it break before then. We don't have a lot of control."

"I know. I owe you."

"You're not kidding."

Hunter hung up. He hadn't realized he had grabbed his glass in his other hand. Nor how tightly he was gripping it.

Not until he felt Shauna's smaller, warmer hand on his, guiding it back to the table.

He put the glass down gently, then turned his hand over, grasping Shauna's hand as if it was an IV line that pumped strength and resolve into him.

And maybe, for the moment, it did.

Chapter 9

They had until tomorrow morning before all hell was likely to break loose. Hunter had to find Andee before then.

But at that moment, he was nearly out of clues. He had done almost everything in his plan and still hadn't found his daughter. That meant he had to work on his strategy, all night if necessary. He'd use the home office in his bedroom. That way, Shauna could get some sleep, even if he couldn't.

He also had one more chance to set things straight in Shauna's story before he sent her home. Whether or not he chose to accept that her stories came true, the one on Andee's abduction was a loose end. One way or another, he had to figure out a way to change the ending. Even if he couldn't do it on paper, he absolutely would change it in real life.

As soon as they finished their meal with Simon, he and Shauna got back into his car. Parked on the street a block from the restaurant, Hunter had Shauna make more calls on her cell phone, in case those on his list who'd been absent earlier had returned to their lairs.

No more success than before.

"He's still not home," Shauna said in frustration when she tried again to call Conrad Chiles. "Or at least he's not answering his phone or returning messages. I really want to talk with him."

Hunter hated delays. Worse, he hated anything unforeseen. This time, he'd anticipated the result of Shauna's call.

That was why he was already headed north, toward Conrad's.

Daylight was nearly gone and the outside light was on at Conrad's, but that didn't mean he was home. Hunter accompanied Shauna to the front door and watched as she rang the bell. Once. Twice. Three times.

"Okay, we tried," Hunter said. "We'll find him tomorrow." He hoped that was true.

Could Shauna be right—that the Chiles fellow was actually three of Margo's neighbors in Shauna's story all rolled into one?

Might he have seen something important without recognizing its significance? Hunter would find out, whether or not Shauna was around.

They were around the corner from Margo's, but he didn't particularly want to see her. He used his cell phone to call—his eyes steadily on Shauna's in the fading late-evening light. Hers were quizzical until he said, "Hello, Margo."

"Have you heard anything?" Margo asked excitedly. Which told him a lot. She hadn't gotten any further communication from the kidnapper.

"No," he said. "I was just checking in to see if there was anything new from you." Anything requiring an impromptu visit.

After the standard stuff with Margo—including her teary entreaties to find their daughter and bring her home—he hung up.

"Is she all right?" Shauna asked.

"Yeah, for Margo," he replied. "No need for us to stop in." He turned the key in the ignition and headed home.

"Do you want something to drink?" he asked Shauna after they arrived. They had entered his house through the door from the garage into the kitchen. He carried the case with Shauna's computer, which she always brought with her.

"A glass of water would be great. I'll get it myself."

He watched as Shauna reached into the cabinet near the sink. She was tall enough that it wasn't much of a stretch for her to grab a couple of glasses—just enough that her blue T-shirt and snug pants hugged her tempting curves more tightly. Curves that Hunter had an urge to caress as her clothes were doing.

Forget it, Strahm. Shauna would go home tomorrow. That would be best for both of them. She wasn't really involved in what had happened, even after writing about it. He didn't need her shrink-style sympathy. Or her insistence on rushing in where he, the P.I., should be handling the investigation.

Plus, he didn't need the distraction of having her with him, teasing his mind away, even just for seconds, from where it needed to be. Teasing his body, constantly, with wanting her.

Mostly he hated her certainty that the ending of her damned story was unchangeable. And that something as bizarre as that might have control over an important aspect of his life.

Like before, when he was with the Phoenix P.D.

Shauna was looking at him.

"I think I'll have a beer," he said. "Want one?"

"Sure." She turned back to his cupboard to put the glasses away. He got another glimpse of material stretching over her taut, alluring behind.

He headed for the refrigerator and removed two bottles from the back of the top shelf. He pried the caps off with the bottle opener attached to the end of a counter, watching the soft sway of Shauna's hips as she crossed his kitchen floor toward him.

"Here." He proffered an open bottle and she took it, brushing his glass-chilled hand with her warm fingers. "Let's toast Andee's safe return."

She clinked her bottle gently against his. "To Andee," she agreed, not quite parroting his toast.

He looked into her eyes. No challenge there. Or sympathy. Instead, their glowing depths surrounded him, cushioned and cocooned him like a warm, whirlpool bath.

She was leaving tomorrow, he again reminded himself, breaking eye contact by tipping his head back and taking a long gulp. He would miss her. Miss talking with her. Hearing her intelligent insight into the search for his missing daughter, despite her not being a law-enforcement professional or P.I.

Having her by his side in this difficult quest.

Having her so near him again...

While another of her stories and its blasted consequences wreaked the worst kind of havoc on his life.

"Why did you do it, Shauna? I mean the last time. Why didn't you tell me about that bank robbery until it was too late?" The words burst from him before he considered them.

Her eyes widened in obvious surprise. "Do you really want to talk about it?"

"Would I ask if I didn't?" He turned his back long enough to walk around his small table and take a seat. He pointed to the one across from him, but she didn't take the hint. Instead, she continued to stand there, watching him.

Studying him, as if she expected him to sprout horns and breathe fire like the devil himself.

"You refused to talk about it before," she said. "That's why I asked. And I'm sure you know the reason I didn't call you sooner back then."

Yes, actually he did.

He'd known when his mother had met Shauna. At first, Elayne hadn't explained why she found the young woman so fascinating. But when she'd introduced Shauna to him, he'd found her more than fascinating. A manager at a chain restaurant at the time, she was the prettiest, sexiest, most wonderful woman he'd ever met. He'd fallen for her. Hard.

And then came the stories that wound up involving him.

She'd helped find a missing child, and afterward had admitted to him—and some other cops he was close to—that she'd written a story about the scared little kid that came true. Only then had his mother told Hunter about the story that had introduced Shauna to her.

He hadn't believed any of it. Coincidence, that was all. Some of his friends on the force, though—a bunch of credulous fools. They believed in her.

Especially after the serial bank robberies started. He'd been put in charge of the investigation. Shauna had called him all excited one day. She'd written a story that had said where the next robbery was going down—at that very instant.

"You know full well why I didn't believe your stories, Shauna. That first one you wrote about those punks who were robbing banks in that northern Phoenix suburb wasn't true."

"Yes, it was," she said, her eyes fixed on his. "The problem with it was that I made a mistake interpreting which branch it was in."

"I'll say." Not really believing, but also not wanting to fail to pick up on a tip that had a chance of being real, he had grabbed a team and run off to the branch she said—while at one six miles away tellers and patrons were robbed at gunpoint.

He'd looked a fool.

"You must have believed me at least a little then," Shauna said, "or you wouldn't have paid any attention at all. And then you were so..." Her voice tapered off as her face reddened.

"I was a nasty SOB," he finished. "I know I gave you a hard time."

"You made fun of me." She looked away. "Since we were so close by then, it really hurt."

"I figured." Damn. He'd felt like a jerk then, and the feeling washed over him all over again. Not for doubting her, but for being so hard on her. He'd known she believed in her stories, and he'd fried them. And her. "But you didn't give up your faith in what you wrote, did you?"

"Of course not," she shot back. Her chin raised defiantly as she regarded him again, more coolly this time.

"So why didn't you tell me about the next story you wrote?" They hadn't talked much about the first fiasco, though he'd remained angry about it. The second was at the dead center of the big blowup between them.

His fellow cops would have believed, if she'd told them. And he, even not believing, would still probably have done something—even if it was just to send a patrol car by to check. But she hadn't said anything at first. Until it was too late to save the three civilians the lousy suspects had blown away before making off with a bunch of the bank's cash.

At least they'd been captured later that day—thanks to good police work, not Shauna's story.

"I did tell you," she replied quietly. "I struggled with it first. That was the problem. I didn't want…" Her voice tapered off, and she looked away. But only for an instant. When she turned back, her eyes were defiant. "I didn't want to be ridiculed again by the man I loved. I had to risk it, though, to prevent the tragedy I'd written about." She took a deep breath before continuing. "But I'd hesitated too long. It was already too late. Things had been set in motion, and—"

Her voice broke. Hunter had an almost irresistible urge to cross the gulf between them—his damned kitchen table—and take her into his arms. Comfort her now, the way he hadn't back then, when he'd taken the heat for failing to listen to her. For even when she had gotten around to telling him, he'd taken his time about sending someone to check it out.

"And that was before I'd become so sure that what I wrote couldn't be changed," she finished hoarsely.

Damn. They'd gone full circle. "It will be changed," he insisted. "This time. Andee will be fine."

"Hunter, you know that's what I wish, too, but I really think you should talk—"

"So, are you ready?" He kept his voice as cool as his drink. Her voice was stronger now, more assured, and though her face was pale, she regarded him with sympathy.

He bet she was going to start some shrink talk about letting his feelings hang out.

The problem was that, even if she was right, if he started describing how he felt, he'd come apart like one of Andee's old stuffed animals where the seam had ripped and mounds of white cotton innards had spilled all over the place.

"Am I ready for what?" Shauna asked.

"To work with your story again. See if you can save any changes."

"If that's really what you want," she said. Her reluctance was as obvious as if she'd shouted "no" right in his face.

"Yeah, that's what I really want," he said. Picking up her computer case, he preceded her toward the guest room.

Shauna wasn't sure what to expect.

But she couldn't just stand around with Hunter in his kitchen any longer, rehashing their painful history—or watching his frustration and pain on his face as clearly as if he spilled it like a patient participating in therapy.

So, without further prompting, she withdrew her laptop from its bag, put it onto the small table in the guest bedroom, and booted it up. She scrolled through menus until she reached the file containing her story about Andee. And opened it.

She scanned it briefly. It read the same as last night, after she'd been able to save the single small change: Andee knew her daddy was already home from his trip.

She still didn't understand why the modification remained. It meant nothing, except to make her look like a liar to Hunter.

But he'd thought her that, and worse, before.

She looked up at him. He stood close to her, just to her right, and now he knelt so he could see the screen, too.

This close, she could clearly see the shadow of his dark

beard deepening the shade of his cheeks. Could watch the way his Adam's apple worked in his neck as he tensed his jaw.

Could breathe in the clean scent of soap, for he must have washed his face when he'd excused himself briefly to go to his bedroom.

"Okay," she finally said. "What would you like me to write?"

"Go to the day after Andee's disappearance and add some stuff about how we looked for her. Stick yourself in the story. You weren't there before, but you're in the thick of it now."

She had tried to insert herself into the story of her father's final illness: talking to his doctors, trying to find some new therapy to help him. Then there'd been her growing grief and her ultimate despair—oh, yes, she had tried to add all sorts of things to that tale.

To no avail.

She had shouted at night, in her own room, to her Grandma O'Leary, who had talked with her often when she was a child about how her very special abilities would mature as she did. Grandma O'Leary's response, in her mind, was always the same:

You can't change your stories, Shauna. They come to you as our family gift. You'll learn to live with them. All the O'Leary women who have the gift do.

And she had. But her "gift" had cost her Hunter once.

She didn't have him now to lose again, but even so, when the ending didn't change but came to pass, his hating her again—even more this time—would be too hard to bear.

"Are you going to try it?" he demanded in her ear.

She'd been staring at the screen in her dismal reverie. Procrastinating.

"Sure," she said. She moved the cursor till she reached the spot he'd mentioned. "Here?"

"Fine."

"Tell me how you want it to read."

"This is your ball game. You pitch it any way you want."

A strange analogy, but she understood it. "Okay. How about this?" She wrote, *Andee's daddy, Hunter, had a friend named Shauna who lived in Arizona. To help Hunter find Andee, she traveled with him to Los Angeles. She had a very special skill: writing stories that came true. She wanted more than anything to write a story for Andee's safe return.*

Shauna looked at Hunter. His head was so close that he could have rested it on her shoulder. She inhaled the warm, musky scent of his short, black hair and the scalp beneath. She resisted tilting her head so that it touched his, instead saying, "What do you think?"

"Not bad. Now, right here—" he pointed farther down on the screen "—stick in a little about going to Margo's, talking to her neighbors, then dropping in on people who didn't like Andee's dad, that kind of thing."

"Okay."

Shauna started typing on the keyboard. At first, she watched the screen, then her fingers, then—

"Hey, are you writing in your sleep?" Hunter's deep voice resounding in her ear caused her eyes to pop open. It sounded vaguely amused.

"Kind of," she said, finding it interesting. She often went into some kind of trance when she wrote, whether stories for Fantasy Fare or her tales that came true.

When she woke, she was often surprised by what she saw on the screen.

Like stories about strangers in emotional situations that roused her now and then. Stories she'd written about Hunter over the years, the way she had kept up with his milestones.

And the terrible story about Andee.

But she hadn't expected to go into a dream state here, with Hunter there, watching what she wrote. Watching *her.*

"Did you read everything as I wrote it?" she asked.

"Yeah. It seemed to track what we did pretty well."

"Just pretty well?"

"All right. You did a damned fine job." He was smiling, his face still close to hers. So close that she could lean over and plant a kiss right on that sexy, grinning mouth while hardly moving at all. If she wanted to. Which she didn't.

"Thanks. Now keep still while I read it."

"But my legs are going to sleep." He rose, and suddenly it was his waist that was directly beside her. If she looked down only a little, there was his groin....

She was obviously being driven nuts by having Hunter so near. And by trying to revise her story for him when she knew how fruitless it was. And by—

"Have you finished reading it yet?"

"Almost," she lied, then focused on the screen once more.

A minute later, she said, "As far as it goes, it reads all right to me. What do you think?"

"Did you change the ending?"

Guiltily she went to the final part of the document and checked. Had she, while in her sleeplike state? "Not yet." She did, made it end with Andee's safe return.

"That's better." Hunter's voice was cooler, as if he was angry he'd had to mention attempting to change the end.

She said carefully, "Okay. I'll try to save everything." She moved her cursor to the icon on the screen, then clicked the left button on the mouse. A tiny hourglass appeared, indicating something was going on. Its disappearance indicated that the computer had done something—or should have. Saved the changes?

Shauna next clicked the little *x* at the top right. The file closed. She waited a couple of seconds, then clicked on the icon that appeared to be an open file folder. She scrolled down the menu that appeared and when she reached Andee's story, she clicked on it.

The story opened at the beginning. No changes there, but she hadn't tried to make any.

Once again, she scrolled through the document—and when

she got to the part that started the day after Andee's disappearance, her mouth opened. "It's there, Hunter," she said in wonderment. "What I just wrote about my coming here to help—it was saved in the story."

"What about the rest?" Excitement pealed in his deep voice, and Shauna felt his arm go around her shoulder as he bent to read along with her.

Aware of his nearness, his touch, she continued going through the story. "Yes," she said slowly. Then, a little louder and faster, she said, "What I wrote about how we both canvassed Margo's neighborhood, talked to people, then started down the list you made—it's there, too."

"Save it on your disk," he demanded. His grip on her shoulder grew tighter, and he held her taut against his leg. "I'll stick it in my computer and print it. Then we'll have even more proof that your stories can be changed."

And then he asked the question she had been dreading—the most important of all. "What about the ending?"

"I don't know."

"Let's look at it now."

She didn't want to. But neither could she say no. Shauna scrolled to the end.

It read the same as before she had tried, once more, to change it. The story still ended badly.

Hunter retracted his arm from her shoulder as if she had suddenly scalded him, and she felt horribly alone once more. Rejected by him—though she knew that was ridiculous. He hadn't done anything to *accept* her, so how could he reject her?

"You changed more stuff that's real but not important, and it's still there," Hunter said. "Why not the ending, too?"

"I've no idea. To me, it seems miraculous that anything's different."

"Some miracle," Hunter muttered. He strode from the room, leaving Shauna staring, unseeing, at her screen.

* * *

Hunter wondered whether Shauna was still awake. Playing with one of her stories. It had been nearly an hour since he had left her. Most likely she was asleep by now.

Not him.

Usually, he liked to work at this time of night. That was why he had his office here, in the corner of his bedroom, so he could get down to business fast, anytime, without disturbing Andee.

His house was quiet at this hour, if he didn't think about background sounds like the refrigerator's motor, the sporadic cars along his street.

The occasional sweet deep-sleep mumble from his daughter's room...

Damn it!

He stared again at his computer screen, at the Web site he had brought up with a database on unsolved kidnappings in Southern California over the past ten years.

None resembled Andee's. Of course.

Why was he doing this anyway? He knew Simon had already checked this site and others, too, and moved on. His assistant was more skilled at this kind of stuff. All he was doing was driving himself nuts. Battering his tired brain against a solid brick wall.

He hated not being able to take control—fast. Find a way to communicate with the SOB of a kidnapper, get the damned money to him, get all of them out of this infernal mess.

Get Andee back.

Too much time was passing. But there wasn't much Hunter could do at this moment but plan and work on Internet searches. He couldn't call on neighbors, friends or enemies in the middle of the night and still expect things to stay covert. He'd already applied for loans that would hopefully yield him the full ransom, but now he waited for approvals. Talking to Banger or Tennyson would only keep them from doing something more productive. Like finding Andee.

He glanced toward the bed. He knew he was exhausted.
Maybe he should lie down for five minutes, try to rest.

Right.

He turned off the monitor but not the computer. Pulled off
some of his clothes. Tugged down the comforter on his bed,
shut off the overhead light, tried to settle on his hard mattress.
And lay there, eyes open.

Shauna lay in bed in Hunter's guest room for the last time.
She was going home tomorrow.

That thought should have filled her with relief. She hadn't
wanted to come. She'd known she wouldn't be able to do
what Hunter wanted her to.

She hadn't even been able to accomplish what *she'd* hoped
to by coming: find a way to help Hunter live through what
was to happen.

She sighed. Readjusted the pillow beneath her head. Sighed
again.

What good had it done anyone for her to be able to save
some changes in her story and not the most important? *Why*
had it happened?

And what the heck was she going to do back in Oasis while
knowing Hunter was facing the most horrible situation anyone
could go through? What would she do in Oasis, thinking
about him? Wondering about him.

Wanting him.

She shifted, uncomfortable in her silky nightgown. She became aware of its stark coolness as it touched her skin in
places where Hunter's caresses once had ignited her.

Where his hot, surreptitious gazes still did.

This time, her sigh was sheer frustration. Why did her
mind—and all her senses—keep sliding back to Hunter that
way?

As if she didn't know. That was one thing Hunter and she
never argued about, when they were together before. They
had shared sex that was the most incredible, sensual, unfor-
gettable—

And then, lying there alone in the barely comfortable bed, she knew what she had to do. For both of them.

It wouldn't solve anything. But, for a short while, it would give them both some solace.

Hunter's eyes blinked open as he heard something unfamiliar. Had he actually slept? He lay still, listening, muscles tense.

His bedroom door was opening.

He reached beneath his bed to where he always stuffed his Glock after Andee was tucked in and he'd retrieved it from the locked drawer where he kept his weapons, on the off chance he'd need to grab protection quick.

Like now. Only…

L.A. nights were always illuminated by streetlamps, lights from the neighbors, whatever. Even when miniblinds were closed tight, some light always seemed to sneak in.

As a result, Hunter had no trouble discerning the outline of the person standing in his doorway. A slender silhouette with long, pale hair.

"Shauna? You all right?" He sat up fast, pulling a sheet over him like some kind of damned prude. He'd kept his boxers on, but it would be embarrassing if she saw what she did to him by appearing unannounced at his bedroom door that way.

"I'm fine, Hunter," came her soft reply. "Except—"

"What?"

She didn't answer. He watched her glide across the room in the faint glow from somewhere outside. She wore a nightgown—blue, maybe? And judging by her bare feet, the soft motion of her breasts beneath the clinging material, little else.

Talk about his body reacting—

"What do you want, Shauna?" His voice sounded as if he'd swallowed sand.

"You," she whispered, sitting on the edge of his bed so he couldn't help rolling toward her.

Hell, he could have helped it—maybe.

But he didn't want to.

Instead, he pulled her roughly into his arms, then rolled on top of her. Felt her ripe curves pillow him, drive him insane.

His lips crushed downward, finding her mouth. He tasted the toothpaste she must have used that didn't mask the sweet and subtle flavor that was simply Shauna. He'd recalled it before with the kisses they'd shared. Lord, how he remembered it now, as he thrust his tongue deep and let it sweep her mouth, bringing back memories of other nights they'd been together. Other burning kisses they'd shared.

Other times his erection had grown so uncomfortable he'd wondered if it could burst from his wanting her so much.

The same way it swelled now, thrusting against her from beneath his shorts. Hindered, too, by that damned piece of silk that she wore.

He reached down, yanked off his covering, felt relieved and frustrated at the same time as he sprang free, pushed against her.

He grabbed for the edge of her gown and started pulling it up as she squirmed—

Was he going too fast?

Had he misread what she wanted?

Trying to maneuver his words out around his heavy breathing, he said, "Is this okay, Shauna? Is it what you want?"

He anticipated a no. A wriggling as she tried to move from beneath his body, which had to be damned heavy on top of her slenderness.

"Yes," she sighed, sounding as out of breath as him.

He muttered something—oath and prayer and gratitude all rolled into one—as he slid her gown over her smooth skin, touching it as his hand skimmed her curves.

She moved to assist him, finally half-sitting so he could pull the thing over her head and off, her hands raised so her breasts were right in front of his mouth.

Eagerly, hungrily, he sucked one rosy tip as he gently squeezed the other.

He heard Shauna's moan, felt her fingers begin to explore his burning flesh. He moved his mouth back up to hers as his hand moved lower.

When he touched her below, she arched and cried, "Hunter. Please."

She didn't need to ask again. He barely remembered in time that he kept protection in a drawer near his bed. He grabbed it, pulled it on.

In an instant, he was inside her, and he felt as if heaven had returned.

Chapter 10

It was over much too soon. Not that Shauna wasn't satisfied.

She lay beside Hunter, her side edged up against his. He breathed heavily. So did she.

"I didn't hurt you, did I?" His rumbling voice held concern so sweet that it dampened her eyes.

"No," she whispered. "It was—I…" Her voice tapered off, for she was uncertain what to say.

That it had been wonderful? That she had wanted it so much she had ached for needing it, needing him, since the moment she had seen him again?

How could she, when what had brought them together this time was so terrible?

"Yeah," he said, as if she had said something profound that he agreed with.

She laughed, then grew quiet. "Hunter, I hoped that you and I could part tomorrow as…friends."

His laughter was even louder than hers. "I considered that more than friendship." He sucked in his breath, as if just realizing what he had said. ''Not that I think we're heading for anything serious again, but—''

''I get it,'' she said, and turned so she snuggled closer against him. He moved his arm, and she was glad when it wrapped around her, drawing her even tighter. She rested her head on his shoulder, put her hand in the center of his chest, where the muscles were taut and the skin was damp and roughened by a smattering of hairs. Though it was too dark to see him, she knew they were dark, as black as the hair on his head. Like the coarser hair below.

Had she made a mistake? Maybe. But she didn't think so. Especially when his breathing quickly grew deeper, steadier, as he fell asleep.

She'd been one heck of a sleeping pill, she figured. But judging by the circles he'd had beneath his eyes, she doubted he'd slept the night before. She'd noted his computer was still on when she'd stood in the doorway, and she doubted he'd been asleep long when she'd come here tonight. She didn't think he'd get much rest for a while, even when the ordeal was ended.

She kept her sorrowful sigh shallow so as not to disturb him. She closed her eyes, hoping that she, too, would sleep.

Much later, Shauna lay in bed still awake. She couldn't believe the lovemaking she and Hunter had just shared again. It had been gentle this time. Slow. And so erotic that her skin still hummed from his touch.

And the rest of her body sang even louder from the way he had felt inside her, the rhythm of him, and of them together.

But once more, not even Hunter's deep, even breathing lulled her to sleep.

Slowly, almost sadly, she disentangled herself from his unconscious embrace and headed for the guest bedroom and her computer.

She always turned to her computer, and to writing, to distract her from anything, everything, that bothered her.

She booted up but stayed far from the story about Andee. She wasn't going to try to change it again. Not now.

Instead, she would work again on the story she had started out to write for little Bobby, the child who had begged her for a story about his dog the next time she read aloud to the children at Fantasy Fare. She had named that file "Duke's Story"—and it had, instead, turned into what she had written about Andee. Now, she began a new file: "A Tale of Duke."

Once upon a time, there was a little boy…

Shauna opened her eyes and shook her head. She hadn't been able to sleep, but she *had* gone into one of her trances. *Once upon a time* no longer faced her on the computer screen.

It was one of *those* stories.

Bracing herself, apprehensive and trembling, she began to read.

Tears flowed down her cheeks, wetting a smile as wide as her face would allow, as sad as all the irony in the world.

This story, too, was about Hunter. And her.

As all her stories flowed from someone's emotions, this one must have sprung from her own, for it was a love story. In the man's point of view—rife with her own wishful thinking.

About two people who'd loved and lost and met once again.

And despite all the odds against them, including a terrible situation that brought them back together, their love was renewed, right along with their passion.

This chronicle, unlike "Duke's Story" about Andee Strahm's kidnapping, had a happy ending.

Sobbing quietly in her realization that this tale, at least, could never come true, she closed the file without saving it.

Of course she knew better, for when she opened it again, it was still there.

When she returned home, she would print it out. Copy it

onto one of the disks on which she now saved all of the stories about Hunter that she had written over the years.

It was a love story. With a happy ending.

Between Hunter and her.

She read it over two more times before closing the file for the night and heading back to Hunter's bed. And his arms.

For now.

For these moments, unlike the story, would be ephemeral.

And she wanted to create as many new memories as she could.

Since much too soon, the ending of her other story would occur. And that would be the ending, too, of whatever it was she now shared with Hunter.

The phone rang.

Hunter was instantly awake. Not surprising.

What was surprising was the feel of Shauna's body on top of him as she instinctively reached over him for the phone.

"I'll get it," he told her in amusement. Her closed eyes shot open, and she appeared shocked to see him there.

But only for a second, as the feeling of flesh on flesh obviously sank into her consciousness, and she wriggled a little on top of him before rolling off.

An anticipatory smile on his face, he answered the phone. "Strahm here."

"Hunter, it's Simon. Turn on the TV—any channel with news."

Hunter didn't ask why. He hung up fast, reached for the remote control beside his bed. He had a television on a stand near the bathroom door across the room. He turned it on.

"What's going on?" Shauna asked. He didn't look at her but turned up the volume as he found a local show.

"Police have not yet corroborated it," intoned a solemn, suited male announcer, "but a five-year-old child has apparently been abducted from her mother's home in the north of the San Fernando Valley. Neighbors have confirmed that the child's mother searched for her two days ago, then later appeared to recant the story of the child's disappearance.''

"Damn," Hunter said. "I know it's already 'tomorrow,' but I'd hoped we'd have till later in the day before Banger stopped being able to hold back the news."

"They haven't named names." Shauna's tone was quiet and quivering. "Maybe the kidnapper will assume it's another incident."

"Yeah, and maybe I'll tiptoe back into the past couple of days and see just who grabbed my daughter. Oh, yeah, sorry. I forgot—you might actually believe someone could do something like that, with your superpowers, Shauna the Storymaker."

"That's not fair, Hunter," she replied quietly.

"You're right. But what *is* fair?" Hell, this wasn't her fault. But she was the nearest person he could lash out at. Because he was damned afraid now for his daughter's life.

He still didn't have any clothes on. Didn't care, right then, if he mooned the woman who'd shared the stars with him last night. He got out of bed and headed for the bathroom, the phone receiver still in his hand.

He pressed in some numbers. The voice that answered didn't sound the least tired. Hunter wondered what shift Banger was on. Voices sounded in the background. He obviously was on duty.

"You've seen the news?" Hunter demanded without preamble.

"Yes, we've been dealing with it for about an hour—the usual. People calling 'cause they're afraid it's their kid. Or claiming they saw something. We're checking into every one."

"How'd it get out there so fast?" he asked. "We need to do damage control, make sure the guy who has Andee understands that we didn't tell the media. That I'll do anything to get her back. I'm hoping to have most of the money together by the end of the day."

"You want to schedule a press conference?" Banger's voice faded a little, as if his cell phone signal was weakening.

"Hell, no. But maybe we'd better."

"You talked to Margo yet?"

"That's next on my agenda."

It wasn't a pleasant experience. He woke Margo virtually the same way as Simon had got him up, then had to deal with her screaming and crying over the phone.

"Cool it," he shouted at her. "No, I don't know how—"

"Please, Hunter, I can't do this," she cried. "What's going to happen to our baby?"

"She'll be fine," he insisted. She had to be. Margo pleaded with him to be with her. Being back in the neighborhood where Andee had been snatched might yet be the best place to be. Especially if the kidnapper called again—hopefully just to make threats. And not to report on what he'd already done to Hunter's daughter…

He turned on the shower to let it warm up a little. He no longer needed a cold one, even with Shauna still in bed.

They'd had their farewell performance. He'd give her cab fare, send her to the airport, get her out of there.

Yeah—and what if she is able to save more changes to her story now? She'd already written that the media got hold of the kidnapping and run with it, so this wasn't new to her.

Only the timing was damned inconvenient. But what timing wouldn't be?

Still, on the off chance she could do something, anything, with this new, miserable turn of events…

He stomped into his room to see her standing by the bed, already dressed in a different outfit from yesterday—another T-shirt, black this time, and slim gray pants. She must have slipped out while he was uselessly talking to people behind his closed bathroom door.

"Can we go back to Margo's, Hunter?" she asked. "I just turned on my cell phone. Conrad Chiles finally called back and left a message. He's demanding to know if Andee's the child in the news. I need to talk to him."

On the drive from Hunter's to Margo's, Shauna gritted her teeth as Hunter kept flipping from one of L.A.'s all-news radio stations back to the other. The kidnapping wasn't the only story on, but it was repeated frequently, with promises of more information when it became available.

"Soon," Hunter muttered after one of those hints of more to come.

"Pardon?" Shauna turned toward him. She'd been staring out the GTO's window at the city's inevitable traffic, wishing she could speed the other vehicles up or get them out of the way.

"Soon. The damned media carrion-eaters are going to love it when Margo and I hold a news conference later."

"Really?" That possibility startled Shauna.

"Yeah. Margo doesn't know it yet, but Banger thought it would be a good idea."

Shauna wasn't sure how to react to the idea. For one thing, that hadn't been in her story. For another… "Don't you think that might make the kidnapper…edgy?"

Shauna watched Hunter's features, as rigid as if encapsulated in ice, as he stared at the road ahead. "He'll be edgier if we don't," he muttered. He glanced toward her, his green eyes expressionless. "This way we can claim we don't know how the information got out there, but we didn't release it." His voice lowered, and Shauna didn't need one of her stories to sense the depth of his emotion. "Maybe he'll buy it, not harm Andee despite his warnings."

He obviously didn't want to talk about it anymore, for he turned up the radio's volume. A while later, she turned her head away from Hunter as they drove up Margo's street. She didn't want him to see her alarm as she counted news vans. Obviously, even though no names had yet been given, they knew who the kidnapped child was.

"Do you think it would be better to park somewhere else?" she asked.

"Yeah," Hunter agreed. He kept driving, slowly enough not to run down any milling reporters, though Shauna had little doubt that he'd like to have scattered them in as startling a way as possible without injuring any. He pulled around the corner and stopped on the street behind Margo's. Near Conrad Chiles's house.

Shauna barely waited for Hunter to turn off the engine before she hopped out. "I'll go talk to Conrad," she told Hunter when he quickly joined her on the curb. "And then I'll check on you at Margo's before I call a taxi."

"Taxi? What taxi?"

Shauna made herself ignore the glower he aimed down at her, even though it hurt, especially after last night. It was, after all, an expression she had come to know well...before.

"We've already talked about my going home today," she said softly, forcing herself to not even touch him, when what she wanted to do was to throw herself into his arms for one last time. "You'll be busy, so I'll need to get my things and—"

"Yeah, well, I've been thinking. You have to stay here, at least until tonight."

"But—"

"Don't you get it? This changes things." He closed his eyes, as if seeking some inner strength. And then he was the one to grasp her—by the arms. Keeping her, still, at a distance.

"My story deals with what happens after the news reports on the kidnapping," she reminded him, trying hard not to wince in reaction to his flinch of pain.

"But nothing in it suggests a press conference," he said slowly, as if she was a not-too-bright child to whom he was attempting to teach a complicated theorem. "It'll add another dimension to that whole fiasco in your story about the media frenzy. It'll show the kidnapper that we had nothing to do with the information leak, but it should get a message to him, let him know we stand ready to do whatever he wants.'' Hunter's expression turned momentarily pleading. "Won't that be enough to change your story, Shauna? To get your computer to at least save the differences. I won't even ask about it allowing for another ending…yet.''

Shauna wanted so badly to take the single step that separated them. To replace his almost-impersonal grip on her arms with a tight and tender embrace. To reassure him that everything would turn out all right.

That would be the woman who had never, really, stopped caring about him talking, though. It wouldn't be the detached therapist who should be trying to help him.

And it certainly wouldn't be the poor fool who was blessed or cursed with the immutable O'Leary gift.

One thing, though, was certain. She couldn't leave him like this, when he wanted her to stay.

She didn't want to leave him, ever…

But she would. If not before, then someday soon, when he would be unable to stand the sight of her.

And though all she could give him now was false hope, she said, ''Okay, Hunter. You know I can't promise changes to my story. But if you want me to, I'll stay.''

''You'll try tonight to change it, won't you?''

She kept her sigh deep down inside. ''Of course,'' she said.

Chapter 11

"I'll meet you at Margo's in about half an hour," Shauna told Hunter. "You go ahead and get things set up."

"No way," he said. "I'm coming with you to talk to our buddy Chiles."

Her going to talk to Conrad Chiles while the media descended on Margo's sounded like a great idea. But not Hunter, too.

"Conrad's not *your* buddy," Shauna reminded him, ignoring the obstinate expression that drew his mouth into an irritated line. The mouth that she had kissed all night. But now they both had things to do. And she had to convince the stubborn man before her that she could handle her part just fine. "If you come along, he's more likely to argue with you than tell us what we need to know. Besides, you can't be two places at once. You need to be there for the press conference. With Margo."

His look segued to exasperation. "You're right. All we need is for the drama queen to get in front of the cameras herself. You win. But make sure you tell me everything he says. And get to Margo's as soon as you can.''

"I will." Shauna turned and headed for Conrad's. She'd actually hoped to miss the news conference but couldn't do that to Hunter. He wanted her there. They'd talked about it in the car. If her story was to change, she had to have knowledge of how reality differed from what she had written.

Conrad's house was a single story, gray stucco with white shutters. The path through the attractive rock garden was no-nonsense straight, from the sidewalk to the plain white panel of the front door.

Shauna found the doorbell button near the jamb and pushed it. She heard nothing from inside but had the odd sensation that Conrad was assessing her through the peephole.

The door swung open seconds later. "Tell me what really happened to Andee," Conrad immediately demanded, as if they were still in the middle of yesterday's conversation at Margo's. He wore a red plaid shirt with the sleeves rolled up to reveal bony forearms, blue jeans, brown felt bedroom slippers, and a fierce gaze behind the glasses perched on his out-sized nose.

"I'll be glad to tell you what I know—" Most, at least. "—if you'll answer more questions. I'm still hoping someone in the neighborhood saw something to help us locate Andee, and I'll bet it'll be a person as caring and observant as you."

His smile slid up one half of his sunken cheek. "Nosy, you mean. Well, come in and let's see." He motioned with a gnarly forefinger for her to follow.

The entry to his house consisted of a platform of yellow tile only a few feet square. The living room was beyond it, with white walls that needed a coat of paint, and shabby furniture that probably hadn't looked much nicer even when new.

"Have a seat." He pointed toward a chair that had a gold slipcover with a stain on the arm. He sat on a rocking chair beside her. A couple of the spindles hooking the seat to the upper part of the back were missing.

"Okay, Conrad." Shauna leaned toward him conspiratorially. "Here's what we know." She gave a rundown of how Andee at first had seemed to have walked away from Margo's yard, then the calls from the kidnapper warning the parents not to go to the police or let anyone know.

"Did the guy demand ransom?" Conrad's eyes narrowed sagely as if he knew the drill. Probably watched a lot of television, since the nicest thing in the entire room was a TV along one wall.

"Yes. Hunter has been working on getting it together while he and others looked for Andee. He's a private investigator, so his assistant has been helping, and the police and FBI, too—discreetly. Hunter told someone he trusted, and the investigation was kept quiet, at least till this morning."

"I get it." Conrad leaned back and rocked contemplatively in the chair for a few moments.

"Now, I'd like to ask you some questions," Shauna said.

"That's the deal. You want a glass of something first—cola? Coffee? All I have is instant, though."

"No, thanks. What I really want is for you to describe what you remember about the morning Andee disappeared, two days ago. Tell me everything, in case there's something that you don't realize is significant." Like the neighbor in her story.

He did as she asked, droning on about how he'd planned to go to the auto-parts store because he thought his car needed oil. He checked it first, in the garage behind his house—in the alley that was also behind Margo's.

"Did you see Andee?"

He shook his head. "No. In fact, I don't think I saw anyone else in the alley. Not when I drove out, either."

Drat. How could he be the neighbor who'd seen something significant without realizing it if he hadn't seen *anything?*

She prompted him to keep talking about that morning a little longer, but he didn't reveal anything helpful.

Her dismay must have been obvious, for Conrad stopped speaking in the middle of a sentence. "This stuff isn't what you want, is it?"

She shook her head. "I appreciate your time, but I'd better go." She rose. "You'll let Hunter know, won't you, if you remember anything else?"

"I'll tell *Margo*," he emphasized. "She's a nice lady. I like seeing her on TV now and then, in commercials and all. When I run into her in the alley, she tells me what she's working on. She's an actress, you know. Auditions for all kinds of roles. She sometimes throws parties for her acting friends and the neighbors. Invites some real famous people— ones I see on TV all the time, though I couldn't tell you their names." Bit-part actors, Shauna figured. "They put on funny skits. You know, she's really good. I tell her she should try stand-up comedy. But she says she likes serious roles better." He frowned. "I know she's done some live theater, too, but I haven't seen any of those plays."

It sounded to Shauna as if this older man had a crush on his neighborhood quasi-celebrity.

"She's invited me, though," he went on. "Problem was, my asthma acts up now and then. But I've seen some of her friends—that John Aitken, for one. He visits her a lot, and I saw one of his plays, a drama. I told Margo how good I thought it was, since she obviously likes the guy, but I was just being nice. Me, I can't stand him. His ego's as huge as the Pacific. He always talks, in that too-too dramatic voice of his, about how he'll make it big in the theater." Conrad exaggerated the last word as if in imitation. "It would help if the guy could act."

"The important thing now," Shauna said to bring him back to the subject, "is for Margo to get her daughter home safely."

"That's for sure. Cute kid. I've seen her a lot when she

stays with Margo. She plays sometimes with a little girl down the street, Sondra Nantes. Her dad Earl's a friend of mine. And when Margo takes Andee for walks around here, she brings her to my place for a lollipop. Margo's told me how much she misses Andee when she's with her father, wishes she had her around all the time but had to give her ex-husband more custody so she could work as much as possible, since she had to give him money for Andee's support. Should be the other way, don't you think?''

Shauna not only thought so but believed Margo had told him the opposite of reality—maybe so she wouldn't look like a bad mother. What Shauna said, though, was, ''I'm sorry, but since I really don't know their situation, I won't criticize it.''

''You're a friend of her ex-husband's,'' Conrad persisted. ''You don't think he staged this whole kidnapping thing to prevent poor Margo from seeing her daughter again, do you?

''No,'' she said firmly. ''I'm certain he didn't.'' She moved toward the door. ''Just please be sure to tell one of them or the police if you think of anything else that might be helpful. And thanks for all you told me. I'll pass it along.''

''Did I say anything helpful?'' he asked dubiously, hurrying ahead of her to open the front door.

''It's hard to say what'll be helpful,'' she hedged.

But as she went around the block toward Margo's, Shauna felt dejected. She'd been so hopeful that her insight about the three neighbors rolled into one was Conrad Chiles.

Yet this time, Conrad hadn't been irritable, just nosy.

And try as she might, she couldn't extract anything from what he'd said that might fit the third criterion: the neighbor who'd actually seen something useful but didn't realize it.

''Any idea how the media glommed onto it?'' Hunter demanded.

Banger shrugged. ''Like I warned you, keeping a mushrooming number of law-enforcement types invisible couldn't last forever.''

They stood inside Margo's front door, along with Lou Tennyson, Banger's trusted FBI crony.

''You want a lot of press in a situation like this,'' Tennyson said, as if delivering a revelation to the uninformed.

''Not when we were told publicity would be hazardous to my daughter's health,'' Hunter hissed.

Tennyson, a suit if there ever was one, wore his federal position like a crown. Hunter had disliked him on the spot. But he knew Banger. And if Banger vouched for this short, pompous Fibbie, then the guy probably couldn't be all bad.

Emphasis on the *probably*.

Bad enough that Hunter had run the media gauntlet getting inside Margo's. He'd been taped and photographed while microphones were thrust in his face and questions hurled at him.

While he was the one who wanted answers.

And now, the law-enforcement types were pretending all the attention was a good thing.

In any event, they had to deal with it now.

''Let's prepare for the damned press conference,'' Hunter said. ''We've got—what? Fifteen minutes?''

''Yeah, I told them nine-thirty,'' Banger confirmed. ''They were supposed to low-key it till then.''

Hunter snorted. ''If that's low key…''

''I've seen worse,'' Tennyson said. Hunter shot him a glare that the guy countered with a wry smile—the first human glimpse Hunter had gotten of him. ''But not a lot,'' he finished. He looked in his late thirties, judging by the depth of the few wrinkles on his face, but his hair was white. Had his job done that to him?

''Great,'' Hunter snapped in response. ''Okay, look, the spin to put on this is that I'm delivering a message to the kidnapper. I don't know how the authorities got wind of this. I didn't tell them. And I've got the money together—which is just as much a lie, though I've gathered enough to get his attention. I'll—'' He had to stop for a moment and swallow, because what came next was almost too hard to say. "I'll do anything to get my daughter back safely. But I need proof she's still alive."

He heard a sudden intake of breath from behind him and turned. Shauna stood there. Whatever the sound meant, her demeanor was calm. A hell of a lot stronger than how he felt.

He wondered if grabbing her and pulling her close would make him feel any better. Hell, yes. But only while it lasted, and that couldn't be for long right now. As a result, he held himself firmly in check.

Had she learned anything helpful from Chiles? He doubted it, or she'd tell him right off, he was sure of it.

How had she gotten in without being pounced on by the media predators outside?

As if she'd heard the question, she said brightly, "I haven't done that kind of sneaking around since I was a kid. I had to pop into the alley, pretend I live around here and was heading for my garage, then double back when no one was looking. Fortunately, the few watching the alley disappeared all at once."

She didn't refer to his last comment about Andee. But even her story allowed Andee to stay alive…until the end, when the kidnapper was caught. Well, that part he'd buy into. They *would* get the guy. But first, they needed to assure him that no one had blabbed to the media.

That the police simply happened on the kidnapping?

Yeah, right.

He noticed then that Lou Tennyson was quietly staring at Shauna, as if sizing her up. As a suspect?

He'd suspect her of something, all right, if Hunter explained why she happened to be here. Her connection to the kidnapping: her magical writing.

Sure, the FBI would buy into that.

He decided to take the simplest route and tell part of the

story. "Shauna, this is Lou Tennyson. He's a friend of Banger's—with the FBI."

"Hi." She approached the man with her hand outstretched. Tennyson didn't look pleased but reciprocated.

Hunter said, "This is Shauna O'Leary, an old friend of mine who's come here to help." An old and dear friend, he thought.

"Do you know how the media got hold of this story, Agent Tennyson?" Shauna asked. "Maybe if we knew that, we'd have a better idea what to tell the kidnapper to protect Andee."

"Could be any number of sources. All we can do now is damage control." Tennyson's tone was all business. As he released Shauna's hand, he looked at Hunter. "So, are you ready to head out front and talk to them?"

"As ready as I'll get," Hunter said, steeling himself as he headed from Margo's kitchen, through her house to the front door.

He stopped as he heard questions being shouted from the front lawn. Followed by the amplified sound of Margo's voice.

Yanking open the door, Hunter was blinded suddenly by a bunch of attacking camera flashes. When he could see, there was Margo, at the edge of her porch, her back toward him— and her face toward a sea of people wielding microphones and cameras. Her friend BillieAnn Callahan was at her side.

Damn! Why hadn't she waited for him? And how was he going to keep control of what she said?

"Ms. Masters," a reporter shouted from the back of the crowd. "Is the information that's now circulating true—it's your daughter who's missing and she's been kidnapped?"

Tears rolled down Margo's face. "If I tell you, will you please let me make a statement?" Her voice broke, and she began sobbing quietly, BillieAnn's arm around her shoulder.

"Sure," called another reporter, holding her microphone toward Margo.

"Give her a minute," yelled BillieAnn. "She's going through a lot."

Which undoubtedly told the reporters their speculations were true. Hunter hurried toward her—first shooting a glance back toward Shauna, whose face was pale and worried.

In moments, he stood between BillieAnn and her. BillieAnn shot him a dirty look but stepped away.

Hunter was immediately bombarded with a barrage of questions, mostly, "Are you the child's father?"

"I'm Hunter Strahm." He projected his voice as if he was in Margo's line of work—acting. "Ms. Masters—Margo— and I used to be married. We have a daughter, Andee, who's five years old. I'm not sure how information got to the media, but we recently learned that—"

"That Andee was kidnapped," Margo broke in, looking beseechingly at him as if wanting him to understand something. He wasn't sure what. He also didn't trust her to say the right words to fix things for Andee.

The problem was, he didn't know what they might be, either.

Reporters hurled questions at them, but Margo held up her hands. Since she was always so concerned about her appearance, he wasn't about to tell her that tears had caused her makeup to streak beneath her eyes.

"Please, let me speak." As everyone quieted, she continued in a voice that cracked with emotion. "What I'm saying now is directed toward the person who's got my daughter. Andee…" Her voice trailed off into a sob.

She looked up at Hunter as if for support. Feeling trapped into it, he put an arm around her.

Blinking, Margo aimed a smile that appeared grateful up at his face, then turned back to the reporters. "Whoever you are, please listen. I don't know how word got out about Andee. We're trying hard to comply with what you want from us. We've got the money together—" She again looked at Hunter, who nodded. He wasn't about to even hint he didn't have every cent available. "As soon as you contact us, we can make arrangements to trade it for our daughter. But, please, don't hold all this against us." She swept her hand around, toward the panting throng surrounding them. "Just take good care of Andee and let us know where you want the money. Please." Breaking into sobs, she turned and hid her face against Hunter.

"Yeah," he said, staring straight into one of the cameras and hoping the expression he stuck on his face looked sincere. "Prove to us she's okay and we'll do anything you want." He tried not to choke on the last part, for it acknowledged that the creep who had their daughter was in control.

From the corner of his eye, he saw Shauna peer from behind drapes at Margo's front window. Aware that his ex still pressed against him, he couldn't help holding her tighter.

He felt like a damned hypocrite. And an utter jerk. Shauna wouldn't care if he pretended to still care for his ex-wife in front of the rolling cameras. She'd expect it of him.

The earth-moving sex they'd shared last night had been an outlet for both of them and their stress. A reaction to being together for the first time in all these years, for the world's worst reason. The feelings they'd once had for each other were way in the past. At least they should be.

Yet even as he forced himself to hug Margo, shield her from the cacophony of shouts from behind them as he led her into the house, he felt like the lowest form of louse. Especially when he met Shauna's gaze. He saw the understanding there.

And beneath the acceptance, did he also see hurt? Or was that only perverse wishful thinking?

They'd looked like a couple united in determination and sorrow, Shauna thought. Which they were.

She sat in a corner of Margo's living room while the others—Margo, her friend BillieAnn, Hunter, Banger and Tennyson—gathered in the conversation area in the middle.

She was, after all, the outsider.

If only she had simply gone home today, as they'd planned.

"What was that all about, Margo?" Hunter began when they were assembled. "Why didn't you wait, so we could deal with that media circus together from the beginning?"

"I...I don't know." Margo sat on her sofa looking both frail and defiant. Not even fear for her daughter or dealing with the onslaught of the press made her appear less than gorgeous. Her eyes were red and sad, smeared around the edges with makeup she'd mostly cleaned off when she came inside, but Margo was the consummate tragic figure. Her face was pale except for color upon her high cheekbones and light lipstick, her complexion flawless, her brown hair a little mussed.

Was Shauna jealous of her?

Not of her beauty...at least not much. But the fact that her loveliness had attracted Hunter in the first place.

And that he was leaning toward his ex-wife in their time of fear for Andee. So much toward her that he had all but shouted their reconciliation to the world, on a hundred news cameras.

The very day after the night he had spent with Shauna.

Well, heck. She had known that all they were doing was taking comfort from each other. She had offered that small bit of solace to Hunter, and he'd taken it. End of story.

But not the end of *her* story.

Margo snuggled closer to Hunter on the sofa. "I'm sorry. I thought it would be best. I mean, I was the one watching Andee when she was taken. It's my fault..."

"Let's not get into fault," Lou Tennyson said smoothly. "Or who should or shouldn't have spoken on camera. The point's been made that neither Hunter nor you did anything intentionally. We have to assume the kidnapper will get this, one way or another. Now that the word is out, he's probably watching the news. You've done what you can. Now—"

Shauna continued to listen as the discussion progressed, but her attention wavered.

She had the distinct sense that she was missing something.

Something in her story? Something that might provide a clue about the kidnapper?

Or was her hopefulness, her fear for Hunter's child, causing her mind to play games?

She wasn't sure. But what she did know was that, as soon as she was able, she wanted to reread her story yet again, every word. Let her subconscious flow with it.

Not that she expected to change it again. Or that the ending would be any different.

But something niggled at the edges of her consciousness.

And somehow she had to figure out what it was.

Chapter 12

A good—and bad—thing about the kidnapping becoming public knowledge was that the public now thought it was involved.

Hunter, having been a cop, wasn't surprised at the sudden influx of information. It didn't deluge Margo or him directly, but the official law-enforcement agencies on the case, the FBI and LAPD, were receiving huge volumes of phone calls and e-mails.

Each had to be checked out, just in case.

Would the initial media barrage result in anything helpful? Who knew? Hunter hated waiting to find out. He hated waiting, period. It made him feel powerless. Especially today, when Andee's life hung in the balance.

While he paced at Margo's, he had Simon run around, tending to business at Strahm Solutions. Checking out the few remaining people on Hunter's list who might have it in for him.

Despite Shauna's hope that her conversation with Conrad Chiles would yield something, it hadn't, except for the fact that Andee sometimes played with neighborhood kids. Hunter had told Simon to check out them and their families, too, just in case.

"Hello?" Shauna answered a cell phone in Margo's living room for probably the twentieth time. It was a special line, activated for this case and publicized among law-enforcement agencies so authorities outside Banger's and Tennyson's offices would have a way to reach them. Margo's home line was left free, in case the kidnapper called.

Shauna sat on one of the two sofas, a cup of tea on the table in front of her. Margo, Banger and Tennyson appeared in the doorway, racing from wherever they'd been in the house.

"Yes, this is Ms. Masters's residence." Shauna turned toward Hunter, who faced her from the other sofa. She mouthed, "LAPD."

He nodded as she took notes on a pad of paper. She had unofficially become their secretary. He appreciated how she had simply jumped in to help when grief-stricken Margo appeared overwhelmed by the sudden information overload. He appreciated Shauna's unobtrusive, soothing presence. Her caring concern for a child she had met only on paper.

It was now nearly seven in the evening. Hunter had insisted on being kept in the information loop. But what he really wanted was to be out there looking for his daughter.

Margo's place was now their unofficial Command Central. The local FBI office in Westwood was probably the official headquarters for the investigation. Unless, of course, Banger and Tennyson were engaged in a turf war. If so, they kept it to themselves. No one knew where Andee was, so they didn't know if her kidnapper had crossed state lines. That would definitely make it the FBI's jurisdiction.

In any event, both agencies were cooperating with one another. Personnel from both kept in touch with their respective representatives about new leads that might be authentic.

They'd all been given the cell-phone number as a point of contact.

So far, no call had been important enough to get the FBI special agent or LAPD detective excited.

"Yes, I'll give the message to Detective Banner." Shauna hung up and looked at Hunter, the expression in her brown eyes neutral. Years back, she'd claimed she could read his thoughts from his face. He hadn't said so then, but he'd sometimes done the same with her.

Now he used her beautiful eyes as a gauge of the importance of what she'd heard, for he had always found them expressive. They'd shouted her anger at him. Caressed him with her love.

Ignited him with her desire.

Damn. This wasn't the time or place for thoughts like that. Though no wonder they perched at the edge of his mind, ready to soar with the slightest encouragement after last night.

"So, anything?" They weren't alone, so he kept his voice as level as if she were just a message-taker.

"What is it?" Margo interjected, sitting on the edge of the same sofa that Shauna occupied.

"Not much." Shauna looked toward Banger and Tennyson, who stood behind Hunter. "Some officers in the LAPD's West Valley Division investigated a call we were told about before."

"Where a bachelor suddenly had a kid living with him?" Tennyson demanded.

Shauna nodded. "Turned out the guy's sister, a divorcée, had to go to the hospital for minor surgery so he's babysitting. It checked out."

"Damn!" Flagellating himself with each new disappointment wouldn't do any good, Hunter knew. But surely something had to come out of all the calls, the public hue and cry. He flexed his hand, realizing from the sudden cramp that he'd had it tensed into a tight fist.

"What I don't like," Banger said, "is that Margo hasn't

heard from the kidnapper. He should be damned mad. Making threats. Whatever.''

''Assuming the kid's still alive,'' said Tennyson.

''Of course she is,'' Shauna snapped. She glared at the special agent as if she'd just scraped him off the bottom of her shoe. Why was she so sure Andee was okay? Because they hadn't come to the end of her story yet? Hunter now believed it was more than that.

''I agree,'' Margo said. She'd been sitting with her head bowed. Now she appeared more animated. ''He made a ransom demand. He took Andee for money. Even with publicity, why would he harm her before he gets what he wants? We've got to hear from him soon. Find out where he wants the money, and when. We'll turn it over to him, get Andee back, and it'll all be over.''

''Let's hope it's that simple.'' Hunter knew it wasn't. He remembered, in Shauna's story, the implication that the kidnapper had a grudge against Andee's parents, or at least one of them.

He may want money, but that wasn't all.

And Andee recognized him. Even when paid off, would the creep let her live?

He guessed Shauna was thinking the same thing, for she didn't respond to the comment. Instead, she stared at Margo, then down toward the phone in her hands, as if urging it to ring.

Hell, he could think of something a lot better for her to do with her hands. And it wasn't her phone that rang, but his.

It was Simon. ''I believed for a short while that I had your answer,'' Hunter's assistant said.

''That tells me you don't,'' Hunter responded, refusing to let himself feel any more discouraged. ''What did you find?''

''I followed up on that neighbor child Shauna learned about—Sondra Nantes. Interestingly, her father Earl has a nice, long felony record. Car theft, mostly.''

''Hey!'' Hunter's mood lifted. ''Let's—''

"Don't get excited," Simon warned. "I telephoned their home, suggested I was one of the authorities looking into Andee's disappearance, and learned Mrs. Nantes has been out of town for a week. Earl's been home with the kiddies along with his wife's mother, who was eager to reveal all her gripes about the man—including that he has been looking over her shoulder the entire week. And Andee has not visited young Sondra during that time."

"Damn. Well, nice try." Hanging up, Hunter revealed the conversation to the group. Despite his resolve not to let any of this get to him, he'd had enough for now. "I'm out of here." He headed for the door. "If anyone hears anything I should know, you have my cell and home numbers. Shauna, come with me. There's something you and I have to take care of."

He pretended not to notice her apprehensive look. He was certain she knew what he wanted from her.

And though he couldn't help feeling tempted, it wasn't another bout of their sensational sex.

They stopped first at Hunter's office. He carried her laptop in but Shauna didn't set it up at first, though he'd told her in the car what he'd wanted them—her—to take care of: her story. But how could she concentrate on anything, with Hunter shouting into the phone and pounding on his own computer?

It wasn't just Hunter that kept her from concentrating, though. It was her own preoccupation. She was trying to grasp something elusive that tickled her mind. What was it?

In the minutes Hunter wasn't dialing someone on the phone, calls came in. He answered each, grumbled something and slammed the receiver down. She gathered most were media people.

"Let's get out of here," he said after a while, his expression so grim that Shauna had an urge to do something, anything to cheer him. As if she could. "Too many distractions.

My office number's listed on my Web site and everywhere else. My home number's not. We'll work there.''

She didn't like the way they sped there in his car. Or that he immediately set up her laptop again in the guest room and insisted that they get to work on the story.

What was it that niggled at her brain? Maybe she shouldn't feel uneasy that Hunter had planted her at her computer. If there really was something, maybe her subconscious mind would spit it out through her fingertips as she revised Andee's story to synchronize with all that had happened that day. And see if it stuck.

She turned on her computer.

''Are you going to try it?'' Hunter stood so close behind her that she could feel the heat from his body warming her. She wanted to lean back, take comfort from his nearness, but it would be a false reassurance.

He hadn't been kidding at Margo's about wanting something from her. But that didn't mean he'd like the result.

''I'll get a glass of ice water first.'' She turned in the stiff wooden chair in Hunter's guest bedroom.

''Stay here. Limber up your fingers or whatever you do to get ready. I'll get your drink.'' He squeezed her shoulders gently, and then he was gone. Not for long, she reminded herself. Still, the room felt empty without him.

She used her laptop's touch pad to open her word-processing program, then scrolled through the menu to the story. Ironically, it was still labeled as it was when she'd first sat down to write ''Duke's Story.'' It didn't, of course, contain what she had started to write, but instead was Andee's story. Other files on her computer also had titles she had started out with when she had sat down to write children's tales. She never changed the names. Why bother? She knew what was in each.

She opened ''Duke's Story.'' It started with the segment in Andee's point of view that had so touched Shauna that she'd begun crying when she first opened her eyes and read it:

Andee was scared. So scared. "Daddy," she cried.

But Daddy didn't come. Instead, the bad man came back into the room.

"Help me, Daddy!"

Bracing herself mentally, Shauna scrolled down to where, chronologically, today's events would fit. In her story, the news media had gotten hold of the kidnapping and run with it, but not for another couple of days. What had changed in real life? Could she save the changes she would make on the computer?

Would it make any difference?

How could Hunter bear it? She didn't even know his child, and she ached each time she read this story. Maybe it was better for him, for he still hung on to his hope.

Hunter returned. "Here's your ice water."

"Thanks." She sipped the cold liquid. She would need every bit of ice in her veins that she could import there. She put the glass down and saw, from the corner of her eye, when Hunter strode from the room again. Was he leaving? Good. She would rather do this in private, and so far he'd hung around each time he had wanted her to change the story.

He came back carrying a folding chair, which he set up beside her. "Don't mind me," he said. "Go ahead."

How could she help but mind him? His presence dominated the room, and not just because he was such a large man, both in height and muscular breadth. His presence dominated her thoughts, too. He wanted a lot from her.

She wished—oh, how she wished—that she would be able to give him what he wanted. Then she could simply slip away, go back to her life, let him go back to his.

Who was she trying to fool? Even if things turned out perfectly, all the blockades she had built up in her brain after losing him before had now been decimated.

Damn. She had work to do. She turned to him, the smile

on her face as false as acrylic fingernails. "Okay, let's see what happens."

She put her fingers back on her keyboard and began to write.

Hunter had seen Shauna write before—over the last few days, at her home before they'd dashed to L.A., and last night, when she'd been able to save the changes to her story.

He wouldn't admit it to her—didn't want to admit it to himself—but she looked damned sexy sitting there, her sensual body poised and slender on the uncomfortable-looking straight chair, her long legs crossed at the ankles, her soft brown eyes scrunched in concentration as she studied what she wrote. Her light, wavy hair swept below her shoulders, moving ever so slightly as she nodded gently to herself.

Her fingers pressed the keyboard in a syncopated rhythm as words he couldn't read from where he sat appeared on the screen.

Her full lips puckered in a pout of concentration. He wanted to concentrate on them. On that pucker. On what she could do—did do—with those lips…

He moved in his chair and looked away, trying to regain control. He hardly noted the bareness of his guest bedroom, except for the bed in its center.

Shauna. Bed. His bed—

He clenched his fists so hard his hands ached. How ridiculous could he be? Like a hormone-crazed adolescent, when what he needed was to concentrate as much as Shauna on her story.

The clues pouring in to the authorities might help. They might not. But what Shauna was doing was damned important, for it revolved around Andee. And, now that he'd been faced with Shauna's stories again, he knew he had to give them credence.

Had always given them credence.

Today's press conference wasn't in her story before. Once she inputted it, would she be able to save—?

At the change in tempo to Shauna's typing, he pivoted back to look at her. And felt his jaw drop. Her eyes were closed. Her mouth was open, but only a little. All color had fled from her lovely face, leaving her complexion pale, fragile looking.

And still she typed.

He'd seen her close her eyes briefly while writing before, go into some kind of daze or whatever, but this was different. Way deeper. As if whatever she was doing had taken control of her body, her mind…

And still her fingers flew over the keyboard.

Was this how her writing changed from tales about kiddies' dogs into the horror stories that came true? If so, where did they come from?

She'd always claimed to consume other peoples' emotions and spit them out, somehow, onto her computer. Whose emotions did she read now?

If he rose and drew closer, would he disturb her?

Disturb her? Hell, she looked as if she'd turned into a sheaf of wheat in a windstorm, ready to blow over any second.

Should he hold her up? Catch her if she fell?

Wake her by shouting her name, the way he wanted to?

Damn, this couldn't be good for her. It wouldn't help Andee. He had to stop it. Now.

But he didn't. As if he was the one who'd suddenly gone into a stupor, he watched for a moment longer. And then another moment. A minute…and then Shauna moaned, a small, mournful sound that made the hairs at the nape of Hunter's neck prickle.

Enough! He stood and rushed toward her as she swayed and nearly toppled. She caught herself before he reached her. He inhaled the soft, sweet-spicy scent that was Shauna's. Grabbed her by the shoulders. She turned her head and looked up at him, a vacant, bewildered expression in those eyes that always drove him nuts with their strength and eloquence.

"Hunter?" Her voice was frail, husky, and he knelt and held her tightly. Pressed his head against her side for strength—his? Hers?

"Are you all right?" he demanded.

"What...?"

"You looked like you were asleep. Really catching some heavy *z*'s—in some kind of trance, but you kept writing. Were you aware of it?"

"Trance? Now? No..." Her voice drew out for a moment, and then she slowly turned her head away from him.

She cringed as she faced the computer, looking at the screen as if creeping up on its contents might make it easier. Every muscle in her body appeared to tense, causing her to shiver.

"What is it?" he demanded.

"I—" She blinked, then faced the screen head-on. Her eyes moved as she began to read. "Oh, no," she whispered.

"What?" He didn't wait for an answer. Still kneeling, he took a few steps on his knees until he was again at Shauna's side. He began reading, too.

"Damn," he swore futilely. "Damn it all."

What the hell was he going to do now?

Big T hadn't counted on this.

Maybe he should have. Everything else had gone wrong since the second he'd snatched the kid.

He'd demanded no police. Police had been brought in.

The person he'd trusted most had betrayed him.

What should have been simple, a game to be won, had turned into a nightmare.

Well, he needed the damned money even more now. He'd set things up, get paid and get the hell out of there.

"Where's my daddy?"

The kid was awake again. She kept interrupting him when he needed to think.

"Shut up."

"That's not nice. Where's my daddy?"

"He'd better be doing what I tell him to." Good thing he'd been able to keep the kid from watching the TV, or she would

know where her daddy was, all right. Her mommy, too. And the cops, and the damned reporters, and—

Hey. He knew how to fix things. Where to schedule the pickup for the money, get rid of the kid and set himself free. He'd think it through, though, before calling again.

If he had to get rid of the kid the hard way to save himself—

Well, even though it hadn't been the plan before, plans change.

Shauna held her breath as she finished reading. Her body was coiled into a tight, trembling mass as it so often was when she finished writing one of her stories. Only this time, it wasn't a new story. It was part of an existing one.

She'd never before lost herself in adding to her writing, only while creating a story in the first place. But, then, she'd never before had Hunter urging her to change things.

"Oh, no," she murmured yet again. She turned in her chair, away from the computer.

Toward where Hunter knelt beside her. He was so tall that despite the height of her chair, his head was even with hers. The muscles at the side of his strong jaw throbbed as if he clenched his teeth hard enough to shatter them.

He was still reading. Saying nothing. He didn't have to.

And then he rose. Dwarfing her. Staring down at her with green eyes filled with the most terrible pain imaginable.

"Scroll to the end," he demanded.

She opened her mouth to say something, then closed it and did as he said. The ending hadn't changed.

"Fix it."

She looked up, but he wouldn't want her to tell him the obvious: even if she changed it, the edits wouldn't be saved.

Instead, she did as he asked. Gave it a happy ending.

"Now, if the other stuff you added saves, that should too."

"We'll see," she said softly. She put the cursor on the Save icon and pressed it. She closed the document. Opened it again. The horrible words she had added in her trance—an addition born of the obvious harsh emotions of the kidnapper who thought of himself as Big T—remained. So did the original ending.

Shauna looked up at Hunter helplessly, hating the cold expression he leveled on her as much as the agony she saw in the churning depths of his eyes.

Without another word, he rose and left the room.

Shauna stayed there, shuddering, her head bowed.

Of course he blamed her for what she had written. For what she could—and couldn't—do.

Don't kill the messenger. The trite expression slammed into her mind, but she didn't voice it aloud.

He wasn't killing her. Physically, he wasn't doing anything at all to her. Emotionally…

Emotionally she was regressing by years. To the anguish of the time she couldn't save her father.

To earlier, when she had lost Hunter. The first time.

The *only* time. She certainly did not have him now.

"If only—" she whispered in the silence.

She didn't finish. There were too many "if onlys."

Instead, Shauna raised her head and looked at her computer once more.

She opened a new file and again began to type.

For a long time, Hunter sat in Andee's room on her small bed, on the frilly gold-and-white comforter his mother had sent for her granddaughter.

He loved the professionally taken photo of the two of them that hung on the yellow wall, their cheeks pressed together, their smiles wide. He thought he could see a lot of himself in his sweet daughter—or at least he'd wanted to. Black hair, though Andee's was as curly as his was straight. But their eyes were both the Strahm green.

Right now, he couldn't bear to look at that picture.

Instead, he stared at the small, white dresser with all the

stuffed animals on top. Andee particularly loved her stuffed kitty cats.

He'd promised, one day, that they could adopt a cat from a shelter, like she'd seen on some show on Animal Planet, her favorite TV station. He had never gotten around to it. Never quite figured out how one took care of a cat, which seemed a good reason not to get one. And now, maybe he would never be able to get his daughter her cat.

The sound that wrenched from deep inside him was too long for a sob, too guttural for a moan.

"Hunter?"

Startled at the interruption, ready to snap at Shauna for daring to catch him like that, he stood, his fists clenched at his sides. "Yeah?"

He didn't want to look at her, didn't want to see the damnable sympathy he was sure he'd find. Not now.

"Look. You have to see this."

Curious, he did turn to her and saw that her cheeks were flushed pink, her eyes sparkling. She held her laptop.

"What is it?"

"I'm not sure it'll help, but I finally figured out what it was that was bothering me."

"And it is—?"

His cell phone rang.

"Hunter, it's Simon. I'm on Margo patrol. She just got another call from the kidnapper. You've got to get over here."

Chapter 13

"Did Simon give any hint of what the kidnapper said to Margo?" Shauna asked. White-knuckled, she clutched the edges of the passenger seat of Hunter's car for at least the illusion of stability. It was just past dusk, and he was driving way over any reasonable speed limit. He barely slowed for stop signs, made sharp right turns instead of waiting for red lights to change, even ran one when they got into a commercial area less than a mile from the freeway on-ramp.

"All he would say was that the call was important, and Margo was on the verge of hysterics again. Banger and he listened in on the eavesdropping devices they'd installed. The guy sounded stressed. Angry."

Like in the revisions to her story. Shauna didn't say it, but she couldn't help thinking it.

Apparently Hunter thought it, too. "But of course you know that from the latest stuff in your story. You wrote about how things changed, how the guy knew how to fix things. Any idea what that meant—other than the part on getting rid of the kid?"

Shauna winced, even though Hunter's tone remained level, conversational. Maybe he really wasn't blaming her anymore. But that didn't keep her from wishing—as always—that she could do something positive to fix what was in her stories.

"No," she said. "I didn't follow his thinking. But I have some theories I want to share with you."

Theories? Heck, they were well-reasoned suppositions, based on her story—how it was written before, and how it had changed.

After Hunter left the room, she had begun to write a sort of flow chart, putting together the ideas that came to her. She'd intended to sort out the odd impressions that had teased her mind, made her think that, if she only could put her finger on it, she had more information than she realized. And now, she thought she'd figured it out.

Was she right? She didn't know. But at least they were heading in the right direction to find out. To Margo's.

"What theories?" Hunter roared his GTO onto the San Diego Freeway, headed north, pulled into the fast lane and pushed the car up to a speed that suggested a street race. He might be remaining civil to her, but his driving evidenced his disturbed mood.

"I'll tell you if you slow down," Shauna said through gritted teeth. "I'd like to arrive at Margo's in one piece."

She saw the glance he shot at her. Great. When she'd asked for more safety, he wasn't even watching the road.

"Please, Hunter," she said. "What I have to say may or may not be right, but at least it'll give us a new angle to explore. It won't do Andee any good if her daddy dies trying to save her." The idea of Hunter harming himself arrowed a pang of sorrow through her. "Slow down, okay? Then I'll run this by you."

She held her breath, waiting for his response. And then he pulled out of the fast lane and slowed.

"Thanks," she said.

"Okay. What's your new inspiration?"

Shauna glanced at him, but neither his tone nor his expression suggested he was being sarcastic. Maybe he was, at last, understanding what she could and couldn't do, and willing to accept her help. "Well," she said, "it stems from my wondering if the four neighbors described in my story were actually only two."

"We talked about that. If Chiles is the nosy neighbor, the irritated one and the one who saw something important without realizing it, all rolled into one, what did he see?"

"I've taken notes on my conversations with him. I entered it all onto the computer, and—"

"If you wrote another story that says Chiles is the kidnapper, it's wrong. I already looked around his place. If he's involved, he has to have an accomplice."

"No, I didn't write a story about Conrad." Despite herself, Shauna was getting edgy. She glanced out the window at the barely illuminated hillsides flanking the freeway, then back at his strong, shadowed profile. "Let me tell this my way, okay? I'm having a hard time low-keying it, because I'm excited. I didn't want to dump it on you too fast and with too much conviction, in case I'm wrong. If you don't want to hear it, fine. I'll tell Simon or Banger or even Tennyson. I'll have to hedge it with the official guys, though, since they don't know the truth about my involvement here. But—"

"Okay, O'Leary. You're driving me nuts." Hunter lifted one hand off the steering wheel in a gesture of surrender. Beneath a quickly passed streetlight, Shauna even saw the ghost of a smile raise an edge of his lips. "What do I have to do to get you to tell me this new theory?" Then, he said more seriously, "If it pans out, if it helps me save Andee, I swear I'll never doubt you again."

"Or my stories?" She should have resisted but didn't.

"Don't push it," he said, though his tone remained light.

Enough so that the other story she'd so recently written, the one about Hunter and her—together—catapulted to the forefront of her mind. Tantalizing her with its impossible "what ifs" that made her squirm in her seat—and not from the way the car hurtled through the night.

Good thing Hunter couldn't read her thoughts.

And that he hadn't seen that story. Bad enough that he knew so much about the one on Andee's kidnapping that he directed her in what to do with it.

With effort, she squared her thoughts back onto what she hoped had been that night's breakthrough.

"Okay, here's what I did." She described the things she'd spoken with Conrad about. How he kept an eye on Margo. Loved parties at her house. Enjoyed seeing plays her friends starred in—sort of. "The guy's got an enormous crush on your movie-star ex-wife. I'm sure of it. He commented about seeing her friends John Aitken and BillieAnn Callahan in some shows. Didn't seem overjoyed that Aitken hung around as much as he did. Seemed to think that Margo and he had a thing going."

"So?"

"I put all that down and more. If Conrad saw something he didn't recognize had significance, then he's key. He's met Aitken and BillieAnn, plus some of Andee's friends and their parents, like Sondra Nantes and her father Earl, the ex-con. I listed them, then ran an online search of everyone's names. That's where I got my theory."

"Yeah? I've done searches, too, and so has Simon, with the names I've given him including Nantes's. Banger's looked for criminal records or any cop database stuff like too many parking tickets. He found Nantes, too, of course. Banger's probably also run Margo and me and even you."

Shauna had anticipated that, but it still made her uncomfortable. One condition of her sharing her stories with the Phoenix Police—including Hunter—was that it remain classified. But that didn't mean it hadn't been entered into a database somewhere and leaked, thanks to hackers or computer specialists, into a place for all law-enforcement agencies to access.

She shrugged off that anxiety for now. "Even if he's run everyone he's met on this case, looking for a criminal record might not help. What if it's not an enemy but a friend? That's who Conrad met—Margo's friends, like John Keenan Aitken. And, Hunter—" Shauna paused to brace herself for his probable ridicule of her idea. "Conrad quoted him. He intends to make it big in the theater." She repeated the words this time in the same manner Conrad had, emphasizing both the "big" and the "theater." "Big," she said again. "Theater. Is it possible John Aitken could be 'Big T'?"

Hunter argued with Shauna for the rest of the dash to Margo's—more to follow her thoughts than because he didn't believe her. It seemed a stretch, yeah, but a logical one. In fact, the possibility excited him. But he needed more than a naked theory, reasoned or not.

Shauna had already asked Margo if she knew anyone whose name began with *T*. Her response hadn't included Aitken, and for good reason. The only T in Aitken was in the middle. It wasn't his initial. But even so…

"What if he thinks of himself that way?" Shauna demanded, defending her theory. "He wants to be a star so much that he could have given himself pep talks about becoming big in the theater, then abbreviated it in his own mind, said it often enough that it stuck."

"I think you want your story to fit reality so much that you may be grabbing at any explanation," he countered.

Since he had just exited the freeway and was stopped at a light, he looked over at her. She didn't appear happy. "I think you know better than that," she said.

"Maybe. But why would John Aitken snatch Andee?"

"Ask him. Or, for now, why not ask Margo?"

First thing when they got to Margo's, though, Hunter insisted on hearing details about the kidnapper's latest call.

Margo's red eyes announced she'd been crying again. "It was horrible." Her voice was so low Hunter could hardly hear her. Maybe he'd be better off not hearing…no way. He had to know, no matter what it was.

They were all back in what had become their official search headquarters—Margo's living room—sitting in the same seats as if they'd been assigned: Margo and Simon on one couch, Shauna and he on the sofa facing it, and Banger and Tennyson on chairs also clustered around the coffee table.

At Hunter's insistence, Simon had been hanging out here when not visiting a potential suspect. Hunter figured Banger would have assigned some peon detectives to watch the place overnight, so his presence was a surprise. Tennyson's, too, but who could ever figure what the FBI was going to do?

"Tell us," Hunter said to Margo, trying to keep his voice firm but insistent, as he did with emotional witnesses on a case.

"He was so mad," Margo said. Moist eyed, she looked down at the coffee table, at photos of Andee that were laid out there. "He was shouting. Screaming, even."

She turned to Simon, who nodded. He'd heard it, too, on the equipment used to tap Margo's phone.

"He said he'd seen the news," Margo continued, her voice uneven. "He reminded me that he'd said no police, no publicity, no Amber alerts—nothing. Just a nice, simple money drop, and he'd even been kind enough to give us time to get it together. But now…" She closed her eyes. Swallowed. Took a deep breath, then looked at him. "Now he says we've spoiled it."

"Did he say what that meant?" Hunter was worried the guy had told Margo he'd already taken care of things. Of Andee.

Where the hell was she? She had to be okay.

He had never felt so helpless in his life.

"He said he's left the L.A. area. He wants another fifty thousand dollars for his trouble, and he'll be in touch tomorrow or the day after to tell us where he wants it."

"Did you ask to talk to Andee?" Hunter couldn't bring

himself to state the obvious. No money if their daughter was no longer alive.

Again Simon nodded.

"He put her on," Margo said. "She said she was okay, then started to cry about the bad man." Tears ran down her cheeks.

Hunter felt like crying, too.

But at least Andee was alive.

For now.

"How well do you know John Keenan Aitken, Margo?" Shauna asked. Hunter turned a frown on her. He wasn't ready to spring her theory on Margo. Not till he'd heard the entire phone call. If Margo didn't buy it, she might not be as forthcoming later.

"He's a close friend," Margo replied, her glare at Shauna a mixture of irritation and puzzlement. "Why?"

"Could it have been him on the phone? Might he have been the one who took Andee?"

"Let's hear the rest of the call first," Hunter interrupted.

But when Shauna met his gaze, she nodded calmly toward Margo.

His ex-wife's eyes bulged. "Oh, my Lord!" she exclaimed after a long moment. "I—he said—I thought I was imagining things, but…this call. I never recognized his voice—he's too good an actor for that. What he said, though—"

Hunter stood, maneuvered around the coffee table until he stared down at Margo. "Is Aitken the kidnapper?" he demanded. "He was in this house the day after the snatch. Acting like your best bud. And all the time—"

"Maybe it's not him," Margo said hurriedly. "I never imagined it before. But this time the kidnapper was so angry. He might have been working off a script in previous calls, but he was definitely ad-libbing this time. He talked about the media leaping in and endangering us all, including Andee. He called it detonated hype, like it was all blown up out of proportion."

"It's hardly out of proportion," Shauna said from behind him. "A child's life is at stake. So tell us why that reminded you of John Keenan Aitken. It did remind you of him, didn't it?"

"Yes." Margo sounded pathetic as she wriggled around Hunter and stood. "John was in a play not long ago where that line was used. A drama named *Public Power,* in which a politician who struck his wife in anger was brought down by the incident when she made a huge public circus of it. It showed both their points of view. Of course domestic violence, even in anger, should not be tolerated, and especially not in someone in a high government position. I'd have loved to have played the wife, but—"

"Margo," Hunter interrupted, "are you saying this term 'detonated hype' was used in that play? And that Aitken played the role and it was a line he said?"

"Yes," she said.

"It's not a well-known play, is it?" Shauna had come around to stand beside Hunter, facing Margo. "I never heard of it."

"It was written by a local screenwriter who wanted to try something different," Margo said.

"Does Aitken ever go by the name 'Big T'?" Shauna asked.

"I don't think so," Margo said. "Why do you ask? Why are you so hung up on someone with the initial T?" Her voice was increasing in intensity, as if she was winding up to blame whatever was happening on Shauna. "That's not John."

"We have reason to believe that the kidnapper uses the nickname 'Big T,'" Hunter said. He caught a furious glare from Tennyson, who stood behind Margo during this exchange. That didn't surprise him. But even Banger looked upset.

"How did you get this information?" Tennyson demanded.

Hunter ignored him, though he knew he'd have to come up with a reason—one that didn't seem ridiculous.

"I never heard him use it but—oh, my!" She edged away from Hunter. "Just a minute." She left the room.

"What the hell is this about, Strahm?" Tennyson demanded.

Shauna rose, blocking the special agent's view of Hunter. He didn't need her protection but appreciated it anyway.

Before he responded to Tennyson, Shauna said, "Please give us some latitude. We're exploring a theory of mine."

When Margo returned, she held a playbill for the play that Aitken had been in. He'd signed it, with love and gratitude and all that. And ended, "We shall both become Big in the Theater." Both the *B* and *T* were capitalized, and as ornate as the man's flourish of a signature, which followed.

Big T.

"I'll be damned," Simon said from behind Hunter's elbow. "I believe we have ourselves a suspect."

But Hunter wanted to be sure.

"Then you do think your friend Aitken could be the kidnapper?" Holding the playbill, Hunter got right in Margo's face. When she tried to look away, he moved again. No way would he let her out of his focus.

"He hasn't been in anything for a while. He quit his job as a waiter a while back, before the play, and I never asked how he was making ends meet. Maybe he wasn't. I thought he was out of town on an audition." Margo was breathing harder now. Looking like the proverbial deer in the headlights—only these lights were Hunter's angry eyes.

"Then the answer is yes?" he insisted. "John Keenan Aitken could be Andee's kidnapper?"

"Well…yes, I'm afraid he could be," Margo said.

Hunter met Shauna's gaze. Her eyes glittered.

If all these people hadn't been around, Hunter would have grabbed her, hugged her, kissed her silly—and maybe even more.

This woman had done what all the experts—professional investigators, cops, feds—couldn't do.

Not only had she written a stupid story that had been coming true, morphing as reality had changed, she'd come up with the only viable lead about the man who'd kidnapped his daughter.

He smiled at her. "Thanks," he said softly, knowing how inadequate it was.

A couple of tears ran down her cheeks.

Damn. He knew what she was thinking and was glad she couldn't say it.

For with all they now knew—or at least suspected—she probably still thought the ending of her story would stay the same.

Well, he'd show her.

He'd fix her story.

For now, at last, he really had reason to hope.

Chapter 14

Despite her exhaustion at this late hour, her unrelenting concern, Shauna felt exhilarated—mostly because of the energy streaming from Hunter.

He had insisted on participating in the convening of law-enforcement agencies at John Keenan Aitken's last-known address. It was in a three-story apartment building in one of Hollywood's seediest areas. Margo had provided the address, but Shauna learned the place's condition by accompanying Hunter. She hadn't given him an opportunity to object. She'd simply slipped into his car's passenger seat.

Tennyson, not surprisingly, insisted that they both stay back while the official investigation was conducted. Banger and he joined the police and FBI agents who approached the building.

While they waited in the car, Hunter took Shauna's hand. Held it as tightly as if he considered it a good luck charm.

She knew better. Still, she gripped him back, reveling, for this moment, in the touch of his warm, rough skin, the unconscious stroking of his index finger attesting to his edginess.

She tried hard not to let such a simple contact ignite embers within her that had been rekindled—had it only been one night ago? She still burned from their lovemaking, ached for more each moment she remained with Hunter.

Once, their holding hands had felt as natural as drinking water during a run together at dawn along already-hot Oasis streets. Tonight, it felt bittersweet. Temporary.

But for now, ignoring all there was—and wasn't—between them, she shared Hunter's excitement and hope. Would it end this easily? Would the authorities find Andee alive and well despite her story, and capture her captor, Big T?

She couldn't believe it would happen that way even as she prayed, for Hunter's sake, that it would.

She watched his profile in the faint illumination as he stared out the windshield toward the apartment building. His eyes glowing with anticipation, his strong chin raised, he had never looked more handsome. If only—

Tearing her thoughts from that useless direction, Shauna watched out the windshield, too, observing the hushed street. Unmarked cars and black-and-whites were double-and triple-parked in a choreographed blockade of vehicles, though pedestrians were not yet kept away. A few locals strolled the opposite side of the street briskly beneath the streetlights, their lack of curiosity either feigned or genuine in this area where oddity was the norm. The homeless, dirty and disheveled, ambled slowly, with no place to go. A couple stopped and stared at the extra traffic on the street and moved on.

At least the media wasn't there yet.

"It's taking too long," Hunter muttered after a while.

"They can't just rush the place, for Andee's sake," Shauna said gently.

"Yeah, but—" He broke off so abruptly that Shauna looked in the same direction he'd been facing.

Banger was leaving the building. His expression was blank. Andee wasn't with him. Neither was Big T.

Hunter abruptly released Shauna's hand and opened his car door.

She joined the men on the sidewalk, along with others who'd gone inside with Banger and Tennyson.

"Well?" Hunter demanded.

Banger gave an angry shake of his head. "He's gone," he growled.

Okay, they'd expected that. Or so Hunter told himself as he opened the car door for Shauna, then got in himself.

Discouraged? Hell, no. Not him.

After all, Banger said that the building manager, after being roused from sleep and shown official IDs, had given up Aitken's forwarding address—unfortunately, a P.O. box in another Hollywood zip code. It would take a little while to get the street address of the person who'd rented the box. Also, steps were being taken to get the information behind Aitken's cell phone number, which Margo had given to them, too. Banger said preliminary forensics had determined Aitken's prints were all over Margo's house, not that anyone had been surprised.

Hunter had sent Simon home to his computer, where he could access all the databases Strahm Solutions subscribed to and some they didn't. He'd soon have all that information available on Aitken, too.

And him? He was going home. With Shauna.

To work, once more, on her story, without the distractions and interruptions they'd have at his office. With Big T now identified, Shauna could change the story and save the changes.

Including the ending.

And he would have the great satisfaction of updating his strategy plan on his computer. Finally he would get some degree of control over this miserable situation.

Top of his list: No matter what the cops were doing, how they were doing it, he would find Aitken. Fast.

Very soon, he would have his daughter home, safe and sound.

"Where are we going?" Shauna swallowed a yawn. He stole a glance at her as he wove through Hollywood streets. Her lovely brown eyes were too wide, as though held open by force of will.

"To my place, to get you some sleep."

She sat up straighter. "I hope you're not thinking you're going to leave me there and go gallivanting off without me."

If they weren't both strapped into seat belts, he might have done something foolish and taken her into his arms. She looked as if she would fall fast asleep in an instant, and she still insisted on helping him.

"I wouldn't dare," he replied. "But you look as if you're going to keel over."

"You've got to be tired, too." She shifted her long, jeans-clad legs as if needing to stretch them in the cramped car.

He ignored his body's instinctive reaction to her unconsciously sexy movements. "I'll sleep when we have Andee back." From the corner of his eye, he saw Shauna's mouth open as if she prepared to say something, but she remained quiet. "I know what you're thinking," he muttered.

"That's supposed to be my line," she said wryly. "Or at least my story's."

"Maybe I've been around you too long."

"Maybe," she agreed, her voice low.

"What you didn't say is that knowing the kidnapper's identity might not change anything," he said in a tone resembling rational conversation. "You want me to understand, so somehow it'll be easier to accept. But you should realize by now that I'll never accept that things with my daughter are hopeless." He braked a little too quickly at a light.

"That's why I didn't say it again. And why I..." Her words tapered off. Instead of finishing, she reached over and lightly rubbed her hand over his cheek.

It felt too good. Too comforting.

And Hunter did not want Shauna to comfort him, for it meant he was giving in. To his tumultuous feelings about Shauna.

And the inevitability of her story.

He grabbed her hand, squeezed it for a second because he couldn't help it, then pushed it away from him.

"The light's changed," he said, as if that explained everything. And then he stepped hard on the accelerator.

Yawning for the umpteenth time that night, Shauna booted up her computer.

Hunter, standing beside her, put an arm around her shoulders. She briefly rested her head against his side, feeling the soft cotton of his shirt against her face, inhaling his clean, masculine scent. She could stay there all night. But wouldn't. She raised her head.

"You can hardly see straight," Hunter said, "and I'm making you revise your story." He sounded apologetic but didn't suggest that she wait until tomorrow. Nor would she, even if he asked. She, too, wanted to see what would happen if she inserted the day's events into her story. Would the changes save?

If so, would the ending be affected?

Please, she begged internally to whatever forces caused her to write stories that came true. This unwanted creation had already been different from all the others. Couldn't it be different that way, too?

She could almost hear Grandma O'Leary warning her, and tuned her out.

The computer finally finished its warm-up exercises. She scrolled through menus. Couldn't help noticing the file called "A Tale of Duke" and felt her mouth twist in irony at her recollection of what it contained.

For this moment, while Hunter and she shared a small truce and an identical goal, she might imagine it could come true. But then there were all other moments.

Quickly she continued on to "Duke's Story" and opened it.

As she scanned it, Hunter bent, and his face practically touched hers as he, too, read the story. Drawn by a need she chose not to question, she leaned toward him till they were cheek to cheek. She felt a grin lift his warm flesh. His stubble rasped against her sensitive facial skin.

She wanted to cry for the fragility of the moment. Instead, she smiled, too.

And changed the story, adding in the identity of Big T.

She also threw in how Big T was thinking hard about where he had Andee now. That it was a good place, and he wouldn't move her from there.

If only she could purposely fall into one of her trances, so her subconscious, or wherever these stories came from, would fill in the blanks. Cause her to write the location where they would find the kidnapper and his hostage. But she had never been able to effect a trance at will. Tonight was no exception. She remained fully aware of what she was writing. At least that permitted her to, once again, change the ending.

She closed the file. Opened it again.

The changes regarding the identity of the kidnapper were still there.

And...how very odd! Had she forgotten she had written in, when Big T considered where he and Andee were, that he had felt at least some relief, despite all the publicity, that he was up in the mountains, where he was known as someone else altogether?

She didn't remember writing that. Had she gone into a trance after all?

Had the story rewritten itself?

"Hunter—" she began.

"Shh," he said. "Just a minute." He was reading it, too.

"Did I write that?" she said when he turned to her.

"Not that I saw." He was grinning. "But I think we now have another clue."

"Maybe, but I've never done that before, and—"

He put his finger on her lips. "I know. Here comes your disclaimer. We won't rely on it, I promise."

"Okay."

"Now, let's look at the ending."

Might the changes have been saved this time? Bemusement and anticipation tickled the base of her scalp. Nothing else seemed to be working quite as it always had with her stories. And she'd wanted so much, this time, for the new and improved ending to be saved. The one where Andee was okay.

She quickly scrolled to the last page and began reading.

The old ending had not been changed.

Shauna closed her eyes for a moment. Sharing Hunter's pain was not enough. She had wanted in the past to fix things for him. It hadn't worked.

Then, it had only been a job.

Now it was his daughter.

She turned and looked up at him. He was reading the screen again, as if he couldn't believe what it said.

"So much was saved," she said. "Maybe if I try—"

"Hush," he said softly, punctuating the word with a brief hug. Then he turned his back and drew his cell phone from his pocket. Shauna heard tones as he punched in a number. "Margo? Yes, I know how late it is. Do you know of anyplace in the mountains Aitken might go? No, I don't know which mountains. Well, think about it. It's important. I'll talk to you in the morning." Hanging up, he still didn't look at Shauna before making another call, this time to Simon. He directed his assistant to do whatever he could to find a connection between John Keenan Aitken and any mountain, anywhere.

When he called Banger and Tennyson, he wound up leaving messages. "Probably a good thing," he said to Shauna. "This way, I won't have to tell them the origin of this new clue. They're both pros and, I think, trust me. They'll run with it using their own resources, and ask questions later."

Only after he hung up from the last call did he return to where Shauna sat, watching him, aching for him.

"Hunter," she began, "I'm sorry. I could—"

"Hey, you know what?" he said, interrupting. "Your story has actually come up with something we can follow up on. That's cause for celebration." His voice rose. "Let's break out the champagne. Fireworks!"

Shauna smiled at his excitement.

But only for an instant, for when he spoke again, it was low and sad. Again. "Of course if we believe that, then maybe we have to believe the rest, too." He turned to leave the room.

"What do you want me to do?" she cried after him, not even pretending the distance of a professional therapist.

He pivoted. He wasn't trying now to hide the pain that shadowed his features. Or if he was trying, he wasn't succeeding. "I don't want to rely on something so impossible," he said unhappily. "Give me back control of my life. Of my daughter's life."

"You know I would if I could," she whispered, then turned to let him go.

Instead, she heard him mutter something unintelligible. An instant later, she was shocked to find him beside her. He took her into his arms. Buried his face against her neck so that she could feel his hot breath there.

"Yeah, the hell of it is that I do know that. How can you live with it, Shauna? Thinking you know the future, and all the miserable stuff you write about there?"

Her small laugh was ironic. "Why do you think I became a shr—?"

Before she could finish, his mouth took hers. Roughly.

Shocked, she wanted to run, not respond. But though she struggled, he didn't release her. And in moments, she found herself pressing against him, kissing him back, no longer wanting to escape.

If this was the comfort he needed, then so be it. *She* needed it. His searching kiss displaced her fears and doubts, set them at the edge of her mind. At least for now.

He nibbled at her vulnerable flesh, upward beneath her hair, to her sensitive earlobe, and forward to her throat. And then his mouth was back on hers, fiery and insistent, his tongue plunging and searching and scorching.

She met his kiss, tasting him, wanting him, as her knees wobbled. He didn't let her fall but held her close, murmuring words against her that she felt without hearing, words that raised sweet gooseflesh on skin teased by his breath against it, contrasting immeasurably with the strength of other burgeoning sensations.

His hands ranged down her back, clasped her buttocks and pulled her even closer against him until there was no doubt of his need.

And hers? "Please, Hunter," she moaned as her hands quested beneath his shirt. His skin was heated tautness over hard, toned muscles. She stroked him, touching, kneading, until her fingers were between them, stroking his chest.

He seemed to mistake her hands coming between them for rejection, for he took a step back. "Sorry," he muttered. "I shouldn't have—"

"Oh, yes, you should," she countered. She couldn't allow him to stop. Not with need raging so deliriously inside her. She threw herself once more against him, unabashedly thrusting her pelvis forward to press against his hardness.

He answered her invitation by reaching down, placing his hands between them, too. Cupping her breasts over her shirt, caressing the nipples until she moaned once more.

"Here." He led her unsteadily to the guest-room's bed. She collapsed onto it, and he gently placed himself on top of her, writhing so she felt every angle of his meeting her curves.

She was exquisitely aware of his drawing away enough to pull off her clothes, for with every place bared, he stroked her until each new touch became a welcome agony.

At first, he refused to let her undress him, and the sensation of being open to him, while he remained clothed, heightened her sense of vulnerability and need.

But then he, too, was bare, and she could touch him. *Did* touch him. Everywhere. She teased his straining erection until it was his turn to moan.

In moments, quickly donning protection, he was back on top of her. Sliding inside her. Filling her once more with a rhythm that reminded her of days long ago and dreams of forever.

Every conscious part of her was centered where they rocked together. All she could think about was Hunter.

The sensation grew and grew until Shauna thought her mind erased forever, exploding in a crescendo that made her cry out loud and long, even as Hunter, too, gave one hard, final thrust, groaned and grew still.

Shauna lay quietly with Hunter still on top of her, their uneven breathing creating a pattern of soft syncopation in the air around them.

She thought of "A Tale of Duke" and the story it told.

Wishing, dreaming, for this moment, that it could come true.

But knowing as certainly as she knew she would write again, that happily-ever-after was a figment of her imagination, and the tale that illuminated a future with Hunter was doomed from the instant her fingers created it.

"Come on," Hunter whispered into her hair. He started to rise. Was it over this quickly?

"Where are we going?" Shauna asked.

"To my bed. It's a lot more comfortable than in here."

"Sure." She nestled close to him as, skin to skin, he led her to his room.

Hunter lay in his bed, holding Shauna close, for a long time.

Inhaling her sweet, exotic scent overlaid with the aroma of

their joining in a sexual encounter that had left him both exhausted yet eager for the next time.

If there would be a next time.

He sighed, but kept it quiet so as not to awaken Shauna. She needed her rest.

So did he, to prepare for the next day. He had a feeling things were going to finally break loose.

He would find Andee. That mountain clue had to do it.

Dawn would arrive soon. He'd immediately begin making calls. See what Simon had found out about Aitken and the mountains. Follow up with Banger and Tennyson, too. Find out if Margo had thought of someplace in the mountains where Aitken might go.

Damn. Hunter knew he wouldn't sleep. He was too wrapped up in pondering. And that little hiccup in Shauna's latest modifications to her story. The part that seemed to have appeared magically, all by itself.

Hell, the whole thing was magic. Sleight of Shauna's lovely hands. Woo-woo, supernatural, way, way out there. No matter how he looked at it, it was surreal.

But somehow it worked and had always worked, even if he hadn't accepted it.

He sighed again. He knew what he needed to do, now while Shauna slept so soundly.

Gently he pried himself away. Stood beside his bed.

Stared wistfully, lustfully down, in the faint illumination spilling between the blinds from the streetlight outside, at her lovely, curvaceous form.

He smoothed the sheet over her and watched to make sure she didn't wake up. She stirred, one slender arm reaching out as if searching for him. But her breathing remained deep, her eyes closed.

He waited for a minute longer, enjoying his observation of her.

He hadn't wanted to start caring for Shauna again, any

more than he had wanted to believe that her writing came true.

But both had come to pass.

For all the good it would do. He had a life here, in California. Shauna lived in Oasis. Had a business there.

Besides, could he really see himself living with a woman who had set his entire belief system on edge, over and over? Who made him feel as if everything was spiraling out of his control?

It wasn't as if she planned it.

Margo had made an effort to exert control. His lovely ex had gone out of her way to make sure everything in their marriage worked exactly as she wanted, or watch out.

He'd taken it as long as he could. Longer, even, for the sake of their daughter. But then he'd gotten out.

It was best for all of them.

Could things be different with Shauna?

Glancing once more at the sexy, sleeping Shauna, he headed for the guest bedroom. He closed the door, put on the light and booted up the computer.

Now that he wasn't disparaging the idea of Shauna writing stories that came true, his curiosity was rampant. Where did they come from?

She'd claimed they couldn't be changed, yet she had been able, in the past few days, to save changes she had made.

This last time, something appeared by itself. Maybe. Had she entered it when he wasn't looking?

But when hadn't he been looking? Was it the computer?

Could *he* do anything with the story?

He had to try. For in some ways, it had proved prophetic.

And he was not about to let that damned ending come true. Not when Andee's life was at stake.

He scrolled through the list of documents, looking for "Duke's Story." He smiled grimly at the name. If only Shauna had simply written the tale she'd started out to, a little fairy tale for her to read at her restaurant, would things be any different? Or would they not have even as many clues as they had now about what had happened to Andee?

He stopped scrolling, confused. Wasn't the title "Duke's Story"? But here was "A Tale of Duke." Had he remembered it wrong? Or was this a different tale, one of Shauna's real kids stories?

He opened the file. And stared.

What the hell was that? A story written as if *he'd* created it, in his point of view.

One that described how he'd once felt about Shauna. How he felt the same about her now, and then some.

How he loved her, wanted to be with her forever.

And this one had a happy ending.

Where had it come from? In some ways, it looked real. Felt real. Felt right.

Only…it also felt as if he was being fed something he had no intention of eating. Having it forced into him, into reality, because it was written.

By Shauna. In one of her damned stories.

His feelings were his own, damn it! No one, and nothing, was going to tell him who to care for.

And this one was as if he had finished his own damned life plan he'd begun once between Shauna and him. Of course, he had tossed it away, unwilling to let it, or anything, control what he'd believed they'd had together.

He rose so fast that the chair nearly toppled, ready to throw the computer against the wall. He needed an explanation. Now he'd go into his room, wake Shauna and—

The last part, was unnecessary. Shauna had already pulled open the door behind him and stood there, her eyes narrowed against the light. She'd thrown on one of his T-shirts and it clung to her curves, reminding him graphically of how it had felt to touch her. To make love to her.

But not even desire for her all over again would divert him from the questions burning inside him.

''What's that?'' he demanded, pointing at the computer. ''Has all this been a plan of yours?''

''I'm not sure what you mean, Hunter, but—''

He refused to let her dissemble, especially when her sleepy, pleading eyes looked so damned sexy. ''I'll tell you exactly what I mean. Isn't it enough that your story about my daughter changes and doesn't change and keeps my head spinning? And now this, too.''

He stalked toward her.

Chapter 15

Furious indignation might not look convincing in a clinging, short shirt, but Shauna asserted it anyway and stood her ground as Hunter closed the gap between them. So what if placing her hands on her hips lifted the hem to an even less modest mid-thigh? "What do you mean?" she countered heatedly.

Hunter had thrown on a pair of boxers, but his well-formed chest was bare, its fast rise and fall as he stopped directly in front of her showing the angry speed of his respiration.

She couldn't help thinking how her fingers had roved over those taut muscles only a short while ago. And now their tension was from anything but desire.

"As if your story about my daughter's kidnapping isn't hard enough to buy into. Did you also have to pretend to dig into my private thoughts? And then stick what you came up with into one of your stories, complete with beginning, middle and end, like it was really going to happen? Forget it!"

"I didn't ask to write this story," she countered. "I thought you finally recognized that I never plan the stories I write about real people. Blame yourself, if you want to blame any-one. I'm a conduit, at least for my stories' beginnings. They're transmitted to me from others' emotions.'' He opened his mouth, and she raised a hand to deflect his protest. ''It's not really how you feel? Fine. Let's pretend it never happened and move on. Now I have a question for you. Why were snooping in my computer files in the first place?''

''I'd intended to read again the description of where Big T was—the thing about the mountains. I wanted to make sure I remembered it right before following up on my calls. Maybe do some checking myself, like I should have earlier before I got distracted.''

A distraction? She'd considered their lovemaking a lot more than that.

A chilliness she had to dredge from deep down, beneath the hurt she refused to show him, dripped from her response. ''I'll bring up that file on *my* computer, and then you can read it. And that way you won't get into anything else that's private.''

Head high, she skirted around him. She didn't want to touch him, not even the merest brush. It might remind her too much, again, of all they'd shared so recently. His *distraction*.

''That story was about me,'' he growled. ''Any confidentiality related to it should be mine. The thing may even be defamatory, the way it lies about what I'm supposedly feeling.''

''I understand that's your position,'' Shauna retorted, wishing she could cover her ears. She didn't want to hear him disclaim what was in that story.

''Is there anything else about me on your computer?'' he demanded.

''Not that I'm aware of,'' Shauna replied icily. And she wasn't aware of any on this one. She didn't keep all those stories she had written about him for years on her laptop's hard drive, for she had never wanted to accidentally read any of them. As long as she'd kept them on disk and in paper files, she'd been able to delete them in their entirety when she was done.

No matter how often she had told herself they no longer mattered—that *he* no longer mattered—they had always evoked an emotional reaction from her.

Now she turned her back on him, sat and brought up the story about Andee. She scrolled to the part in which Big T thought about where he held the child, in the mountains.

"Here," she said, and rose.

"Fine. Just a minute." He left the room, returned quickly with his cell phone and made a call.

Glancing at the corner of the computer screen, Shauna noted the time: five-thirty in the morning. Still early for most people to rise, though Hunter might be calling Simon or Banger, both of whom had struck her as diligent enough about their responsibilities that neither might have even seen their beds this night.

"Hi, Margo, it's me." Hunter's body was rigid beside Shauna, his eyes on the screen. "Yes, again. Yes, I know what time it is now, too."

Staying quiet, Shauna filled in the other side of the conversation without hearing Margo. She rose, crossed the room and sat on the edge of the bed, both feet on the floor.

"Have you come up with any ideas of where Aitken might head if he went to the mountains?" He paused, then said, "I'm using my resources to track him down, and you should use yours, too. What about BillieAnn? Have you called her yet? She's a friend to both of you. She might know something."

This time, after a short pause, he muttered, "Damn."

Shauna wanted to ask what was wrong but stayed silent. Hunter probably wasn't even aware she was still in the room.

She half wished she wasn't. She wanted to be home.

But even after the soul-twisting ups and downs of yesterday and this morning, she wouldn't go before the story's end was reached. Whatever way it played out, she had to know the finale.

Hunter continued, "How long will BillieAnn be gone? No, obviously a week'll be too long. She doesn't have a cell phone? All right. If you hear from her, be sure to ask if she knows about any place Aitken has in the mountains. Or a cabin he might borrow or a quiet resort—anywhere he might not be known well and could take a child who isn't his without anyone questioning him."

When he hung up, he continued to stare at the computer, as if the answers were written somewhere behind the screen, and if he watched it long enough, they would appear.

"I gather she still didn't have a clue," Shauna finally ventured.

"Yeah," he said without looking at her. He pushed a couple buttons on his cell phone. "Simon? Found any other addresses for Aitken yet? Great! Oh. Well, let's check them out anyway."

He slid onto the empty chair. Squeezing the phone between his neck and chin, he opened a new document on the computer and typed some addresses onto it. "None more recent than last year? Damn. What about something that connects Aitken to the mountains? Yeah, it popped up in the damned story. So don't rely on it, but— Sure, keep going. I'll stay in touch."

He hung up, then called Banger and reached him this time. He professed that the clue about a mountain connection had come from something Simon had found online, but changed the subject fast, obviously so he wouldn't have to answer questions. But Shauna figured Banger hadn't found a mountain connection yet, either. Neither, when Hunter called him, had Tennyson.

And then he rested the cell phone beside the computer, saved the three addresses that Simon had apparently dictated to him, and brought up Shauna's story about Andee. Again.

He didn't look at her, didn't ask her permission, simply ignored her, even as she drew closer.

She watched silently over his shoulder as he went right to the end of the document, deleted a bunch and began typing.

Once more, he inserted an ending in which his daughter was saved, this time alluding to Big T's mountain hangout being located and the kidnapper being caught.

He saved it, closed the file, then opened it again.

No matter how angry Shauna was with him, how hurt and eager to be anywhere but here, she had an urge to approach and put her arms around his bare, shuddering shoulders as he stared at the screen reading the same old ending.

But knowing nothing she could say, nothing she could do—especially now—could help Hunter, she resisted the impulse and left the room.

Hunter was aware as Shauna slipped out.

Should he go after her? He'd been too hard on her. Again.

As he'd acknowledged yesterday, it was thanks to her story about Andee that they had any kind of break in the case.

And that other story? Hell, he still believed in free will. But he also felt out of control where Shauna simply picked scenarios out of the air and they came true.

Yeah, he felt something for her again. Still. But that didn't mean he'd go anywhere with it, like the sweet little ending she had written that locked him into marriage with her. And where was Andee? She hadn't been in *that* story at all.

"It's my life," he muttered. He'd do what he wanted with it, stories or not.

Or could he…?

His cell phone rang. He snatched it up from the edge of the table, glad for the disruption. Looking at the display, he smiled grimly. "Yeah, Simon?"

"I have something." Hunter's assistant sounded excited.

"On Aitken and his mountain connection?"

"You got it," Simon replied.

* * *

An hour later, Hunter tried to keep the GTO to a speed fast enough to hit the San Bernardino Mountains, and the area known as Big Bear, in as short a time as possible, and slow enough not to get pulled over by the cops. They were already out of the LAPD's jurisdiction. Banger wouldn't be able to help him out of a ticket, even if he wanted to take the time.

But he wanted to get there himself before the feds and Banger arrived. He'd called to let them know where he was heading, and the connection to Aitken that Simon had found.

Shauna rode shotgun yet again. He was surprised when she'd insisted on it. He had only argued a little bit.

Actually, he was glad for her company. Especially after the way he'd come down so hard on her. No apology this time. No discussion, either.

They'd grabbed something at a fast food drive-through. Shauna's only comments since they'd left his house were to thank him for the food, and to remark on how much nicer driving in Southern California was at this time of day, too early for much traffic.

"Does Aitken own property at Big Bear?" Shauna asked, almost startling him as she broke her silence. "Is that what Simon found out?"

Hunter glanced toward her. "Someone close to him does."

She wore an unbuttoned white shirt over her navy T-shirt that was tucked into tight jeans. She could have worn a shapeless, waistless gunnysack and still looked beautiful. In this outfit, she was lovely, but the slender curves that he had molded in his hands last night were all but obscured by the looseness of that overshirt.

It was as if she was telling him *hands off.* Which he deserved.

Plus, it was what he wanted. Otherwise, he just might cave in to the gooey, loving stuff she'd written about the way he felt about her. And that too-pat ending.

"Who owns the property?" she persisted. "A friend? A member of his family?"

"The latter." Hunter stopped himself from grinning at her irritated look. Obviously, she wasn't satisfied with short answers.

"What family member? And how did Simon find out?"

"He is a genius with computer searches," Hunter said. "It turns out John Keenan Aitken's mother was named Esther Keenan."

"So that's where his middle name came from."

"Exactly. The Keenans lived in Fresno while John was growing up, but his granddad was originally from the L.A. area. He was a skier and owned a place up at Big Bear. John's grandmother passed away while he was in high school, and his grandfather a few years ago."

"So John owns the place now?"

"No, his sister does. She's married, and the title is in her married name. That's why I say Simon's a genius. What with accessing birth records, court probate records and all, he tracked down this place that Aitken has access to. In the mountains. A place he's not likely to have gone often, so he could tell anyone he ran into that he's got his sister's permission, and he's there with his own kid. Who'd bother to check it out?"

"Probably no one," Shauna said. "Not even now that there's been publicity about Andee's kidnapping."

"Right. The good thing is that he won't know we're on to him, either. So hopefully, we'll catch up with him nice and quietly, and rescue Andee, before Tennyson and his guys arrive. Banger doesn't have jurisdiction so far from L.A., but I figure he'll be along anyway."

"That sounds wonderful."

He shot another look at her to see if that had been sarcasm. After all, it didn't follow her precious story. But she was looking out the windshield, not at him. Her smile lit her face in what appeared to be genuine anticipation and pleasure.

Appeared to be? Hell, he knew it was. Her facial expressions had once more become as readable to him as her Andee story. More so.

He enjoyed every nuance of her soft, radiant skin, her high cheekbones, her proud, small chin.

Watching those brown eyes that spoke volumes, even when—especially when—her full lips were still and silent.

And he'd again learned her face tactilely, with his fingers and his mouth. Tasted her…

Damn! If he wasn't careful, that second story, which had blown his mind, just might come true.

"Have you ever been to Big Bear?" she asked.

That seemed a neutral enough topic. He told her of a trip he'd taken there to go boating on Big Bear Lake shortly after arriving in L.A. "It was a big change from Oasis, Arizona."

"I'll bet."

They continued to talk about stuff that didn't strike sparks in either of them, stopping for lunch and a rest-room break.

Hunter checked out the map Simon had downloaded from the Internet and faxed him, then he headed that way up the mountain and into a thick, wooded area not far from the lake.

Eventually he stopped near a small, winding road through the trees and looked around. Made sure the landmarks on the map were those he saw around him.

"This is it." He intentionally sounded as impassive as if they'd just gotten to another restaurant, not the place he believed his daughter was being held.

"Okay," Shauna said, equally neutrally.

He aimed the car down the road and stopped outside a rustic-looking wood cabin that had "Keenan" on the mailbox.

Hunter didn't bother to suppress his grin, especially since an old truck squatted right beside the building.

That had to be how Aitken had transported Andee here.

Only then did he notice the white car parked beneath some trees. It had gold lettering on the side: Police.

"Damn!" he said. He got out of the car and approached

the cabin as a couple of guys in uniform came around the side.

"Are you Hunter Strahm?" called one.

"Yes." Hunter drew closer to them, knowing Shauna was right behind him.

"Detective Banner from the LAPD called, said to check out this place," said the taller, more senior cop. "Said you were on your way, but you might as well have stayed home. No one's here."

Hunter swallowed the invective that sprang to his lips. He was angry with Banger, but what the hell? These guys might have been able to catch Aitken—if the guy had actually been here.

"Any indication anyone was here recently?" Hunter asked.

"Yeah. Looks as if they left in a hurry."

"Is it okay if I look in the windows?"

"Sure. We'll hang around while you do." To make sure he didn't break in, Hunter figured.

With Shauna beside him, he peered in the front window. Just typical rustic furniture there. As he looked in the kitchen window, he saw dirty dishes on the table. And when he went around to the back and looked in a bedroom window, he saw a familiar-looking stuffed animal on the floor.

Andee's.

"I'm so sorry, Hunter," Shauna said from beside him.

"Yeah." He felt as if all the substance had spilled from his body, draining from his punctured heart.

And despite their argument, the way he hated her stories, he didn't object when she came toward him, put her arms around him and held him close.

He rested his head on her fragrant hair, shuddered in frustration…and fought the urge to yell.

Shauna almost cried at the unvoiced despair that shuttered Hunter's expression, pursed his lips into a grim line as he navigated the narrow, tree-shrouded roads toward the highway down the mountain.

She had to get him talking, planning their next move.

Focusing on optimism, not defeat. At least until the time for optimism ran out.

"It looked like they left in a hurry, don't you think?" When he didn't answer, she continued, "Do you suppose someone alerted Aitken?"

She held on as they navigated a particularly sharp curve.

"Yeah, I've supposed that." His tone was an ironic growl.

"Do you think the police somehow warned him they were coming, or that we were?"

"Who knows?" Hunter replied gruffly.

"Well, someone must have," Shauna said. "And I don't imagine it was Banger. Did you tell Tennyson where we were going?"

"No, but it's possible he found out the same way Simon did."

Still, Tennyson's alerting Aitken made no sense. And after Hunter had called him to let him know what had happened, he'd told Shauna the guy sounded truly pissed off and had promised Hunter he'd have a team up there soon anyway to scour the place for evidence and clues on where the SOB was headed now.

No, Hunter didn't believe it was Banger or Tennyson or Simon who would have let Aitken know. The local police? Could be, if he had a friend on the force, but Hunter had assumed he'd chosen this place because no one knew him here and would question his having a child with him.

But— "Hunter, I hate to suggest it, but Margo was Aitken's friend before this. Could she have accidentally let on what we were up to the last time the kidnapper called?"

"Or intentionally?" He held up a hand as she formulated a halfhearted protest. "I know—sour grapes against my ex-wife. I'm grasping at straws. And any other kind of stupid cliché you can think of. But it'll be easy enough to eliminate her as a possibility.'' He pulled his cell phone from his shirt pocket, glanced at it and pushed a couple of buttons. ''Banger? No, nothing new here. Have you gotten any further word from Simon?''

He looked toward Shauna and shook his head, then turned back to the road. They'd reached the main route down the mountain.

''I don't suppose Margo's spoken to the kidnapper or anyone about what's going on, has she? Maybe she inadvertently told someone who's still in touch with the guy where we were going.'' A slight pause. ''She's not been on the phone at all then—her house or cell? And Tennyson and you have had people in her place the whole time? The monitoring system's working? Okay, thanks. And I don't suppose your guys have found anywhere else yet where Aitken might go. All right. See you soon.''

He hung up and replaced the phone in his pocket. ''They're checking out Aitken's old addresses,'' he said to Shauna. ''He and Tennyson have people out canvassing everyone Aitken might have talked to in the last few years—people Margo suggested, studios and theaters where he's worked or even auditioned. A couple of restaurants where he's waited tables while waiting for his big break. It's not been long enough for most to have reported in, but so far there's nothing.''

Shauna's heart went out to him. As usual. That particular part of her body always seemed to be engaged around Hunter, whether she liked it or not.

''I'm so sorry,'' she said, tired of the inadequate sentiment.

She wished she could say something that really would make him feel better.

And then it dawned on her exactly what that would be.

''Tell you what,'' she said. ''Do you feel like taking a breather?''

''What, do you want to drive?''

''I will if you'd like, though I'm not wild about L.A. area freeways. But what I meant was that if we stop for a while, we could get my computer from the trunk, and I'll add into my story the fact that when we got to Aitken's place in the mountain, he wasn't there.'' She tried to speak lightly, as if their wasted time wasn't a big deal. ''Maybe my fabulous flying fingers will add something else that'll be helpful.''

Chapter 16

It wasn't like he'd really expected Shauna to come up with something good.

But Hunter, sitting in the fast-food restaurant's booth clutching a foam coffee cup as if it was the only thing that could warm him on the inside, still couldn't melt away the icy steel vise that had attached itself to his gut.

"Ready to give up yet?" His voice was gruff enough to be a challenge.

He had to hand it to her. She met that challenge by giving back as good as she got. "Want me to?" Her brown eyes flashed her continued anger, which was better, he figured, than the sympathy he hated to see. Her long, light hair was wispy, maybe from the humidity in the air up in the mountains.

Most women he knew—like Margo—would have headed straight to the rest room and combed her hair. Fixed her makeup.

Not that Shauna needed anything artificial to make her soft, pink skin look any better, or to bring out the color of her eyes.

"Hell, no," he answered her. "I'll never give up, and I won't let you, either."

Her ironic grin was only directed at him for an instant.

Then she directed it to her laptop set up on the table.

He'd waited until they'd gotten off the mountain and onto the freeway before stopping at a busy exit to take Shauna up on her proposal to mess with her story again. Foolish, maybe, but he was pinning some of his hopes on that story.

Changes to it had sent them to where Aitken had been.

Next time, they wouldn't be too late.

Shauna had immediately set up in the booth while he got them coffee. By the time he'd gotten through the line and joined her at the table, she'd told him she had already entered the part where Big T wasn't there when Hunter and she reached his mountain cabin.

"It saved," she'd told him. "But my change to the ending didn't. And I didn't start writing anything I wasn't aware of."

He'd given her a couple of suggestions on things to add, like a generic inclusion that Simon's research led to more places Aitken might hole up.

It didn't save.

Neither did anything that might lead them to some unnamed conspirator who'd tipped Aitken off.

Nothing much seemed to be working here. They had to get back on the road to L.A.

Maybe.

Would Aitken have been stupid enough to return there, where he was more likely to be recognized than somewhere far away?

But if he had kept going, how could they possibly learn where?

"Damn," he muttered.

"Do you want me to add that?" Shauna eyed him sideways.

"If it'll help."

She was pulling his leg, trying to lighten his mood. Of course, right now, nothing would help.

Would it?

He got out of his side of the booth and slid in beside Shauna. He saw a couple of teenage girls look at him from the next booth and giggle together. He ignored them as he got close to Shauna to read the screen.

Got so close that her body heat, radiating through the long-sleeved white shirt over her T-shirt and jeans, curled around him and warmed that metallic clamp around his insides—just a little.

It also reminded him of other heat they'd shared during their brief reunion.

It fired up, all over again, his resentment of that other story on her computer.

Before he pulled away, she said, "Here," and typed the word "Damn" where the cursor was blinking. The paragraph around it must have been what Shauna had just added, as it said that Big T's cabin was empty.

The part after that he'd read before. It got into Andee's thoughts.

How scared she still was.

He felt his body tighten, his muscles contract until he shook.

Shauna turned toward him, soft curves brushing against him. He shouldn't be noticing her nearness that way, not now.

Not when all he cared about might be so close to being lost.

"Hunter," she said, "let's—"

He turned toward her. "Don't say it."

One edge of her mouth turned up in a half smile. "Okay, I won't tell you I'd like to speculate on how you think Andee would react to your frustration in finding her gone. If I can somehow tune into her emotions that way, then—"

"Then you'll fade off into one of your big, bad writing z-states?"

"Interesting way to describe them. And probably not. They never show up when I want them to. But it doesn't hurt to try."

"What the hell. Okay, Andee's only five, but she's smart for her age. She knows her dad's got a temper. She has one, too. If she knows I'm mad, she sometimes pulls a tantrum of her own to distract me. Other times, she's sweet as can be. Shames me out of my mood."

Shauna smiled. "I can't wait to meet her."

Hunter shot her a look. Did she mean it? If her story unfolded as she wrote it, she would never meet his daughter.

"So here," Shauna said, "where she knows you're mad at Big T, not her, and you're really worried about her, what would she tell you?"

"The only thing I can think of that'd be similar is when she knows Margo and I have had words."

"And what does she say to that?"

He had to take a moment before he could respond. When he did, his voice was thick. "She says, 'I love you, Daddy.'"

Hunter almost didn't catch Shauna's slight reaction—a twitch of one index finger on the keyboard. But he knew the woman was touched by his words.

She kept her voice level as she repeated slowly, while typing it onto the screen, "'I love you, Daddy.' And your reaction would be—?"

"I'd grab her, fling her up in the air and laugh with her, and tell her I love her, too." He spoke in a harsh monotone. He wasn't used to describing personal moments like that.

Especially not when he feared they'd never happen again.

His eyes lit on a couple of kids about Andee's age at the other side of the crowded restaurant—a little boy in a Dodgers T-shirt. A little girl in something pink with lace on it.

He drew his gaze away. Fast.

"And then," he continued without looking at Shauna, "I'd—"

She was still typing. He edged a glance toward her face.

Her eyes were closed.

Hot damn! Had she gone into one of her writing states just like that?

She looked fragile, her skin pale and translucent, as if every ounce of blood, every gradation of her existence was centered in her fingers. She still sat straight in the booth, though, not slumping at all.

Still, worried about her, he put an arm around her.

She felt cold.

If he lent her his body heat, would it break the spell?

But could he let her freeze anyway?

He compromised by not drawing too close. Instead, he watched the screen. Read the words she wrote.

And grinned.

"It's okay, Daddy," Andee said. *"But you have to come and get me."*

"I will, honey. Tell me where you are, and I'll get there just as soon as I can."

"I don't know," Andee cried.

"Is it someplace you've been before?" her daddy asked.

"Uh-huh," Andee agreed.

"With Mommy?"

"Yes."

"And with the man who's with you now?"

"No, Daddy."

"Is it a house?" Daddy asked.

"A great big place," Andee said. *"And it's cold and yucky."*

Shauna stopped typing.

"No," Hunter whispered. "Keep going. Please. We need more to find her."

But Shauna's hands dropped from the keyboard as she slumped on the seat beside him.

He gathered her into his arms, holding her close. She felt as cold as the top of the San Bernardino Mountains in skiing season, and she shook as hard as if she were out there, in the snow, in the light clothes she had on now.

"Hang on," he said, kissing her eyelids, which remained closed. "I have a jacket in the car. I'll go get it."

But her eyes popped open and regarded him with shock, as if he were a complete stranger. The sensation of her not recognizing him kicked him right where it hurt. Especially when she began struggling in his arms.

"Shauna, it's me. Are you all right?"

Recognition dawned on her face, and she stopped moving. Looked up at him in what appeared to be an agony of embarrassment as she tried to pull away in the booth.

"I'm sorry, Hunter," she said. "What happened?"

"You went into one of your big, bad writing z-states," he replied. "And it was a doozie."

"Did it say how to find Andee?"

"No, but it gave a damned good clue or two." And without regard for the anger he'd felt for her earlier, or the fact they were in a restaurant crowded with kids, he leaned toward her and gave her one big, grateful, sexy kiss.

They were nearly at Margo's when Hunter, stopped at a traffic light after hopping off at the final freeway exit, looked at Shauna and asked, "Did you try to change the story's ending again at the restaurant? I mean, when you started writing about Andee and me together. I know you said you did earlier, but nothing happened."

He actually looked curious, not incredulous or mocking… or angry.

Shauna loved that particular expression on his handsome face, which only got better-looking with time—even when shadowed with worry. His straight, black brows were raised just a little, his green eyes quizzical, and he appeared interested as he waited for her reply.

"Not then," she said. "Weren't you watching me and what I wrote?"

"Mostly. But when I kept an eye on you, I couldn't be certain what you were writing."

"Neither could I," she said ruefully.

"Tell me more about how your writing z-state goes. Do you think hard then about what it is you want to write? Or are you vaguely aware of what your fingers are typing? Or is it like your mind goes somewhere and your hands are someplace else?"

"All three, at different times. And sometimes none of them. Mostly, it's like the last one—I'm not conscious, like I'm sleeping. My hands are awake, though, and write automatically, like they and not my mind are what's tuning into…whatever. The emotions of the people I'm writing about, at least initially, though it goes beyond that since I usually type out a whole story—beginning, middle and end—and the subjects I'm writing about can't possibly know what's going to happen in the future."

"But your fingers do?"

Shauna had been watching Hunter, though his eyes had returned to the road as they'd proceeded when the light turned green. "I honestly don't know how I get to the stories' endings. I generally can guess how they start, thanks to the descriptions of the emotions of others at the beginnings. The ends, though—"

"Can be wrong." He made it a statement, and she saw the stubborn set to his broad jaw.

"All I can tell you is what I've seen, Hunter. They've always come true. On the other hand, I've never been able to save even a single change before, so this one is, somehow, different. If only I understood what caused that difference, maybe I could say with certainty that the ending to this one could be changed."

"Or couldn't." His voice was hard again, but before she could think of how to reply he turned the steering wheel, and they went around a corner a little too sharply. She braced herself—and wished she had mentally, too. "So the story you wrote about you and me was caused by someone else's strong emotions, which I'd guess you figure were mine.''

"I—"

"And then you expect it'll come true like the others?"

Shauna had never thought she would be glad to arrive at Margo's, but there it was, the two-story blue house that dominated the street's residential skyline.

And there was the horde of media vans parked along the street, undoubtedly waiting till something happened to excite all the reporters inside them.

Like a glimpse of anyone connected with the kidnapped child. Such as her father.

But maybe even braving cameras and microphones would be better than responding to Hunter's last question. Expectations were so very different from impossible dreams.

"Is that Simon's car?" She pointed toward a foreign model almost as sporty as Hunter's GTO.

"No, he drives a black sedan that's nearly invisible on stakeouts," Hunter said. "And you're changing the subject." He pulled into one of the few empty spaces, behind the vehicle in question, and turned off the engine. He reached over and put his forefinger gently beneath Shauna's chin, turning it toward him.

She kept her eyes level as she considered her response, trying to ignore the fact that his hand hadn't left her face. His closeness, his touch, made it even harder to speak in a monotone, but she did.

"If you're asking whether I wish that story tracked reality, you know I'd be lying if I said no. As to the ending, though—that's a trap. If I say yes, that things will happen that way, you'll say it's impossible. If I say it won't come true, you'll remind me I believe that the ending to Andee's story will come to pass, so why not this one? I'll put it this way. I want Andee to come back safe and sound. Whether I believe it'll happen is irrelevant. And the story about our relationship? We don't have a relationship, Hunter. Not one that could go where that story implies. I wrote it, but I have to distinguish it from the rest without a really good explanation.''

He appeared ready to interrupt, but she didn't let him.

''We were thrown together again because of circumstances neither of us could control. When we have Andee back— hopefully safe, well and unharmed—I'll go home, you'll stay here, and I'll sometimes recall that particular story nostalgically in years to come, just as I wished for a long time that things hadn't ended between us before the way they did.'' She reached for the door handle. ''And now I'm ready to question your ex-wife about all the places she's taken Andee that your daughter might recognize.''

Hunter hadn't actually intended to let Shauna handle the latest round of questions for Margo, but she'd stormed right by the herd of reporters who'd leaped out of the vans parked along the street, ignoring them all. She'd kept her head high, ignoring their shouts and Margo's tearful criticism when she opened the door.

In fact, Shauna had stalked into the house as if ready to take on the world.

Or at least Margo.

Now he stood leaning against the kitchen wall while the two women faced each other over Margo's table. Shauna had a pad of paper in front of her that she'd pulled from her computer bag, and she kept her pen poised above it as she began to quiz Margo.

''Assume Aitken has taken Andee someplace that she's been before with you, but not in his presence. Just start naming places you've been recently with your daughter that fit that description.''

Margo sighed and swiped at her eyes. ''What's this about? I'd tell you anything to help find my daughter, but I don't understand. I mean, there are thousands of places I might have gone with Andee when John wasn't along. Why are you asking your question like that?''

"Humor me," Shauna said.

"This is ridiculous," Margo cried. "A waste of time. My poor Andee. She must miss her mommy and daddy." She sniffled, then grabbed a tissue. Her snug, sleeveless sweater was a shade of red that Hunter had always thought looked particularly good on her. She looked at him pathetically, as if for support.

"We got an anonymous tip that was really cryptic, Margo," he said. He wasn't about to explain the origin of that tip. "We can't afford to ignore any possible lead to Andee, can we?"

"Of course not." Barely glancing at Shauna, Margo rattled off places in the neighborhood first—supermarkets she went to with Andee, fast-food and sit-down restaurants they'd gone to, a movie theater.

Shauna made notes, but after a short while she interrupted. "You're on the right track, but those aren't places Aitken could hide Andee on a long-term basis. What about—" Shauna's face lit up. She turned toward Hunter. "I was going to ask about mutual friends, but it's obvious. BillieAnn!" Looking at Margo again, she said, "Didn't you tell Hunter she's out of town somewhere shooting a commercial? Where does she live? That could be the perfect place for Aitken to take Andee."

"But BillieAnn has a roommate," Margo sniffed.

"Does the roommate know Aitken?"

"How should I know?"

Shauna looked at Hunter. "We should check there anyway, roommate or not." Turning back to Margo, she said, "Who else do you know in common? Anybody who's also out of town?"

Margo's list of mutual friends and acquaintances was a lot shorter and didn't pour out as fast as the places she'd mentioned. When she was done, she'd come up with half a dozen names.

"If you ladies will excuse me for a minute," he said, and nodded toward the hall leading to Margo's guest bathroom.

Not that he was so desperate to use her facilities, but it gave him a way to steal off and contact Simon fast.

In the small powder room that smelled of herbal air freshener, Hunter used his cell to call his second-in-command.

"Any other addresses on Aitken?" he immediately asked Simon.

"Still working on it, but I've already given you the easy ones."

Hunter had checked in with Simon before even leaving Aitken's sister's cabin at Big Bear, letting him in on his frustration. "I've got some new stuff for you to check out. People Margo and Aitken know in common. We've reason to believe the guy's holding Andee somewhere she's visited before with her mother, but not when Aitken was with them."

"And we think this because—?"

"Because of a new twist in Shauna's story," Hunter admitted. "We made a little stop on the way here and it appeared then."

"Yes! Any suggestions from Margo?"

Hunter, who'd also taken notes, gave Simon a rundown. "See if you can find alternate addresses for a BillieAnn Callahan. She's out of town. Only problem is, she's got a roommate, so it's unlikely that Aitken stashed himself and Andee at their place."

"Sure thing. And you want this info the day before yesterday."

"Yeah, but I'll settle for half an hour from now."

"Right. And you won't take into consideration that I'm twenty miles from the office? I just talked with one of Aitken's former landlords—from about three years ago."

"Anything useful?"

"Not really."

"Then, no, I won't take into consideration that you're not

near the office. Not when my daughter is counting on me to figure out where she is, and fast.''

''That was in the story?''

''Yeah,'' Hunter said. ''In Shauna's latest version.''

''So you think John Keenan Aitken kidnapped Andee and started this entire mess just because he needs money?'' Shauna wanted to make the best use possible of her time alone with Margo.

She'd run through most things she could think of to remind Margo of other people she and Aitken knew in common. Now she needed to delve into the emotions behind what happened. Aitken's emotions, perceived by someone who really knew him and not just her keyboard impressions.

''I'd never have believed it of him,'' Margo said sadly. ''How could he do this to me?'' Even under interrogation by a woman she despised, and especially in her obvious distress, Hunter's ex managed to look distressingly beautiful.

''But money is his reason?'' Shauna pressed.

''I can't imagine anything else.'' Margo stood and began pacing the limited space in her designer kitchen. ''When you find him, tell me. I want to ask him why he'd do such a terrible thing. He's my friend, or at least I thought so. Sure, he needs money, but that's a terrible motivation to steal any woman's child, particularly mine.''

''Hopefully we'll be in a situation where you can ask him,'' Shauna said carefully. She couldn't make any promises that Margo would be able to confront Aitken, for in her story the kidnapper died.

''So Hunter and you are back together,'' Margo's soft comment ripped into Shauna's thoughts. She had stopped pacing and stood behind the chair next to Shauna's. So close that Shauna felt smothered by her expensive perfume.

''Excuse me?''

''Don't play games,'' Margo said. ''It's okay with me.

We've been divorced for years, and things weren't great before that.''

"All that's between us now is related to finding Andee,'' Shauna told her.

"Then I might try to salvage something with him when this is over,'' Margo said thoughtfully. "For Andee. She'll need extra TLC. Having both her parents there for her should help.''

"Of course.'' Shauna's heart rolled slowly over inside her. "But right now, I'd like to ask you—''

Hunter burst through the kitchen door. A jubilant smile lit his features and elicited an involuntary mirroring grin from Shauna, despite her not knowing its origin.

"What is it?'' she asked him.

"You were half-right.'' He addressed his comment not to Shauna but Margo. "BillieAnn has a roommate. What you didn't know was that her roommate got her the role in this commercial. They're both out of town. But BillieAnn's place would fit right into the criteria: a place Andee's been with you before, but without Aitken. Right?''

"Yes, but—''

"And Shauna, get this—the apartment building is a converted warehouse.''

Though Margo looked puzzled, Shauna recalled immediately the last scene of her story…which took place in a warehouse.

"I'm going to take a look, and I'll let you both know what I find,'' Hunter continued. "And if Andee's there, you'll be the third I'll notify—after Banger and Tennyson. I don't want to tell anyone else, not even the cops, right now, after what happened up at Big Bear. I don't want to take any chances on Aitken hearing that I'm on my way.'' He looked at Margo. 'You're not going to tell him, are you?''

"Of course not,'' Margo replied, sounding indignant.

"Anyway, keep your fingers crossed.''

Shauna's fingers, usually so independent, crossed tightly together.

Chapter 17

"See any?" Hunter demanded.

From the corner of his eye, he watched Shauna, beside him in the car, swivel and peer out the window. Her soft blond hair swayed about her shoulders. "No, I think you lost them."

"Good." His tension eased, though just a little. It was one thing to lose a bunch of media cattle who'd tried to stampede him as he left Margo's. But the bigger hurdle was yet to come.

That was why he'd allowed Shauna to join him. She'd reminded him quietly, before he'd dashed from Margo's, that the more things that were different from what they expected—meaning her story, though they didn't mention that in front of Andee's mother—the better chance they'd have for an alternate ending.

Of course Margo, confused, had asked what they were talking about.

Good thing Shauna had some tact, one of her admirable traits from the old days that had become even more pronounced with time and her shrink's training. He had none.

He let her make up something about scenarios that the authorities anticipated in similar kidnappings. And then they'd left together.

They were followed by a bunch of microphone-wielding reporters who wouldn't take ''no comment'' for an answer.

''Where is BillieAnn's place?'' Shauna asked. Her voice was low and conversational, as if she discussed L.A.'s sunny weather and smog.

He heard anxiety beneath the surface nonetheless. He didn't try to smooth it over. Much as he would have liked to sugar-coat the situation for Shauna's sake, she'd see right through it and call him on it. He'd treat her as he would Simon—like an equal.

Yeah, an equal that he had an overwhelming urge to touch. And hold against him. Even make love to again, just once more, for when this day was done, his life would be different. He'd have his daughter back.

He had to.

But to do it, he would most likely have to kill a man.

That part of Shauna's story he believed.

''Her address is in Burbank,'' he said. ''We're only about fifteen minutes away.''

''In real time or speed-limit time?'' Shauna asked wryly.

''Guess.'' He shot her what he hoped passed for a grin.

''I figured.'' She was silent, then said, ''Shouldn't we talk strategy?''

''Not necessary. Backup's on the way. I told Simon to let Banger and Tennyson know where we're going, but I wanted to get a head start.''

He felt in control again. Finally. So many of their clues, helpful and not, had come from Shauna. But Simon had found this address for BillieAnn. And Hunter would be the one to get his daughter back.

''When we get there, it'll go like this. I'll check out the area, then knock on the door. If Aitken answers, I'll insist on coming in and I'll try to talk to him—not that I expect his cooperation, but I'd like to try to get Andee back the easy way. If he doesn't answer, I'll still go in. And then, assuming they're both there, I'll still get Andee back.''

"I'm figuring on Andee not being there, Hunter, even if Aitken is.''

"Yeah. Right. Your story. That's why it'll be better if I at least try to force the guy to talk to me first.''

"Before you shoot him?'' Her voice, though still soothing, rose a little. She glanced down at his pant leg.

After leaving Margo's, they'd sneaked out the back to avoid reporters. At his car, he'd taken a snub-nosed .38 from the locked box in his trunk and stuck it into his ankle holster. It hadn't been till they'd gotten on the road that they'd been spotted again.

He sucked in his breath. "No matter how much I want to do damage to him, I'll only fire my weapon in self-defense, or to protect Andee or you.''

"Don't try to be my defender in this, Hunter. I don't want you harming anyone on my behalf, even if you think I'm in danger. I especially hate the idea that you may be endangering yourself without being sure you can save Andee this way.''

His fists clenched on the steering wheel, and he forcibly relaxed them. "This is real life, Shauna. Not one of your stories.''

"And you're following my story like you believe it,'' she retorted.

Of course she was right.

But that ending—

He glanced at her. Her eyes were downcast and misty, her lips dipping sadly at the edges.

"Yeah, I believe in it,'' he told her softly, dampness in his throat coating his words. "But it's changed some, and I'm going to change it more. Whatever it takes to get my daughter back.''

"Whatever it takes?'' she repeated. "So you won't shoot Aitken, the way it says in the story? He wouldn't tell where Andee was, and then he couldn't.''

"You think I don't remember that? If I can avoid shooting him, I will, as much as I'd love to see the SOB rot in hell."

Shauna almost mouthed the words as Hunter said them. "Stay in the car. I'll come and get you soon as it's over."

Her insincere nod was toward his disappearing back.

She got out of the car. She couldn't let him go alone. She wouldn't. For her own sake, as well as his and Andee's.

She carefully shadowed him up the sun-baked concrete walk to the large warehouse in this run-down industrial area. This was where BillieAnn Callahan lived? As Hunter said, it had apparently been converted into apartments. Someone had a sense of humor, for the old concrete building had a sign on the side: Jardin del Valle Apartments. Shauna hurriedly translated in her mind—Garden of the Valley. The name was evocative of greenery and pretty colors.

Sure, and it had probably once smelled like a cesspool.

She stopped when Hunter paused at the entry. Despite its industrial origins, this apartment building must have a security entrance like most these days. He scanned the directory, then pushed a button.

She wished she could hear what he said. She'd have bet anything he didn't simply press the button for BillieAnn Callahan's apartment, identify himself to the voice that answered, and get let in. But whoever he'd talked to did, indeed, unlock the front door. Hunter slipped inside.

How would she get in?

She looked at the directory and found BillieAnn's apartment number—6. Wondered how much she'd sound like a pizza delivery person if she started ringing everyone's bell.

She heard a footstep behind her. Though it was midafternoon, a guy who looked like a real delivery person was walking up the path, a large box in his hand. As he got there she smiled and shrugged. "My friend probably can't hear me over her hairdryer. She said she was washing her hair when I called her before."

As it turned out, she probably could have stood there with a knife in her teeth and the guy would have paid no attention when she slipped inside after him.

She hurried to the end of the drafty corridor, which opened into a courtyard of sorts—with a concrete floor, open metal-beamed ceiling, and dirty glass walls at the two ends. The apartments had apparently been constructed inside the shell.

Shauna headed for the door marked 6. BillieAnn's.

When she got there it was closed, but she heard voices inside.

She tried the door. It was open. She pushed it slowly at first, watching for movement, listening.

"I don't give a damn why you took her," Hunter was saying. "I just want my daughter back."

"And I want my money," growled a voice that Shauna didn't recognize. Of course she'd only met John Keenan Aitken once. And he might sound different in the heat of the moment.

She cautiously sneaked inside. And stared.

The two men were in a large, open room that looked as if a portion of the old warehouse had been simply walled off from the rest. Mismatched furniture formed a couple of conversation areas, and appliances and shelves formed the kitchen. Along one end was a wall with a door in it. Did it lead to a bedroom? Another apartment?

The two men faced each other in what appeared to be a testosterone-charged battle of wills. Thank heavens neither pointed a weapon at the other.

Hunter towered over the other man, much broader and more well toned beneath the beige buttoned shirt he had worn with black denim trousers that day. He remained several feet from Aitken, but dominated the room with his anger.

Please, stay cool, Shauna silently commanded him. The man had Andee. And, according to her story, the man had a gun.

Not only his daughter's life was in danger. Hunter's was, too.

They hadn't noticed her yet. She tried to slip by to hunt for Andee.

"Ah, Shauna, isn't it?" Aitken demanded. Even if she didn't recognize his voice, he was definitely the man she'd met a couple of days earlier at Margo's. He was of medium height, and more slenderly built than Hunter. Once again, he wore a muscle shirt that emphasized that the guy worked out. His face was almost debonair, and Shauna figured he excelled at roles playing royalty, the rich, or high-placed government types.

He didn't look like a kidnapper.

But he also hadn't told Hunter he hadn't the foggiest idea what he was talking about.

"Hello, John," Shauna said, coolly joining them in the living room. "The game's over. How about letting me know where Andee is. I'll go make sure she's all right."

"I didn't expect you," Aitken said. He sounded awfully cool for such a tense situation, but of course the guy was an actor. "Especially not you, Shauna."

Which was a good thing. In her story, Hunter and Aitken had faced each other alone.

"If I'd known you were coming, Strahm," he continued, "maybe I'd have brought the child to make sure you followed my instructions this time."

"What instructions?" Hunter growled. Shauna could see, by the heaving of his chest, that he was having a hard time controlling his temper. But he wouldn't do anything rash while his daughter's whereabouts remained unknown.

And that was the biggest fallacy in her story. For at its ending, Aitken had been shot. In a warehouse—one converted into an apartment? By Hunter, after "Big T" fired at him.

Hunter simply wanted his daughter back. There was no reason for Aitken to shoot at him.

Was Aitken's weapon behind the couch, like in her story?

But there were two couches. Shauna slowly approached one, intending to hunt for the gun herself. But what if she chose the wrong one?

And how long could Hunter remain calm enough not to attack the man who had stolen his daughter?

"Stay where you are," Aitken snapped at her. Actor or not, he was losing his cool.

Shauna froze in place. "John, you know this is over," she said in the most placating voice she had learned as a therapist. "We just want Andee back safely. Let's go where she is, okay? Then we'll help you as much as we can."

"I want my money," Aitken repeated. His voice was louder still, with a whine at the edges. He was definitely no longer in character.

"We understand," Shauna said. "And Hunter has most of it together. If we get Andee back safely now, he'll give you what he's got on him and make sure you get a head start, before the authorities know what's happened."

"The authorities? There weren't supposed to be any. No police. No publicity. That was how it was to be." What was left of Aitken's suave demeanor crumbled, and his expression turned wild. "Where's my money? I need to get out of here."

"After we get Andee back." Hunter spoke through gritted teeth. He edged closer as if trying to get around Aitken—toward the couch farthest from Shauna.

"If you get her back, what's my leverage?" Aitken's voice grew strident as he blocked Hunter. "I don't think so."

"What I think is—" Hunter began.

Shauna approached and touched his arm warningly. "We'll work it out as a fair trade. I'll stay with you, John, while we go get Andee, and Hunter will join us with the money. Let's do it now, since we may have been followed by some reporters, and possibly even the police and FBI."

"What?" Aitken's hazel eyes bulged, and he looked panicked. "Why did you tell them? Oh, no, it's going to be too late. I was afraid that was happening. I'm trapped!"

"No, you're not," Shauna soothed, her heart sinking. He *was* trapped. So were they.

Without Andee.

"Let's go get Andee right now, and do the exchange," Shauna said again.

Aitken ran his hand through his hair, and only then did Shauna realize that it had been cut so expertly that it had hidden the way his hairline was receding.

"I don't know. I need to ask…" His voice trailed off.

"What are you talking about?" Hunter demanded, but Aitken only shook his head. "Where's my daughter?"

Hunter's rage combined with Aitken's indecision would only make things worse. "It's the best way, John," she said. "Once Andee's okay, no one will have any reason to harm you."

"Yes, they will," he cried out. "This isn't how it was supposed to be. It's—" He seemed to look beyond Shauna. And then, without any warning, he dove behind the sofa that Shauna had tried to check out earlier.

He came up holding the biggest gun Shauna had ever seen, and she remembered the ending from her story, verbatim:

Big T swooped down and reached behind a couch in the middle of the warehouse floor, lifting his Uzi. Before he could begin spraying bullets, Hunter ducked, rolled and came up shooting. His first volley got the guy in the gut.

The kidnapper fell to the hard concrete floor, moaning, as Hunter ran to kneel beside him, his weapon still leveled on him.

"Tell me where Andee is, you perverted bastard. Now."

Blood spurted from between Big T's fingers as he clutched his middle. "Too late." His gasp was a ghastly laugh. "Good luck finding her."

Only, he didn't shoot.

Hunter ducked, grabbed his gun from his ankle holster and aimed, but unlike in the story, he didn't shoot, either. Aitken pointed his huge weapon toward Hunter but looked somewhere over his shoulder. "Margo, why didn't you c—"

He was cut off by the sound of a weapon firing from behind Hunter, behind Shauna.

Aitken went down.

Only then did Shauna turn to see who had shot him.

It was Margo Masters, holding an automatic pistol larger than Hunter's in a stance worthy of a police officer—the way Shauna had seen the Phoenix police do years before, when Hunter was part of them.

Margo was crying hysterically, and the weapon in her hands shook. "He took Andee. He was going to shoot you, Hunter. I couldn't lose both of you. I love you, Hunter."

"How the hell did you get here, Margo?" Hunter demanded.

"She came with me." Banger stalked out from the hallway that Shauna had assumed contained bedrooms or an exit from the apartment. "I should have known better, damn it all." He knelt at Aitken's side. "I didn't think about checking her purse for weapons."

"Is Andee back there?" Shauna pointed behind him.

"No. I looked."

Shauna's mind whirled. Why were things so different from in her story?

And what had Aitken been saying when he was shot?

She thought she knew, and it made perfect, if horrifying, sense.

"It's over now, Margo," Hunter said. Shauna watched Hunter put an arm around his ex-wife reassuringly. Or was it? She saw his cold expression as he reached for Margo's gun. "By the way, where's Andee?"

He knew, too.

"How should I know?" Margo wailed.

"Were you supposed to call and warn Aitken?" Hunter asked quietly. "Is that what he was about to say when you shot him?"

Margo pulled away, swinging her weapon so it aimed at Hunter. "No, of course not."

"You were in this with him, weren't you?" Hunter's voice remained soft, but the glint in his eyes told Shauna how angry he was. "You've warned him the other times."

"How can you say that? Andee's my daughter. I would never put her in danger, or help anyone who did."

"Then give me your gun and we'll talk about it."

"No." Margo moved quickly, and Shauna hadn't anticipated it. Margo threw an arm around Shauna's neck and held the gun against her temple. "You can't say such terrible things about me, Hunter, not with Banger here. He'll believe you."

Shauna could barely breathe, let alone think, with the hard, cold metal digging into her. When she spoke, it came out in a rasp because of the pressure against her throat, "We need to find Andee, Margo. Then we can sort this all out."

"You come with me." Margo's voice was flat. "I'll let you go when I'm free, and then you can find the kid. You two, put your guns on the floor and stay out of the way."

Shauna saw Banger take his place beside Hunter. Both men laid their weapons down. And then Margo started pulling Shauna, by the throat, toward the apartment door.

Shauna had to do something. Margo wouldn't let her go unharmed, no matter what she'd said.

She met Hunter's eyes. There was fear in them, but encouragement, too. He glanced down toward the floor, where Aitken lay, motionless, then back toward Shauna.

She thought she understood. "No, John!" she shouted. "Don't try it."

Margo swung the gun away from Shauna's head and toward the floor, at Aitken. That was distraction enough for Shauna to slam her heel into Margo's shin and tear out of her grasp.

The two men dashed forward and grabbed Margo before she fired a shot.

It was over.

But not all of it.

Shauna had, in fact, noticed Aitken move, but ever so slightly. She ran and knelt beside him as Banger took Margo into custody.

Shauna expected the worst: *"Too late."* His gasp was a ghastly laugh. *"Good luck finding her."*

His eyes closed. He was dead.

Somewhere close by, but not near enough for Hunter to find her, Andee Strahm weakly cried "Daddy" for the last time.

But Shauna wouldn't give up. For Hunter's sake. And Andee's. She gently shook Aitken, and his eyes opened.

"Margo?" he rasped.

"They have her," Shauna said. "And now we have to help Andee. I'll bet all you wanted was the money, and to help Margo. I know you didn't want to hurt a child. Please, tell me where Andee is."

"My car," he rasped. "Sleeping pills. So she couldn't cry. Would give me away."

Oh, Lord. Had he given her an overdose? Shauna looked up and met Hunter's bleak gaze. There were tears in his eyes.

It was midafternoon. Even a child who hadn't been drugged who was locked in a hot car could die quickly from dehydration. "Where's your car, John?" Shauna asked.

"Three blocks." He shuddered and looked up at Shauna. "So sorry I—"

And that was all.

Shauna bent her head. Tears rolled down her cheeks. No matter what he had done, someone needed to mourn this man. It shouldn't be her. She'd hardly known him. But he'd been a living, breathing human being—

And a kidnapper.

"What did he say?" Hunter demanded. "I couldn't hear. Did he say where Andee was?"

Shauna repeated John's last words, including the apology.

"Let's go find her," Hunter shouted.

"Yes." Shauna rose to her feet.

She only hoped they wouldn't be too late.

They'd quizzed the sobbing Margo before rushing out of the warehouse-apartment.

She wasn't saying much, but she had described John's seventies-vintage, dented car. Banger and Tennyson sent their troops out with Hunter and Shauna, along with some local Burbank cops.

The next problem was finding the car in this industrial area, where cars that should have been junked ages ago sat in parking lots and along the streets. They had already run a check and had his plate number.

"Can you write something?" Hunter whispered in her ear after the first futile ten minutes of looking.

"No time," she told him. Even if she could produce on demand. Plate number or not, she peered into back seats of one car after another. Most were empty, though some held junk.

None contained a small child.

Ignoring the cops who had scattered for the hunt, Hunter dashed from one car to the next. His face was a frozen mask of determination, yet Shauna saw the fear in his eyes.

Shauna heard a shout and pivoted to look at Hunter. He'd pulled open a car door.

Could this be it?

But he pulled out a pile of clothes and slammed them to the ground. He kicked the door shut.

Rested the top of his head on the grungy old car's roof.

Shauna's heart ached for him. But the best thing she could do was keep looking.

She looked inside cars parked nearest her on the street.

Nothing in this old sedan. The wrecked SUV. The stripped late-model luxury car.

And then—a few cars beyond, she spotted one from the seventies.

What really caught her attention, though, was that it was cleaner than the heaps surrounding it. And the plate number? Yes!

She rushed toward it. Peered into the back seat.

Shauna screamed jubilantly, "Hunter! I've found her!"

A child lay on the floor, her head propped on the seat—a beautiful child with curly, dark hair. She looked asleep.

Please, just let her be asleep...

The car was a four-door. The rear passenger-side door didn't open. Neither did the front door. By the time Shauna had rushed to the other side, Hunter was there.

"Andee!" he shouted, pounding on the window.

He couldn't get the driver's-side rear door open either, for he grabbed at the driver's door. Nothing.

Ignoring the approaching cops, Hunter hurried to a piece of metal on the ground. The old axle was big and heavy, and he carried it to the car where his daughter lay.

Unmoving.

He used the metal bar to smash in the windshield, far from where the child lay. Though pieces of safety glass rained into the vehicle, they didn't reach the back seat. Hunter grabbed the edge of the roof and used it to lever himself in, feetfirst. He dove over the console between the two front seats and lifted the child, at the same time opening one of the rear doors.

He exited the car cradling Andee.

Shauna ran to Hunter's side, afraid to reach out.

Almost afraid to ask, "How is she?"

She looked at Hunter, and his huge smile gave her the answer she'd craved.

"She's alive," he said, pulling Andee up so he could kiss her cheek. And then he shouted so loud the whole world could hear, "She's alive!"

The little girl stirred in Hunter's arms. Thank heavens! Another hour, even another minute, she could have been gone. They'd found her not a moment too soon.

Tears rolling down her cheeks, Shauna stayed back, watching the reunion between father and daughter as Andee's eyes opened.

She swallowed sobs of emotion and relief when the little girl looked right into Hunter's face, gave a wide smile that was the image of her father's happiest, and said in the sweetest voice Shauna had ever heard, "I knew you would come, Daddy."

Chapter 18

"So what are you doing back here?" Kaitlin asked the next afternoon.

"I own this place," Shauna retorted.

They were seated at a booth at Fantasy Fare, sipping hot and fragrant herbal tea. Since it was midafternoon, between lunch and dinner, the restaurant wasn't busy, so Shauna intended to catch up with all that happened in her absence.

Instead, she'd wound up spilling the tale of Andee's kidnapping and rescue to her friend and manager.

Not to mention the evolution of her story about the saga.

And that other little story she'd written about Hunter and her.

Shauna crossed her legs beneath the table. Because she planned to tell stories at her regular story time that evening, she wore a long yellow skirt and white peasant blouse that she would spruce up with a pinafore later to look like a Bo-peep shepherdess outfit.

"Of course all this is yours." Kaitlin swept the restaurant with a flippant gaze. She wore one of her typical short skirts and tank tops that worked well in Oasis desert weather. Her long chestnut hair was drawn into a pearly clip at the back of her head, and the look emphasized the oval shape of her face and ethereal glow in her pale blue eyes. One finger swirled about the rim of her teacup as she studied Shauna critically. "But you know full well I could handle it for another few days. Weeks or months, for that matter. Why didn't you stay in L.A. to settle things with Hunter?"

"Things were already settled." Shauna spiked her voice with cheerfulness when what she wanted to do was fade into a puddle of grief.

Losing Hunter once had been hard enough. Twice was an unbearable agony. But she would survive it. Somehow.

"Sure they were settled," Kaitlin scoffed. "You want him, he wants you, and here you are."

"It's not that simple," Shauna protested.

"You're telling me," Kaitlin agreed. "Remember who you're talking to. I can't tell you the number of times I felt you over the last few days, heard your emotions go gaga. But if I'd called more, I knew I'd interrupt some pretty hot stuff. 'Simple' isn't the word for what's between Hunter Strahm and you, honey. Wasn't before, and certainly isn't now."

Shauna suddenly saw a slide show of herself and Hunter in her mind, a mélange of one scene after another of yelling at each other, ignoring each other…kissing each other and more.

Courtesy of Kaitlin and her ability both to read others' emotions and implant images in their minds.

"Cut it out," Shauna demanded.

"Okay."

The last vision, one of Hunter and her sharing a long, hot, sex-laden kiss, suddenly popped like a balloon and disappeared.

Leaving Shauna feeling as bereft as if the real Hunter had suddenly stopped kissing her and run from the restaurant.

"Better?" Kaitlin asked slyly.

"Yeah. Sure."

"So, like I asked before, what are you doing here?"

Shauna sighed, glancing around Fantasy Fare. The main restaurant room had potted plants everywhere, like Shauna's home, and the story-telling room had even more. There were more customers than usual at this hour.

"I couldn't stay," she finally said to Kaitlin. "Once everything was over, I just added to the confusion. So, I came home."

Was it the right decision? Of course. But she reviewed it quickly in her thoughts—for both Kaitlin and her to consider.

After he'd rescued Andee, Hunter took her straight to the nearest hospital to be checked over. Other than disorientation from the mild sedative Aitken had given her and minor dehydration from being left in the car that long, she was fine. She was kept overnight, though, for observation.

Shauna had sat with her for a while in the hospital while Hunter gave his official statement about Margo's shooting of Aitken, her subsequent actions and the search for Andee.

Andee was every bit as adorable and precocious as Hunter had said. Shauna talked as a therapist and friend to the small imp with curly black hair. She told Andee that her daddy loved her and that soon a very nice person she didn't know yet—a counselor—would want to hear all about her adventure over the last few days. She urged the child to talk about it, and even draw pictures about it.

"Okay, Shauna," Andee had said. A small frown darkened her face, and she said, "Johnny said I should call him 'T'. He wasn't nice to me. I didn't want to go in his car but he made me. A lot." And then she smiled. "But he gave me lots of cookies to eat."

"Do you like cookies?" Shauna had asked.

Andee gave a decisive nod, then her expression grew solemn again. "T said bad things about my daddy."

"I'm sorry to hear that. You know your daddy's a very nice man."

Hunter had returned while Shauna was in the middle of telling Andee one of her favorites of the tales she had written for story time at Fantasy Fare. He had waited while she finished, then hurried to the bed to fuss over his child.

Shauna had gone through an agony of indecision. She figured that returning as soon as possible to how things were before would be best for the child.

She had left for Hunter names of noted child therapists in the area. She'd borrowed his car keys and removed her computer from the trunk. In the note she left for him there, she urged him to get counseling for Andee and asked him to ship the rest of her things when he got around to it. She left cash in the glove compartment to cover the cost.

She'd returned his keys to him, then slipped away on another pretext, called a cab and headed for the airport.

Her story's ending hadn't come true, and no one could be happier about it than her. She wished, though, that she understood why this story had been so different from all others she'd ever written.

Or maybe she knew.

And now she was home.

"What about the story about Hunter and you?" Kaitlin interjected. "Where'd it come from? What do you think it meant?"

"I've struggled with that," Shauna admitted. "I don't know."

"Sure you do." Kaitlin cocked her head admonishingly. "Think it through aloud. Right now."

Shauna sighed. "Sometimes I wish you were just a normal human being."

"Then you wouldn't have hired me to keep you in line. Now, don't change the subject. I think you know not only why you wrote that story, but also why you could save all those changes to the tale about Andee. Tell Auntie Kaitlin."

"Okay, it's Hunter," Shauna stormed.

"What about him?" Kaitlin prompted.

"Everything!" Shauna stared at the liquid in her teacup and said, "You know I've always written stories about milestones in his life. I somehow pick up on his emotions, even from this far away. Before, the emotions of bad guys he was responsible to stop got my fingers tingling. This time, it wasn't his feelings that triggered my writing about Andee's kidnapping, but hers—probably since she's his daughter. I gathered the kidnapper's emotions, too, once I started writing."

"And Hunter's?" Kaitlin asked.

"That's…it's never happened before, but I was able to save some changes I made to my story about Andee. I think it was because they emanated from Hunter's emotions. I couldn't change the ending, though, which of course generated most of his emotions. But I knew my caring about what happened to him and his daughter wouldn't have been enough to do it, since I could never save changes I made in the story about my father."

"I still think that, by then, your dad was ready to die, don't you?" Kaitlin asked gently. They'd discussed this before, but Shauna had never quite accepted Kaitlin's theory.

"I know you believe that if my emotions were the important thing, he'd have rallied under treatment and survived longer."

"Don't you?"

"Yes," Shauna blurted. "I've never wanted to give you the satisfaction of admitting it, but—"

"But you know I'm right."

"I guess I do. And now, Hunter's emotions were the important thing, so by his force of will he changed my story. Even what was supposed to happen at the end. You know, I think I'll take one more stab at that story. See if I can save the ending as it really turned out, just for closure."

"Why not?" Kaitlin agreed. "And that other story you mentioned, about the two of you. What's your current theory about it?"

"I know you want me to say it was completely a result of Hunter's emotions. That he cares for me enough to want a happy ending. But when he read it, he despised me for it. Hated that my stories suggested control over their subjects, and he's always rejected anything out of his control." She took a sip of hot tea, then looked into Kaitlin's sympathetic blue eyes. "If for no other reason than to prove he's in charge, I figure he's convinced himself that the opposite of what I wrote is true."

"Did you purposely let him read the story?"

"No, but I could have guessed he'd see it."

"And do you want its ending to come true?"

"To be with Hunter forever, happily ever after?" Shauna shook her head and gave an unladylike snort. "Talk about fairy tales."

Kaitlin reached over the table and patted Shauna's arm beneath the peasant blouse's bouffant sleeves. "Honey, you may be able to convince yourself you haven't let yourself really care again, but you can't fool ol' Kaitlin."

Hunter sat back on his living room sofa and turned on the television low. And sighed. Largely from contentment, since he had just tucked Andee into her own bed for the first time in more than a week.

First, there had been his business trip, and his having to leave a job undone for the first time ever. Fortunately, his client had been very understanding after hearing of Andee's kidnapping on the news.

Then there'd been Andee's kidnapping. Thank heavens he had gotten her back safe and sound, Shauna's story notwithstanding.

Shauna.

She was another reason for his sigh. She had taken off 'thout saying goodbye. She'd just left a note in his car and— nd made him crazy. He missed her, damn it.

His cell phone rang. He checked the number before answering, and felt his muscles tense.

As if his thoughts of her had summoned her call, it was Shauna.

"Hello?" he said briskly, as if his gut wasn't spasming inside him. The woman had driven him nuts. Still did.

"Hi, Hunter," said the soft, familiar and much too welcome voice of the woman he wanted out of his life. Maybe.

"Did you make it home safely?" he asked, the way he would of one of his mother's friends who'd come for a visit.

"Yes."

He heard the hesitation in her voice. Well, the heck with it. He wouldn't make it easier for her, even as he pictured her soft brown eyes regarding him sympathetically as he backed as far from her as he could over a telephone.

"Great. Glad to hear it. Thanks again for coming. Say hello to my mother for me."

He started to hang up, then heard her call, "Hunter? I just wanted to let you know that I rewrote my story the way it actually happened and all the changes saved."

"That's good."

"Have you learned anything about why Margo did it?"

"Revenge. And money. Our divorce wasn't that friendly, and I only paid her child support for times when Andee was with her. She wanted more."

"Oh," Shauna said. "But—"

"She enlisted Aitken to help, for a cut of the ransom. Everything was to be kept quiet, no cops, no media. When reality changed, Aitken freaked, but she used it to her advantage. She played up her media interviews like the great little actress she professes to be—the frightened mother, the brave heroine. She was already approached with a couple of offers to sell book rights and do a movie."

"But she won't be able to profit like that if she's convicted of killing John Aitken and kidnapping Andee."

"Right. The cops are gathering evidence as we speak.

Turns out her neighbor Conrad Chiles overheard some discussions between Aitken and Margo that he hadn't realized were about snatching Andee and extorting money from me. No one picked up on her calls warning Aitken as she'd rented a prepaid cell phone in an assumed name. BillieAnn Callahan suspected what was going on, though since she'd figured Andee actually was safe in Aitken's hands, she hadn't spilled it before. And who knows what Aitken would have done to Andee at the end, since she could have identified him.''

"I'm just glad she's safe," Shauna said. "Thanks for the update. It was nice talking with you, Hunter. Goodbye."

"Wait!" he shouted into the phone. She wasn't simply going to end it like that, was she?

He still needed some answers.

"Yes, Hunter?" She sounded distantly cordial, as if they were total strangers.

"You said you were tying up loose ends. Revising the story about Andee's kidnapping." He paused for a moment, then asked, "What about the other story?"

"What about it?"

"Isn't it a loose end? Are you trying to tie it up?" He realized his voice had turned cool.

"That's not a loose end," Shauna said softly. "It's one that's all tied up and tossed away. Goodbye, Hunter."

"Duke ran out of Bobby's house barking at the kitty cat," Shauna read aloud from the pages on her lap as she sat cross-legged on a mound of colorful pillows on the floor, her long skirt tucked under her, in the Fantasy Fare story room. "Bobby ran after Duke. And Bobby's mommy ran after Bobby."

Dozens of children sat on other pillows on the floor surrounding her. They laughed now, and so did Shauna. She ⌐⌐⌐d up, meeting delight in one young face after another, ⌐⌐ ⌐e was amusing them.

Glad there were people around her who were lighthearted enough to laugh in the unrestrained way children did.

Maybe someday that would be enough to lift the heaviness from her heart.

Eleven days had passed since she had left Los Angeles. Had left Hunter and his adorable daughter Andee.

Ten days since she had last spoken with him and sworn that she had left no loose ends.

That the story she'd written about them living happily ever after hadn't mattered to her any more than to him.

She was sure now that what she'd talked about with Kaitlin had been correct: those two stories, and all others she'd written in which Hunter was a character, had sprung from her fingertips because on some level she was so attuned to Hunter.

The man she had loved so many years ago.

The man she still loved.

His emotions had been the impetus for all the changes to the story about Andee, and her ability to save them.

Including, afterward, the ending that told the true story: Andee had been saved, restored to her loving daddy forever.

But her mommy was going far, far away.

Poor Hunter. Even more, poor Andee.

But Shauna hadn't only left the names of suggested therapists with Hunter. She'd talked to Elayne, too.

Elayne had been a good friend before, when her son had left Oasis and walked out on Shauna and her stories and the love they'd shared. Elayne had made it clear she loved her son, understood his actions, but she'd nevertheless remained close to Shauna.

And now, though Shauna had tried not to reveal how hurt she was, Elayne had also expressed sorrow that things hadn't worked out differently for both her son…and the woman who still cared for him so deeply.

Yet Shauna still felt blessed. She had friends like Elayne and Kaitlin.

She had Fantasy Fare, and the adoration of all the kids who

piled into her story room, like now, and raptly listened to her spin tales she'd written about funny animals, including her favorite, Buster the Barker, and princes and princesses who were as strong and smart as they were beautiful, and mean ogres who got their comeuppances.

She even had a better understanding of her other stories now, and her abilities and limitations when it came to altering the realities they predicted.

"Duke didn't know that the next-door neighbor's sprinkler was stuck. Duke was a doggy, and doggies don't worry about stuck sprinklers. He didn't worry about it, either, when he fell into the neighbor's humongous mud puddle. Bobby was close behind, and he fell into the mud puddle, too. And Bobby's mommy was close behind him, so…" She looked up to ask, "What do you think happened to her?" Only the words came out much softer than she'd intended.

For as she raised her head, she saw who was standing in the doorway: Kaitlin, of course, since she always liked to listen in on the stories when she had a spare minute.

Elayne Strahm was there, too. And she wasn't alone.

A little girl's voice shouted out with all the other kids', "Bobby's mommy fell into the mud puddle, too." An adorable little girl with green eyes and curly hair the same shiny black as her grandmother's…and her daddy's.

Hunter was there, too, holding Andee in the curve of his arm.

As he caught Shauna's eye, he put Andee down and whispered something. His daughter, dressed in matching magenta sweatpants and shirt with a purple flower embroidered on the front, picked her way around the other kids sitting on pillows on the floor. When she got to Shauna, she raised her arms to be picked up.

Shauna obliged, lifting the minimal weight of the five-year-snuggling the child against her, inhaling her bubble-gum scent. "Hi, Andee," she said.

Shauna." Andee pulled back. "My daddy and

grandma said you tell the best stories in the world, so we had to come to hear you tell them.''

"You can thank your daddy and grandma for me, honey.''

"Oh. I'm supposed to thank you," Andee said. She looked a little puzzled. "For your very special story. Is it the one about mud puddles?''

"Kind of," Shauna said, meeting Hunter's gaze among the crowd.

Oh, heavens. He was looking at her with eyes filled with desire. And something more.

Something deeper.

Suggesting forever.

Or was she just reading her own wishes into his smiling stare?

The children in her audience had begun to wriggle and whisper. She still had a story to finish.

"Andee, I see a pillow right over there." She pointed a little to her left. "Would you please go sit down so we can finish the mud puddle story?''

"Okay, Shauna." Andee straightened her legs as Shauna put her on the floor.

Somehow, Shauna managed to finish reading the tale of Duke, Bobby and the mud. She must have done okay with it, for the kids laughed in the right places and, afterward, cheered and clapped and asked for more.

"Tomorrow," she assured them. "We'll have another story time then.''

As they rose and scampered away, Shauna saw Elayne take her granddaughter's hand and lead her from the room with the rest. She smiled over her shoulder at Shauna.

So did Kaitlin, after shooing all the remaining children from the story room toward the restaurant.

And then only Shauna and Hunter were left.

He came toward her, then stopped a foot away. Shauna inhaled, hoping for fortification from the air around her, b··

all she got was Hunter's clean, male scent along with what felt like insufficient oxygen.

That had to be the explanation of why her equilibrium seemed off.

"Good story," he said, his deep voice full of some emotion that Shauna didn't even try to identify.

How would it translate into one of her stories? She didn't know.

"Thanks." So banal was their conversation. So full of an undercurrent that she didn't dare to name. Or did she?

Only to herself.

Love.

"I enjoy your stories," Hunter said. He closed the space between them, pulling her into his arms. "All of them."

"No, you don't," she began, but he stopped her by a long, sweet kiss that, had her equilibrium not been affected merely by his presence, would have made her dizzy.

It *did* make her dizzy…with hope.

"Why are you here, Hunter?" she asked when she could force her lips far enough away to speak. Which was an effort. For all she wanted was to continue to kiss him. For now.

Maybe forever.

As long as she didn't have to think about what it meant. What the future could be. What—

"I'm here because that's what the last story you wrote about me said would happen. I'm here to tell you how much I love you, and to ask you to marry me so we can live happily ever after."

Shocked, Shauna pulled away. Sure, that was what her story said. What she wanted. But it couldn't really happen.

Not so easily.

"Do you think I wrote the story to keep you off balance and out of control?" she demanded almost angrily—the only way she could keep herself from running from the room after

rse yet, crying.

"No, though maybe sometimes being a little out of control's not a bad thing."

"Maybe." Shauna, shivering, couldn't draw her gaze from his eyes. What she saw reflected there was all that she'd ever hoped to see. Caring. More.

Surely he didn't love her. She could be misreading it all.

"Then that story about us," he continued. "You didn't just write it to play mind games with me?"

"Not intentionally." Her voice was too hoarse. Her legs too weak. But she couldn't leave.

And not just because he once more held her close.

"You wrote it because it was there, inside me, and your big, bad writing z-state sensed it, right?"

"Yes," she whispered. "But—"

"And years ago, the stuff you wrote was possible because it affected me. Even though I refused to believe it."

"You were a down-to-earth cop. You wrote plans based on facts and strategy. What I wrote didn't seem real to you."

"Stop defending my shortsighted stupidity," he commanded, pulling back just a little. His glare was tempered by a smile, one of his genuine smiles that drove her nuts with wanting him. "Anyway," he continued, "I'm done fighting it. Fighting you. Here's the deal." He didn't have to work hard to pull her back against him, so she could feel every hard, muscled part of him. His obvious need strained against her abdomen. She wouldn't have spoken then, even if she could.

She had to hear him out.

"I've told Simon he's in charge of the L.A. office of Strahm Solutions. I'm opening a Phoenix branch here, in Oasis. Andee and I are moving here—away from L.A. and all the nasty stuff that could touch her when her mother's put on trial for everything she pulled. It'll help for Andee to be near her grandmother. Don't you think, Lady Shrink?"

"Yes," Shauna agreed, speaking against his shirt. Oh, lord. He'd be here, in the same town as her. What did that me

"Now, in that story you wrote about us, I asked you to marry me, and you said yes."

"That doesn't mean anything," Shauna began. "It was—"

"It was exactly right. What was inside me, what I wanted, but refused to think about. I love you, Shauna."

She looked up into his face, and saw what she hoped for—confirmation of what he was saying.

"I've always loved you," she responded huskily.

"Then let's make that story about us come true," he commanded. "Marry me, Shauna. And then we'll live happily ever after, right? It's what you've written, so it's got to be true."

"It will be now," Shauna said, pulling Hunter's head down for a long kiss to seal their future.

*   *   *   *   *

researching the cure

The facts you need to know:

- **One woman in nine** in the United Kingdom will develop breast cancer during her lifetime.

- Each year **40,700** women are newly diagnosed with breast cancer and around **12,800** women will die from the disease. However, survival rates are improving, with on average 77 per cent of women still alive five years later.

- **Men can also suffer from breast cancer**, although currently they make up less than one per cent of all new cases of the disease.

Britain has one of the highest breast cancer death rates in the world. Breast Cancer Campaign wants to understand why and do something about it. Statistics cannot begin to describe the impact that breast cancer has on the lives of those women who are affected by it, on their families and friends.

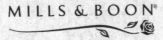

MILLS & BOON®

**During the month of October
Harlequin Mills & Boon will donate
10p from the sale of every
Modern Romance™ series book to
help Breast Cancer Campaign
in *researching the cure*.**

Breast Cancer Campaign's scientific projects
look at improving diagnosis and treatment
of breast cancer, better understanding how
it develops and ultimately either curing the
disease or preventing it.

Do your part to help

Visit <u>www.breastcancercampaign.org</u>

And make a donation today.

researching the cure

Breast Cancer Campaign is a company limited by guarantee registered in England and
Wales. Company No. 05074725. Charity registration No. 299758.
Breast Cancer Campaign, Clifton Centre, 110 Clifton Street, London EC2A 4HT.
Tel: 020 7749 3700 Fax: 020 7749 3701 www.breastcancercampaign.org

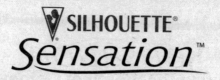

SILHOUETTE® *Sensation*™

UNDERCOVER MISTRESS
by Kathleen Creighton

When Celia Cross escaped Hollywood's spotlight, her only refuge was the beach. Then Roy Starr washed ashore, bleeding from an assassin's bullet. With the killer determined to finish the job, would this be their beginning—or their end?

EXPLOSIVE ALLIANCE
by Catherine Mann

Wingmen Warriors

Air force captain Bo Rokowsky had been haunted by Paige Haugen and the part he played in her husband's death. But when Paige began receiving threats, he'd risk everything to keep her safe.

IN BROAD DAYLIGHT
by Marie Ferrarella

Cavanaugh Justice

When Detective Dax Cavanaugh started following the trail of schoolteacher Brenda York's missing student, it was an all-out war between duty and desire…

Don't miss out! On sale from 21st October 2005

❖ SILHOUETTE®
Sensation™

RUNNING ON EMPTY
by Michelle Celmer

Pregnant and alone, Sylvie Mitchell was in hiding. And when Jon Cahill appeared, she had to lie to the one man she truly loved, even though he was the only man who could keep her—and her baby—safe.

SAFE PASSAGE
by Loreth Anne White

When a terrorist turned agent Scott Armstrong's safe mission into a deadly battle, he had to keep beautiful scientist Dr Skye Van Rijn safe. But would Skye's secrets jeopardise their lives?

DECEIVED
by Carla Cassidy

Bombshell: An Athena Force Adventure
Someone was lying to retrieval specialist Lynn White, but could it be Nick Jones, the intriguing head of security? With the FBI on her trail, she had to find her betrayer.

Don't miss out! On sale from 21st October 2005

Available at most branches of WHSmith, Tesco, ASDA, Borders, Eason, Sainsbury's and most bookshops

Visit our website at www.silhouette.co.uk

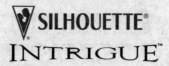

▼ SILHOUETTE®
INTRIGUE™

FULL EXPOSURE by Debra Webb

Colby Agency: Internal Affairs

Cole Dane's investigation revealed the unimaginable –
Angel Parker had been leaking information about the agency.
But the more time he spent with her, the more he came to
believe in her innocence, and to realise their attraction could
prove fatal.

PATERNITY UNKNOWN by Jean Barrett

Top Secret Babies

A year after their passionate night together, Ethan Brand
was back to find Lauren McCrea, the woman he couldn't
forget. When Lauren's daughter was kidnapped, Ethan began
a desperate search. But would he forgive Lauren when he
learned the child was his?

BRIDAL RECONNAISSANCE by Lisa Childs

Dead Bolt

When Evan Quade tracked down his amnesiac wife, Amanda,
he got the shock of his life – she'd given birth to his son. Now
she was determined to face the threat of a madman's revenge
alone. But Evan couldn't abandon his family…

SPELLBOUND by Rebecca York

Eclipse

Someone was trying to frame Andre Gascon for murder,
so he turned to the Light Street Detective Agency for help.
But PI Morgan Kirkland realised she would have to unearth
enigmatic Andre's secrets, before they became the next
victims…

All these thrilling books are on sale from
21st October 2005

Available at most branches of WHSmith, Tesco, ASDA,
Borders, Eason, Sainsbury's and most bookshops

Visit our website at www.silhouette.co.uk

Three new stories to make your heart race – with suspense and passion

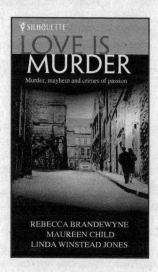

TO DIE FOR *by Rebecca Brandewyne*

When a loveless couple attends a party that ends in murder, Paul becomes the leading suspect while Lily, his soon-to-be ex, must find a way to prove his innocence.

IN TOO DEEP *by Maureen Child*

When the lawyer daughter of a mob boss is threatened, she's not sure who is more dangerous – the unknown assailant or the gorgeous mobster sent to protect her!

CALLING AFTER MIDNIGHT
by Linda Winstead Jones

When her advice to a late-night listener results in murder, DJ Veronica Gray finds she needs some help herself – from sexy detective Eli Benedict.

On sale Friday 16th September 2005

F36729

4 FREE

BOOKS AND A SURPRISE GIFT!

We would like to take this opportunity to thank you for reading this Silhouette® book by offering you the chance to take FOUR more specially selected titles from the Sensation™ series absolutely FREE! We're also making this offer to introduce you to the benefits of the Reader Service™--

- ★ **FREE home delivery**
- ★ **FREE gifts and competitions**
- ★ **FREE monthly Newsletter**
- ★ **Exclusive Reader Service offers**
- ★ **Books available before they're in the shops**

Accepting these FREE books and gift places you under no obligation to buy, you may cancel at any time, even after receiving your free shipment. Simply complete your details below and return the entire page to the address below. You don't even need a stamp!

YES! Please send me 4 free Sensation books and a surprise gift. I understand that unless you hear from me, I will receive 6 superb new titles every month for just £3.05 each, postage and packing free. I am under no obligation to purchase any books and may cancel my subscription at any time. The free books and gift will be mine to keep in any case.

S5ZED

Ms/Mrs/Miss/Mr ....Initials ....

BLOCK CAPITALS PLEASE

Surname ....

Address ....

....

....Postcode..............................

Send this whole page to:
UK: FREEPOST CN81, Croydon, CR9 3WZ